HABEAS CORPUS

AND OTHER STORIES

BY

PETER GREEN

THE WORLD PUBLISHING COMPANY

CLEVELAND AND NEW YORK

Published by The World Publishing Company
2231 West 110th Street, Cleveland 2, Ohio

Library of Congress Catalog Card Number: 63-7244

FIRST EDITION

CONTENTS

ACKNOWLEDGMENTS

Acknowledgment is due to the Editors of the *Cornhill*, the *New Strand*, and *Pick of Today's Short Stories 8*, in which some of these stories originally appeared.

HABEAS CORPUS

Two hundred yards ahead, on the corner by the cross-roads, stood a freshly painted telephone booth: the only positive splash of colour for miles around in the flat, neutral East Anglian landscape. Jack Newhouse, known to his many pub acquaintances as J.J., and described by his wife Sarah (rather too often) as God's gift to women, eased his foot off the accelerator and eyed the scarlet oblong with mingled apprehension and excitement. He took one hand off the wheel, fumbling in his waistcoat pocket. If no coppers, forget it. If four pennies, then. Well. Fingers scrabbled over-eagerly through pocket detritus. Spare car key (always losing them), nail scissors (got an obsessional thing about black rims, rising cuticles), rosary (try not to think about Confession), all jumbled up with odd half-crowns, half-pennies, worn tanners, nubbly twelve-sided threepenny bits to which you couldn't ever get acclimatised. And pennies. Two, three—nearly there now, crawling at twenty-plus, the powerful engine juddering in protest—*four*, change into third (a neat double declutch despite the synchro-mesh gearing), decision made, turn into kerb, right foot firm on brake.

Switch off engine. Wind thundering across the Fens, a tangible noise, sharp-edged, like sheets flapping in the wind. Sheets. Sarah with pegs in her mouth, straining at the line,

thin body irritably anglepoised, cheeks flushed under the
blown strands of auburn hair. Bones, Newhouse thought,
are uncompromising things. And Sarah wears hers too near
the surface for comfort. The blood pulsed and sang in his
head; the first surge of familiar excitement came crowding
up. Not too late. Think. Quickly.

Newhouse fiddled with the ignition key for a moment,
then eased his long body out of the car and stood, for a
second or two only, by the roadside: somehow an ineffectual
figure despite the carefully calculated raffishness—bottle-
green corduroys, the old tweed jacket patched like a prep
school master's at elbows and cuffs, blond hair not so thick
as it had been, too fine anyway to be worn quite so long by
a man in his over-late thirties, blown now every which way
by the tangling wind. Goya might have drawn those elon-
gated hands, that melancholy profile—but in a hurry; the
features were roughened and blurred, as though the artist
had used his thumb impatiently, creating a sort of plausible
fuzz in gouache. A fair if fashionable judge of College
wine; slightly suspect politically, and apt to appear on tele-
vision programmes rather more often than the unspoken
norm allowed; a sound archaeologist nevertheless (as his
colleagues admitted, magnanimity and surprise jostling for
front place in their voices), and a model family man, father
of two small grave daughters who regularly, on his behalf,
battered away at the stony hearts of professors, Faculty
Board members, and various species of the visiting great.

Also a Catholic: and worse still, a convert, something
which had to be played down (though not too far down) in
the liberal, rational, sensible, post-Keynesian, shades-of-the-
Cavendish, tight-knit, shibboleth-ridden, exotic-provincial,
bitchy, gossip-tangled, scandal-hungry, Geiger-sensitive,

underpaid, wine-and-car-snobbish society that was post-war academic Cambridge. Well J.J., and how's Original Sin working out in the Mesolithic communities? Tell me, Jack, how do you reconcile—oh I'm sorry, I shouldn't bring up things like that. And those neither so kind nor so tolerant, the rationalist Savonarolas ready with the verbal fire-and-faggotry of their secular puritanism, probing not only for logical flaws but fleshly weakness, eager to expose *l'homme moyen,* or more than *moyen, sensuel.*

In which, Newhouse thought, the bastards had something. He hooked long fingers into the slot on the stubborn phone-box door, tugging it open to a faint odour of bad breath, urine, and cheap tobacco. *Peccavi nimis cogitatione, verbo, et opere.* By thought word and deed, regularly and unremittingly. I'm sorry, Father, you might call it chronic infidelity, and it's no use telling me about the syndrome of protracted adolescence, I know that bloody well and it doesn't make a damn of difference. Not when you're up against nature, instinct and a long, long habit. I'll grant you it's something of a liability in Cambridge, there you have a point, Father. But. All right, then, I'm like Augustine, I'm sorry I'm not sorry, and maybe when I'm feeling really low and defeated I'm sorry period. But it doesn't often get that bad.

Newhouse stood in the cramped booth, four pennies still clutched between thumb and forefinger. He glanced at the coins, was bothered by a vaguely blasphemous symbolical association, and quickly put them down on the black metal box. Still playing for time, he lit a cigarette. Half past two. Then he shoved the four pennies into the slot and dialled a number.

'Celia? Jack here. Are you free?'

A*

'Oh darling—how wonderful to hear your voice! I thought you'd never ring.'

Why the hell is it, Newhouse wondered, that women are bloody well incapable of giving a direct answer to any question?

'You know how it is,' he said.

'Of course I do. I'm not complaining——'

Like hell you're not.

'—it's just such a lovely surprise, that's all. *Tu sais?*'

French, too. What would you think if I blew a gigantic raspberry into the mouthpiece and then, very gently, replaced the receiver?

'Look, Celia honey, can you manage this afternoon?' If I don't get out of this phone-box soon, Newhouse thought, perspiration gathering on his forehead, I shall throw up.

'Well, I'll have to find someone to keep an eye on Rachel,' Celia said. 'It's Mrs Jarvis's day off—didn't you remember?'

Well no, actually, since you ask, I didn't, and what the hell leads you to suppose that every detail of your daily domestic routine is indelibly stamped on my memory?

'Sorry, Celia—you know how it is.'

'Jack darling—' this with a gay but rather jagged laugh—'if you tell me I *know how it is* just once more, I swear I'll throw something at you.'

For God's sake, Newhouse thought, she's getting more like Sarah very day. But his voice was warm and bantering as he said: 'Through the telephone? You have unsuspected talents.'

'Oh lord. Now I'm getting tetchy. That's what comes of not seeing you for a month, darling.'

'Well,' Newhouse observed, his half-smoked cigarette wagging up and down as he spoke, 'no one would guess you were in a tearing rush to see me now, the way this conversation's going.'

'You *are* a bastard, Jack, aren't you?'

Ah. That's better. Much better.

'Of course I am. You love it. My true intent, sweetie, is all for your delight. Now what about this afternoon?'

There was silence for a moment; he could hear Celia's quick, shallow breathing.

She said: 'Well, I suppose I could drop Rachel over at Janet's for a couple of hours——'

Newhouse said, in quick relief: 'You do that, darling. Janet's always glad to see children about the place.'

'Luckily for us.' Celia gave her special private Jack-and-Celia giggle, a sexy, conspiratorial noise that always struck Newhouse as the sort of thing a St Trinian's schoolgirl would produce if she stepped out of her cartoon.

'Poor Janet,' Jack said: it was the expected response. Poor Janet be damned, he thought: the coy, glucose, over-weight, under-screwed, chattering, corseted, exophthalmic cow. If they made it a competitive sport she'd bore for England. He choked on a mouthful of smoke.

Celia said: 'Look, honey, I'll have to ring her up and make sure it's all right—where are you, by the way?'

Newhouse told her.

'All right—you wait by the box and I'll call you back.'

Newhouse groaned inwardly, but aloud he said: 'Right-ho. Don't be long.'

'What do *you* think, sweetie?' and with a click and a whirr, the line went dead. Newhouse thankfully shoved his way out of the box and drew in a deep breath of fresh air. He got back into the car, wound the window down, wiped his forehead, and lit a fresh cigarette from the stump of the old one. I could drive on now, he told himself, virtuously. Resisting temptation. Or (not so flatteringly creditable) plain boredom.

During the past couple of months he had more than once considered ditching Celia. Celia, frankly, was getting a bit of a bore, and not the way Dean Swift thought, either. The clinging tendrils of possessiveness, at first barely noticeable in their snatched and passionate meetings, had now begun to spread at an alarming rate. Newhouse sucked hard on his cigarette as he thought about this. But in the end (as he was always forced to admit) there were certain rather special advantages about Celia, which entitled her to special consideration.

It hadn't been a bore at first. But then it never is, is it? Newhouse reflected, staring at a sparrow perched on the telegraph wire overhead. That's right, you bastard, preen yourself, he told it. What the hell have you got to worry about? Celia, dark Celia at that first fatal tennis party, so elegant in white linen, but not playing, oh no, not Celia, stretched out in a deck-chair under the Bowmans' deodar with a long gin-and-lime and the local male talent dancing attendance. June sunlight on the court, the astringent tang of dried sweat, *lucky the rhododendrons,* Janet calling that mouldering pigeon-box a doo-cut, a *doo-cut,* my God, and the quick amused eyes that met and flicked away again, the dark creamy body curled like a cat's.

Celia Sanderson.

Sarah had cried off the party, she was in one of her *noli*

me tangere, I-hate-all-people moods, and had the first wiry shadows of a migraine scratching at her eyes. Sharon and Miriam were at school. Footloose Newhouse driving up to the Old Rectory in a swirl and a crunch of gravel, blazer, new racquet, clean white shorts, Charvet scarf, the lot. Janet fussing around in that pop-eyed elephantine way of hers—'Jack, *so* glad you're here, I've got a wild hairy man who's creating absolute *havoc* with us poor rabbits, *couldn't* you have a single while we use the other court?'—and introducing him to Colin Sanderson, Sanderson the estate agent, with his Midland accent and leg-of-mutton arms and the black hair bushing out at the V of his sweat-shirt, yes, a wild hairy man was about it, he ought to have shaved three times a day but clearly didn't. The five o'clock blues, Celia called it. Oh the instant male prickliness, cocks sharpening claws on dunghill, such fluffing of feathers from the baseline: ridiculous looking back. Yet not, perhaps, all that ridiculous, with Celia sitting there, long legs crossed in an elegant swirl of petticoats, while the rival males fought and sweated, paladins in the lists.

Sanderson had been good, too, better than Newhouse would ever have guessed from that beer-heavy barrel of a body: a wicked, killing serve, a series of grunting smashes and volleys at the net. Against this storm Newhouse deployed the devious holding tricks he had learnt, long ago, as a Wimbledon junior, in the bright dead days when tennis mattered: high lobs, sliced cross-court drives, savagely spun passing-shots chopped just inside the chalk of the inner tram-line. Little by little Newhouse had slowed Sanderson down, worn him out, forced him on to the defensive. In the end he drew level at five games all, broke Sanderson's service, and clinched the set with four successive aces, the last of which was a showy high kicker down the centre line.

Afterwards Sanderson had been brisk and wary, gulping lemonade, towelling his face and neck, eager to get away. Newhouse was left to talk to Celia while her husband strode off to soothe his wounded ego in a mixed doubles. Yes, it had been wonderful at the beginning, all right: the first recognition of desire, the almost unbearable excitement, the urge to touch, discover, explore, possess. Sanderson had gone home early: Celia insisted on staying, impervious to hints. She had a car of her own: this, Newhouse felt, was profoundly characteristic of that marriage. Drinks with Janet, phone-call to Sarah, don't keep supper, love, I'll pick up a sandwich on the way home.

Janet, very pickled, saying an hour later: You want to watch Colin Sanderson, Jack.

—Because I took a set off him?

—That, and other things. He thinks you're a prize shit, period.

—Such language, Janet.

—His own words. I heard him telling Roger.

—All right, what did Roger tell him?

—Roger said you were a bastard for the women.

—Oh to hell with Roger.

—Jack, why can't you be a bastard with me sometimes? I'd give you a bloody good time. Truly I would.

Breath coming fast now, tiny veins under the powder, big breasts heaving. Oh God.

—I'm a respectable married man, Janet, whatever sods like Roger say.

—Oh all *right,* Jack, go and make Celia if you want to,

you can't keep your eyes off her, can you? Get her out of your system. But I'm telling you, *watch Colin*.

—Take it easy, Janet.

—Funny you should say that. It's Celia's watchword. Weak heart. That's why she doesn't play tennis.

—Poor girl. I'm sorry.

—There are compensations, Jack.

This with a glance of confidential lubricity.

—Meaning? Newhouse asked, inquisitive now.

—Meaning, no more kiddie-poos. All legal and above board. Signed, sealed and knotted.

That would be old Owen Barclay. Very profitable practice Owen had, a fair mint of dollars he made out of liberal, rational, freethinking, etcetera etcetera as before Cambridge. Ha.

—Floreat Fallopia, eh, Janet?

—That's right, that's just it, laughing in that hostessy way, bloody Janet, only half getting it.

—Well, thanks for everything. Thanks a lot.

—Don't mention it, Jack.

—Don't you, either.

What a hope. But what a prospect, too.

And all that, thought Newhouse, hunched over the steering-wheel, was what the little Welshman called a grief ago.

> *You cannot cage the minute*
> *Within its net of gold—*

Never so good again, never again the aching, laughing, wind-driven tumult of that first time, turning off the main road in a dazzle of summer sunlight, thrusting the Humber hard up that rutted, stony hillside track in third, parking under the trees and waiting, waiting, knowing the little Morris would follow.

Oh Celia. Celia——

If only it could always have stayed so simple, so uncomplicated: the secret existence carved out of time, the private and unsuspected passion, the exhilaratingly double life.

Running, breathless, in a yellow summer dress and tan sandals, unable to speak, gasping with the impatient agony of her desire. Down together in a tangled flurry of bodies and brushwood, clothes shed anyhow, black burning hair and coffee-brown nipples, so hot, so engulfing that dark arched body with its thirsty tongues of liquid fire, my pentecostal Celia, riding blind in your pride and your ecstasy, drawing me with you to the burning point of no return.

But afterwards Newhouse, obscurely burdened by his secret knowledge, and at the same time nervous that his motives might be open to unflattering interpretation, and under all this wondering if he were not perhaps the victim of a really diabolic joke by Janet Bowman, circled the dangerous subject with wary persistence.

—Celia, was it all right?

—Ah, wonderful. Better than I could have dreamed, my darling.

—No, I mean—*will it* be all right?

—Why ever not, Jack? All we have to do is to take reasonable precautions.

Now there was an Eighth Type of Ambiguity, if you liked.

—Precautions?

—Well, of course. Be your age, darling. What's eating you?

—Janet—Janet said you had a weak heart.

—Bless you, sweet, I'm not going to die on you, if *that's* your trouble. Nice of you to worry, though. Now lay off and kiss me—we haven't got much time, God knows, so why waste it? That's better, that's much better—Ah God, yes, *yes*——

Nothing solved, problem shelved indefinitely. Was she shy about being sterile—always supposing she *was* sterile? Why couldn't she look you in the eye and say, straight out: I know your sort, you want an easy lay without awkward consequences, and that's the beginning and end of it. Oh yes, and your bloody Catholic conscience prefers one mortal sin to two, though what difference contraception makes to a good screw *sub specie aeternitatis* I've never fathomed? But she didn't say that, she wouldn't, no woman ever would. They wanted it all mixed up with declarations of undying devotion, they had to have it both ways. For a mixture of sentimentality, ruthlessness, and large-scale self-deception, Newhouse reflected, women were bloody hard to beat. In the end, of course, she'd admitted she couldn't have a child, but not till their liaison had been going long enough to let her believe that *that* wasn't its main *raison d'être*. Three cheers for *das ewige* bloody *Weib,* and why the hell was Celia taking so long?

With the anxious and uncomfortable sense of timing which she invariably displayed over anything to do with their relationship, she chose this precise moment to call back. Newhouse sat on in the car for ten long seconds while the bell shrilled at him. A fussy, neurotic noise, he thought. Very appropriate. With a sigh, he heaved himself out of the car again.

Celia's voice said: 'It's all right, Jack—I've parked Rachel.'

'On Janet?'

'Yes.'

'What did she say?'

'She sounded a bit suspicious—I mean, Rachel's got a cold, that's why she's away from school, and Janet knows damned well I could leave my Cambridge shopping till Colin gets back——'

Ignoring Rachel's cold (some comment on this was obviously expected) Newhouse said: 'When *will* Colin be back?'

'About seven this evening. He had a job on over the other side of Newmarket.'

'Doesn't leave us much time.'

'No.'

Newhouse glanced at his watch. 'Usual place, then? In about twenty minutes?'

'All right, darling.' Then, after a pause: 'Jack darling, I do love you so. You know that, don't you?'

'Yes, Celia. I know that all right,' Newhouse said. 'You know how I feel about you, don't you?'

'I think so,' Celia Sanderson said. 'I think so. I'll be there as soon as I can.'

'I'll be waiting,' Newhouse said, and quickly put the receiver down. As he started the engine up and shifted into gear he felt the old familiar excitement sweep through him. But by the time he reached the top of that wooded crest— scene of so many briefly passionate meetings during the past eighteen months—he was resigned and melancholy. '*Ante coitum triste omne animal,*' he said aloud. A rook cawed sardonically in the tree tops overhead.

The little black Morris come bouncing up the track five minutes later. Celia Sanderson got out, awkwardly as always, showing a remarkable amount of leg in the process. She smiled and blinked at Newhouse, her myopic grey eyes defenceless without their habitual dark glasses. She was wearing an old heather-mixture tweed skirt and a thick black fisherman's jersey, and her dark hair was concealed under a yellow scarf. As Newhouse moved towards her he saw that she was wearing more make-up than usual, and that under it her face looked heavy and tired.

They kissed where they stood, in the middle of the track, pressed hard against each other, silently repeating the first movement of a ritual sequence that had become refined and stylised with much repetition. The wind whipped through Newhouse's long fair hair; over Celia's shoulder his eye traced fold and convolution of ground, the grey hills that had seen Roman and Saxon come and go, leaving behind rampart or road to sink back with time into the anonymity of mere earth. Leaves blew round their feet and lay strewn against the split-wood palisade that stood between them and the trees.

> *Today the Roman and his trouble*
> *Are ashes under Uricon,*

Newhouse thought, and kissed Celia more hungrily under the leaden sky, hands moving over her body with the unthinking skill of a surgeon.

Presently she broke from his embrace, and hand in hand they walked up the path, stooped through the gap in the fence, and moved into the uneasy privacy of the wood. They knew where they were going. Twigs crackled underfoot; no silence here, but a furtive multiplicity of tiny sounds, burrowing insect, hesitant leaf-fall, a wood-pigeon that whickered away at their approach, its wings clapping like an umbrella when the rain is shaken out of it.

In the dry concave hollow between three bushes Newhouse took off his jacket and spread it over the heaped dead leaves. Then he held out a hand to Celia. This, too, was part of the ritual. She lowered herself slowly, with a faint hiss of nylon as her long legs rubbed against each other. But instead of moving into his arms she sat apart, arms folded, staring up at the black tracery of the trees overhead.

Newhouse slid an arm round her shoulders, cupping his hand lightly under the swell and sag of the heavy breast that rode out from the soft cage of her ribs. He could feel her grow tense at his touch, willing him away, remote in her cocoon of melancholy isolation.

‘What is it?’ he asked, dismayed at this sudden change of mood, already seeing her as problem rather than lover, the secret magic of their intermittent togetherness splintering into sharp jagged fragments under some unknown external pressure, the mood of desire imploding, lost.

‘I don’t know, Jack. I’m sorry. I’m being a bore. It’s just—oh, I don’t know. Give me a cigarette, darling.’

You’re stalling, Newhouse thought as he snapped his lighter, watching her inhale awkwardly, blowing the smoke in fierce jets from nostrils and mouth. You don’t want to. That’s all it is. You don’t want to. Now there’ll be words, words, words to wrap round your refusal, explaining, making it palatable, excusing yourself.

‘Jack,’ Celia said, quietly and wearily, ‘what does this affair of ours mean? Where’s it getting to? Where can it ever get to?’

‘Oh for God’s sake,’ said Newhouse. ‘We have an hour

together—an *hour*—and you have to waste it asking rhetorical questions. What's the point?'

'That,' said Celia, with the ghost of a smile, 'is a rhetorical question itself, in case you hadn't noticed.'

Newhouse, anxious only to steer her clear of the messy emotional storm his practised eye saw gathering, caught instantly at this softening of mood.

'Darling, you're tired to death,' he said. 'Come here and relax.'

'Relax?' Celia twisted sideways, cigarette in mouth, squinting up at him through a haze of smoke as she exhaled. 'Oh Jack, when have I ever *relaxed* with you?'

Newhouse said, running his fingers through her dark hair, irritation and boredom subordinated to more immediate and pressing ends: 'I haven't noticed you wanting to relax much.'

She pulled away from him again, angrily, almost despairingly. She said: 'You know what you are? A sort of sexual blackmailer, Jack. Oh, I don't mean you'd put pressure on me in any crude sense—you've got too much sense of self-preservation for that. No, maybe sex-peddler's the word. Like dope-peddler. You got me to a point where I couldn't do without you——'

'Past tense, Celia?' With a slow, deliberate gesture Newhouse ran one hand across her breasts, then sat back and watched as she struggled to control her breathing.

'Oh you bastard,' she whispered. 'You *bastard*.'

'No,' Newhouse said. 'Just honest.'

'Doesn't it mean any more to you than *that*?' Celia asked. 'Do you ever think about me as a *person*, Jack? Or do you put me out of your mind the minute you drive down that lane?'

'You know I could never get you out of my mind for long,' Newhouse said, grinning.

'Well, *what* do you think, then? Oh, I know. "Good old Celia, always handy for a quick lay, doesn't make any fuss, no chance of a little accident, no need to fork out two hundred quid to some smooth abortionist, everything under control, *just the bloody job*." I can almost hear you saying it.'

Not bad, Celia, not bad at all, Newhouse thought. Glimmerings of realism will keep creeping in behind that romantic front. Oh you stupid self-flagellating bitch, why can't you get wise to yourself, stop reaching for some non-existent bloody moon?

You can never tell them the truth, he told himself. That's the hell of it. Truth is a commodity they won't buy. And if it comes to blackmail, who's talking? Look at that face. It's got 'I dare you to hurt me' written all over it, with 'Please preserve my illusions' as a sub-heading. And you're soft, boy, soft. Keep everyone happy, that's your motto, isn't it?

'We seem to have run out of conversation,' he said, after a moment's pause.

Celia said: 'When in doubt, quote. First rule in the academic *Kharma Sutra*. Put up someone else's umbrella and hope to high heaven it'll keep the rain off.'

'What's the point of quarrelling, Celia? It won't get us anywhere.'

'No,' said Celia. 'I suppose it won't. But since we aren't getting anywhere anyhow, why worry?'

'I thought we were,' Newhouse said.

'Did you, Jack? Did you? We meet once a week if we're lucky. Sometimes only once a month. I'm pretty low in the order of your priorities, Jack. Two hours if you can manage it.'

'We had all this out long ago. Neither of us wants to break up our marriage. That means sacrificing a lot we'd like to have. You know that as well as I do.' The phrases slipped out, dull and meaningless, echoing countless other awkward scenes over the years.

'We could have more than *this*,' Celia said. 'Just making love, and then—nothing. Goodbye till next time. You can't see your face, Jack. You can't see that look of creeping boredom that comes over your face when you've had me. Even if that's all you want, oh God, why can't you pretend you care for me, just a little, Jack, just a little?'

The tears were very close now.

'Jack, have you any idea how you humiliate me? You make me feel like a tart.'

A cold, detached voice in Newhouse's mind said: Well, if the cap fits— And then sniggered at the *double entendre*.

He said: 'You'll say you've never enjoyed it next.'

'Oh no.' Celia's mouth twisted bitterly. 'I enjoy it all right. I enjoy it. That's the hell of it. Every time I look at you I want you. When we're at a party I have to hold on to myself not to touch you. I ache for you, you bastard. That's the most humiliating part of the whole bloody business. And afterwards—afterwards I feel so sick, so ashamed of myself, I could die.'

Newhouse, vulnerable now, hurt in his pride said: 'Was it like that always? Right from the beginning?'

'No. I'll be honest. No, it wasn't. You took more trouble at first. You wrapped it up. And I believed you, I wanted so desperately to believe that smooth line of yours, even when it came out like a worn record, a scratched old disc that's been played too often, and with a blunt needle at that.'

'It was true, Celia. It is true, love.'

Her eyes searched his. 'Those poems you quoted—so apt, so slick, that Wyatt sonnet, that thing by Day Lewis, all part of the bag of tricks, weren't they, Jack? Select the right stimulus and apply pressure. You might as well have slipped a dose of Spanish fly in my gin and had done with it.'

Newhouse pushed the hair back off his forehead with a weary gesture. 'If you want to believe that I can't stop you,' he said. 'It isn't true. But if you want to believe it——'

'Want? *Want?* Of course I don't *want* to believe it. You give me no option. You've got me on the hook, Jack, and you never let me forget it. How many times do you think I've said No, no, I *won't* go again, I'll stand him up, I'll finish it? But I couldn't. I couldn't. It's as though you brought me out here just to show me your power.' She clenched her fists hopelessly. 'Sometimes I think you hate me, Jack,' she whispered.

Newhouse stared out at the bare fields, the black, circling rooks, and said nothing. A dry leaf detached itself and came drifting down between them.

'Oh, I know what we used to say,' Celia went on. 'That we were sensible, responsible people. That—quotation again—they ordered these things so much better in France. But in France, Jack, a mistress has a *lover*. Do you know what the word means? I doubt it. What you want, a Frenchman would get in a high-class brothel. No, don't interrupt me. I said a brothel and I mean it. You've never taken me out or bought me presents or even treated me as a special person, someone you cared for deeply, someone you had a relationship with. To you I'm an object, a *thing*. You don't make love *with* me, you use me as a sort of—of——'

'Target for Tonight?' Newhouse suggested.

'You think you can get out of anything by making a cheap joke, don't you?' Celia snapped, eyes glistening. 'Oh you cold fish, you emotional cripple! There's something missing in you, Jack, you simply don't respond to a whole range of normal human feelings, they don't touch any part of you. God help me, sometimes I feel almost sorry for you. That blank terrifying bewildered look on your face, Jack —you're like a child who's thrown the switch and set a machine going, and hasn't a clue what it all means, let alone how to stop it. All this is just a tedious noise, isn't it? A sort of impersonal tornado that may blow over if you're lucky.'

Newhouse said: 'If you mean I think you're making a hell of a fuss about nothing, I wouldn't argue with you, darling.' He glanced quickly at his watch. Oh hell and damnation. Over half an hour wasted already.

'Oh Jack, is that all you can say?' The appeal was naked in her eyes. For God's sake prove me wrong. Tell me. Tell me I'm wrong, that you love me, that I can touch that cold self-sufficient heart of yours. Newhouse, seeing the signals, recognising his moment of strategic advantage, gathered her fiercely into his arms, kissed unresponding lips, said: 'I'm sorry, Celia. I've been a stupid bastard. Forgive me.'

Still, desperately, she held back, searching his face, rigid, agonised.

'Say you care for me, Jack. Say you care for me just a little. I couldn't bear to be humiliated again, now, not now Jack.'

He said: 'I care for you, Celia. I care for you very much,' and at that her breath came out in a great sobbing gasp, and her body relaxed, and her mouth opened to find his.

'Christ, I love you,' she whispered. 'I love you. I love you.'

Twigs and dry leaves cracked beneath them. Burning, burning. To Carthage then I came. Gently now, deep now, the mind a blinding dazzle, ah now, *o lente lente*, I'll burn my books, dear love, how like you this? Off, off, you lendings. Keep crotchet time, time's winged chariot, annihilation, extasis, exolution, liquefaction, transformation, the kiss of——

'God, God, God,' Celia moaned, and then, with appalling suddenness, her face turned purple and she began to choke and heave for breath, lips blue, eyelids fluttering.

Newhouse rolled over, staggered to his feet, stood helpless as Celia writhed and whooped in agony. Her weak heart—hell and damnation, a heart attack, now, here, of all impossible bloody times and places. He bent down towards her, the ice-water of terror flooding his bowels; and as he did so she went stiff and still, the purple flush faded to a waxy pallor, the harsh breathing died away.

Oh God. No. *No*. It can't be.

Another leaf detached itself from the tree overhead, spiralled slowly down, and lay between Celia's breasts, skeleton-thin, a still brown dab of colour.

'Celia.'

No answer.

'For Christ's sake, Celia, *are you all right?*'

A cold November wind stirred through the branches overhead. Newhouse began to sweat with panic. Must *do* something. Pills. Quick. Bound to be pills. He stumbled clumsily out of the wood, leaves scattering around him, ran down the track, tore open the door of the Morris, fumbled in the locker, breathing a mixture of stale cigarette smoke and Celia's sweetish scent, chest heaving in sudden revulsion. Handbag. Ah. Lipstick, compact, old letters, comb, photographs, nail-scissors, nail-scissors, *nail-scissors*. Empty bag over seat. No pills. Nothing.

Nothing.

He stood on the track, heart pounding, mind in a daze. He tried to light a cigarette, but his hands shook so violently that the flame went out three times running. Half-past four. The sweat on his forehead began to dry in the chill breeze. Then, without warning, his stomach contracted and he retched again and again, sharp tearing spasms that brought tears to his eyes, leaving him at last aching and empty.

The light was fading fast now.

He wiped his mouth, and slowly walked back the way he had come, ducking under the gap in the fence, feet dragging through the leaf-drifts, a faint residual hope still left in his mind that Celia would be all right when he got to her, that the whole ugly incident would soon be erased.

But she was still spreadeagled in the same awkward, tell-tale position, supine, legs apart, knees slighty raised, skirt thrown back round her waist. Newhouse could scarcely bring himself to look at her, so sickeningly did that dead marbly stillness mock the lascivious disposal of her limbs. Head averted, he bent over her, straining to catch any sign of life. But the thought of touching her body, of rolling up that heavy jersey to listen for a fugitive heart-beat, left him weak with disgust and fear. (Once a big tabby he owned had been run over, and he could not, literally could not, touch it, even with a spade; it had been Sarah who did what had to be done, seemingly indifferent to the flaccid horror, the dead carrion weight of it, the quick-glazing fishy eye robbed of all movement and meaning.) A mirror, then: wasn't that it? A mirror placed to the lips. But this would have meant going back to the car, searching through Celia's handbag yet again. Nausea surged back at the thought.

He stepped back, for the first time allowing his mind to frame the unspeakable words.

It was at this point, facing openly the idea of Celia dead, that Newhouse's mind cleared, and panic was slowly ousted by the instinct of self-preservation.

There's nothing I can do for Celia now, he thought. Hold to that. That's your sheet-anchor. On that justification all else hangs. No amount of scandal or noble renunciation can bring her back. There are other, more important things now. Sarah. The children. They're alive, their futures matter. You've got to be realistic, face facts.

The scandal wouldn't be very good for your career, either, would it? Enough trouble in that quarter already without giving the wolves something like this to sink their teeth in. Be sensible. Committing professional suicide won't help Sarah, or Colin either, come to that. Would it make *him* happier to know the truth? Would Sarah thank me for wantonly wrecking our marriage? There are times when the truth helps no one, and this is one of them.

In fact, he thought, snatching eagerly at the idea as it brushed his mind, to go to the police now would be mere self-indulgence, luxuriant purging of guilt. *I've got to take the hard way, for everybody's sake.*

Already he was seeing himself, in some unacknowledged back-kitchen of his mind, as the master-criminal, skilfully covering his tracks, working out alibis, keeping a cool head. But this mood lasted only a few moments, defeated by the hideous presence beside him in the wood.

She can't be left looking like that.

Christ, though, I can't touch her, *I can't*.

He bent down hurriedly, tugged at her skirt, turned her gingerly till she was lying on her side.

Lucky we didn't bother to—take anything off.

'Oh my God,' Newhouse whispered, 'what have I done?' And then he was running like a madman, breath sobbing in his throat, away, anywhere, brambles ripping at the tweed of his jacket, out of the wood, quickly, quickly, hysteria fountaining up behind the precarious barriers of his self-control, till he reached the Humber, flung himself into the driving-seat, and with blind, automatic gestures switched on the ignition and took the big car lurching and swerving down the track.

Faster, always faster along the black ribbon of road into Cambridge, the needle flickering up past eighty-five.

How long before they start looking for her? Someone's bound to find the Morris soon. Questions. You were, I believe, a close—might I say an *intimate*—friend of the deceased, Mr Newhouse?

They'll do a post-mortem.

Pathological evidence proves conclusively that——

Sancta Maria, ora pro nobis.

Newhouse changed down into third to overtake a loitering bus, engine and mind racing in time, the subdued roar of cerebral overdrive thundering through his brain.

What was that bloody stupid thing Blake said somewhere about a whore always having the lineaments of gratified desire?

Ahead of him down Hills Road was the Catholic church —large, blackened, ineluctable, hideously arresting in its Victorian Gothic. Newhouse hesitated an instant, then swung the Humber round by the traffic-lights into Lensfield Road, and turned in at the dismal, tree-shadowed parking lot, crammed every Sunday morning with the Jaguars and Bentleys of the well-heeled faithful, empty now except for Father Livesey's battered shooting-brake.

Five o'clock.

Newhouse marched through the big dim porch of the church with its multitudinous notices—parish meetings, the Knights of St Columba, the Legion of Mary—a tall, stooped, familiar figure in this context, long fair hair blown untidily across his forehead, hands shoved deep in the pockets of his green corduroys, eyes on the ground. As he passed through the inner door he straightened himself, removed his hands from his pockets, crossed himself quickly at the stoup.

Someone, a woman, passed him before his eyes had become accustomed to the gloom, greeted him by name, was gone. Before him a bank of lit candles flickered. He genuflected, knelt down, and took out his rosary.

Confiteor Deo omnipotenti—He ran quickly through the familiar words of the General Confession, mind detached now, emotions remote, the three self-accusatory taps of the forefinger—*mea culpa, mea culpa, mea maxima culpa*— a faint summons only, such as Macbeth's porter might have heard in dreams. Then, methodically, he set himself five decades of the Rosary. Newhouse was very matter-of-fact about the outward liturgical disciplines: Sarah had once told him, irritably, that this was because he lacked a genuine religious instinct, a charge which at the time he had disarmingly admitted.

Newhouse had been converted to Catholicism at the time of his marriage to Sarah, and even now there lingered an ineradicable association in his mind between religion and physical desire, between passions and the Passion—an association which (and again he had told Sarah this) the metaphors and imagery of Christian doctrine did nothing to dispel.

—When I married you, he told her once, I had to take on God as well. A jealous God. It's like having your ex-lover as a lodger, Sarah, I always feel I might be *cocu* at any moment. An Eternal triangle, that's what we've got, capital E.

Sarah, a rigidly devout cradle-Catholic (though her mother had been a convert from Scottish Presbyterianism, which gave Newhouse some sort of psychological comfort) told him, shortly, not to be blasphemous. Newhouse had then annoyed her further by reading and absorbing more Catholic theology in six months than she had learnt in her entire life, his sharp academic mind ripping like lightning through centuries of complex Church history and whole Sargassos of heretical disputation. He once, out of sheer experimental curiosity, spent an evening convincing Sarah she was a Pelagian. Sarah went off in a panic to Father Livesey, who was highly amused (Sarah found this unforgivable) and told Newhouse he mustn't tease his wife.

—Why not, Father? She was at Newnham.

—Her mind may have been, Jack, Father Livesey said, but her soul wasn't.

Now Newhouse knelt and prayed, efficiently, mechanically, as though engaged upon a routine business deal with God, the detached part of his mind contemplative but obstinately blank. He was aware of a need in himself to confess: but this need was quasi-physical, akin to the vomiting up of tainted food, a discomfort to be eliminated by the prescribed forms. During the period of his instruction he had just managed to bridge the gap between his intellect, with its enjoyment of theological pyrotechnics, and his instincts, which remained baffled not only by the *vita mystica*, but also by the elementary notion of conscience.

—The trouble with me is, Father, I lack a sense of sin.

—Don't be so conceited, Jack.

—It's true, you know. Too much Freud and comparative anthropology.

—*Nous allons changer tout cela,* my son.

But they hadn't. Not deep down they hadn't, Newhouse thought, looking at his wrist-watch, desperate now with the need to unburden himself, sick and afraid, impatient for the panacea that he did not understand, and could only judge by its effects.

Confessions began at six o'clock. Another forty minutes to go. Oh God.

A dark shadow paused in the aisle beside Newhouse, and he glanced up.

'Father—would you hear my confession now? I'm in—' he was about to say 'serious trouble'; but then the vigilant private censor that watched over his mind moved into action, and he changed the phrase to 'rather a hurry' instead.

Father Livesey eyed Newhouse impassively for a moment, as though in some way troubled by what he saw. Then he smiled and nodded, and moved off towards the confessional, cassock swirling.

Following him, Newhouse thought: There must be the intention to commit a sin. My sin was making love to Celia. Her death was an accident. I probably wasn't even un-intentionally responsible for it. She could have had an attack at any time. Alone. With Colin. She'd very likely have had this one even without our making love. *Ergo*—Satisfied by his own argument, Newhouse knelt down in darkness by the grille, and confessed to having committed, on one occasion, an act of adultery. For this he received Absolution, and two decades of the Rosary by way of penance.

When he came out it was quite dark. He got into the Humber and sat there for a moment, limp and drained, his mind a snakepit of uneasy foreboding.

God may be satisfied, he thought to himself, but the C.I.D. won't be. Finger-prints on the door of the Morris. Patient enquiries. Foul play is not suspected, of course, but —*Or isn't it?* Christ. It *could* look like a rape-and-murder case. Those bastards, there's nothing they'd think of quicker.

He lit a cigarette, considering this danger that now threatened the frontiers of his secret world.

Suppose I take a chance, he thought. No one *knows* I was with Celia. But I can't prove I wasn't, and I've got plenty of loving friends who'll be only too damned glad to drop broad hints in the right quarters. *Funny about poor Celia, wasn't it? Passed out on the job, by the look of it, old boy. Wonder who the man was? Confidentially, I heard she went around on the quiet with Jack Newhouse. New-house, eh? Well, well. Can't say I'm surprised. No, have this one on me.* And the whispers would spread, and

B

eventually it would get to the ears of the Faculty, and the College, and, ultimately, to Sarah.

Newhouse shivered.

It's no use kidding yourself the police won't catch on, either, he thought. Celia's going to hit the local headlines, all right, and the *News of the World* too, I shouldn't wonder. The situation's bad enough as it is, it'll look a bloody sight worse if I sit quiet till they come for me.

He frowned in concentration, weighing up pros and cons.

Look, he told himself, you haven't done anything criminal within the meaning of the act. If you go straight to the police now you'll be in the clear.

But oh Christ, the publicity. Everybody would know, it couldn't be kept quiet. Newhouse had a vision of scrawled newspaper posters in Oxford Street: *T.V. Don—Sensation.* The coldly polite request for his resignation. Averted eyes in the street. Facing Sarah and the children.

And Colin Sanderson.

Newhouse saw again Sanderson's heavy, angry, blue-jowled face on the tennis-court, the charging, baited bull, fifteen stone of bone and muscle. Janet Bowman's words came back to him: *He thinks you're a prize shit, period.* Well, Newhouse reflected bitterly, you can't say she didn't try to warn you off, boy. A bloody fine fix you've landed yourself in. Sit tight, and the odds are you'll find yourself up on a charge of rape and manslaughter. Go to the police, and even if they believe you, your career's finished anyway. Unless, unless they can be persuaded, somehow, to hush the whole thing up. But there'll have to be a coroner's inquest. They couldn't withhold material evidence. No, you're bitched, Jack, he told himself. Well and truly bitched. So what to do?

No choice, really.

He started the engine, eased the Humber out into the evening traffic of Lensfield Road, and drove to the nearest phone booth.

'Sarah? Look, I may be a bit late. Got to see a man.'

'How late?' Sarah asked.

'I don't know. Something turned up.'

Sarah said, wearily: 'I see.'

'You don't, you know,' Newhouse said. Keep it normal, he told himself. You're not done for yet. Take it all the way.

Sarah said: 'Are you quite sure it's a man, Jack?'

Newhouse shut his eyes. 'Oh yes, darling. It's a man all right.' A bloody meat-faced, nasty-minded, pig-eyed, sneering sod of a copper. Ha.

'It did occur to me,' Sarah said, carefully casual, 'that you might be with Celia Sanderson. Not,' she hastened to add, 'that it's any of my business, of course.'

Watch it, Newhouse thought. You never made any secret of your meetings with Celia, did you? Not all of them, anyway. Chamber concerts. The occasional film. All beautifully above board, chat about it afterwards, Celia said, etcetera, etcetera. England has nothing to hide.

He drew a deep breath and said, equally casually: 'What makes you think that?'

'Janet rang up a few minutes ago. She's running round in small circles because Celia dumped Rachel on her at five minutes' notice this afternoon, and hasn't shown up again to collect the poor kid.'

'So you thought of me.'

'That's right, Jack: I thought of you. So, I may add, did Janet.'

'What a poisonous gossiping bitch that woman is,' New-house said. He was sweating again now, and had difficulty in keeping his voice under control.

'Look,' Sarah said briskly, 'I don't give a damn if you've been holding Celia's hand in a tea-shop some-where——'

'Oh for God's sake, Sarah, don't be childish.'

'—what *I'm* concerned about is Rachel. Someone ought to take care of the poor kid, preferably her mother if she isn't otherwise engaged.'

'I'm not with Celia, and I'm not seeing Celia,' Newhouse said, a thin edge of hysteria creeping into his voice.

There was a slight pause at the other end of the line. Then Sarah said: 'All right, calm down, Jack: I'll believe you. Do you want me to leave you some supper in the oven?'

'Don't bother. I'll get a sandwich. I must go now, darling——'

'Goodbye, Jack,' Sarah said, and put the receiver down. Newhouse was left with the angry buzzing of a discon-nected line.

Despite its strip lighting and general air of efficiency, the police station was a dim, solid old-fashioned building, stone-walled, stone-flagged, and smelling faintly of Jeyes Fluid. Newhouse walked up to a constable scratching away laboriously in a ledger with a J-nib pen and said: 'I want to see the Duty Inspector, please.'

The constable looked up, appraising Newhouse carefully. 'Oh yes, sir? What might be the trouble?'

Newhouse swallowed. 'It's a—private matter,' he said.

The constable, who knew this kind of approach from long experience, grunted non-committally. 'The Inspector's busy just now, sir. Would you care to call back tomorrow morning?'

'No,' Newhouse said. 'I wouldn't. It's urgent.'

The constable raised one eyebrow, and reached for the phone on his desk.

'What name?' he enquired.

'Newhouse. Dr J. J. Newhouse.'

'All right, Doctor. See what we can do for you.'

You never know, Newhouse thought, when a Ph.D. will come in handy.

Two minutes later he was shown into a small office where a short, plump, uniformed man sat, ball-point in hand, staring despondently at the *Evening News* crossword.

'Dr Newhouse? My name's Potts. Anything I can do for you?' Cropped grey hair, red face, big spatulate fingers. 'Cigarette?'

'No thanks,' Newhouse said, and then hesitated, wondering how to begin. The Inspector's small, shrewd eyes never left his face.

Newhouse said, abruptly: 'There's a dead woman up in a wood on the Gogs.'

'Oh hell,' said Potts cheerfully, 'and I thought it was going to be a quiet evening. What happened, Doctor?'

'Look,' Newhouse said, 'you don't understand. I'm not that sort of doctor——'

'Ah,' Potts said, in a noticeably less amiable voice, 'something to do with the University, then, I take it?' He reached out one hairy paw for a scratch-pad.

Newhouse nodded. Christ, he thought, the bloody man looks like Sanderson. He's even got Sanderson's accent. I'm going to have a rough passage here.

'Now then, Doctor Newhouse,' Potts said, 'let's get this straight. When did you find the body?'

Newhouse said: 'I didn't find it, Inspector. I was there when—when she died. She was a friend of mine.'

'H'm,' Potts said, his face impassive. 'You'd better tell me what happened, then, hadn't you?'

Newhouse did so. When he had finished Potts said: 'I see.' He pressed a bell on his desk, and a young constable came in. 'Have a car brought round, Richards. Tell the Duty Surgeon and a photographer to stand by. And Sergeant Wilkins.'

When the constable had gone, Potts looked at Newhouse, an expression of sour distaste on his face. 'All right, Newhouse,' he said, 'let's go.' As they passed through the doorway he trod, heavily and excruciatingly, on Newhouse's heels. 'Sorry,' he said. 'Clumsy of me. This way.'

In the corridor Newhouse said: 'Inspector—does there have to be a lot of publicity over this business? It wouldn't do anyone any good—' His voice trailed off uncertainly.

'Some people,' Inspector Potts remarked, 'want to have their bloody cake and eat it. Christ, on your own account you've been screwing around for months with another man's wife till she bloody well died of it, and now you've got the nerve to ask me if I'll keep your dirty nose clean for you! There ought to be a law to keep bastards like you away from women. But there isn't, worse luck. So the least we can do is make damn sure the public's adequately warned, if you get my point.'

In the police car Newhouse sat hunched and silent, chin resting on his hands, with Potts on one side of him and the photographer on the other. *Qu'allais-je faire dans cette galère?* he wondered. How the hell did all this happen?

It's not true, it can't be true, oh God damn and blast it, why *me*? The car purred on through the darkness; the photographer lit a cigarette. Only when they turned off the main road on to the rough track did Potts say: 'Now then, wake up, sonny boy. It's all yours from now on.'

Newhouse peered ahead down the cone of light slashed by the Wolseley's powerful headlamps. Then he sat up, rigid, incredulous.

'The car's gone,' he said.

Potts was not impressed. 'If you left the bloody ignition key in it,' he said, 'I'm not surprised. Are we there yet?'

Newhouse nodded.

'All right, driver,' Potts said. They all got out. In the darkness Newhouse could hear branches creaking and scraping as the wind caught them. Somewhere an owl hooted.

'Here's a torch,' Potts said. 'On your way. We haven't got all night.'

Newhouse turned the sharp, narrow beam towards the fence, flickered it along till the gap showed, black and jagged.

'After you,' Potts said.

Newhouse scrambled through, and moved cautiously forward. An odd numbness had invaded his hands and features, similar to that induced by a dentist's injection. He ran his tongue over the dry roof of his mouth. Sounds seemed to come from a great distance, the wrong end of a long funnel. Nothing was real any more. Like a sleep-walker he advanced through the brushwood, barely conscious of the heavy-footed procession behind him, till he reached the three tall bushes where Celia and he had so often made love.

Now.

He dipped the torch. Its beam picked out dead leaves, moss, black humus, bracken.

'Well, well,' said Inspector Potts. 'Someone would seem to have been here before us, *Doctor* Newhouse. That is, if your imagination hasn't been working overtime.'

He took the torch from Newhouse and turned it, blindingly, into his face.

'No, you don't look very much like a practical joker, I'll give you that. Just take a dekko, will you, Wilkins?'

The big sergeant dropped down on hands and knees at the edge of the hollow. The photographer set up his tripod and took a couple of flashlight photographs.

Potts lit a cigarette while this was going on. 'Well,' he said to Newhouse, 'does your educated mind have any explanation to offer?'

Newhouse shook his head.

Potts blew out clouds of smoke. 'You disappoint me, *Doctor* Newhouse. I doubt if you're the only bright boy who comes up here for a quick bash on the quiet. If you ask me, which you haven't, some Good Samaritan's stumbled over your girl-friend and run her down to Addenbrooke's. That'll make another witness for the inquest, *and* a good juicy front-page story when the reporters get hold of it.

He walked over to the photographer, feet crunching through the leaves.

'Any joy, Wilkins?' he said.

'*Someone's* been here, all right, sir,' the sergeant said.

'Yes. Doesn't help us much, does it?'

'No, sir.'

'All right, back to the car. Unless we've got an amateur

body-snatcher on our hands, whoever shifted this lot'll be on the blower to us before the evening's out.'

'Right, sir.'

Half-way back to Cambridge Potts woke up from some unimaginable private reverie and said to Newhouse, almost chattily: 'I read a ghost story once, never forgotten it.'

Newhouse blinked, speechless.

'This ghost,' Potts said, warming to his theme, 'sent a message to some chap, in Latin. How did it go? Oh yes— *"Si tu non venies ad me——"*'

'*"Ego veniam ad te"*' Newhouse said. 'M. R. James.'

'What it is to be well-read,' Potts said. 'Know what the Latin means, eh, *Doctor* Newhouse?'

Newhouse said, in a low voice: '"If you don't come to me, I shall come to you".'

'That's it. Appropriate, don't you think?'

No one said anything else till they were back outside the police station in Regent Street.

'Now then,' Potts said, rubbing his hands, 'we'll see what's been happening.' He led Newhouse into a drab little waiting room. 'Stay there till I call for you,' he said, and vanished. Newhouse sat down, sick and exhausted, almost beyond coherent thought. The electric clock on the wall caught his eye. Half past seven. Sanderson must be back by now. By tomorrow the news would have broken. At this very moment, in all probability, Celia was lying on a mortuary slab, while a pair of proletarian lovers explained, over and over again, how they'd just happened to be walking through the wood, like, when they saw—Oh yes, Newhouse thought grimly, we know what they saw, all right. No, on second thoughts, *not* proles, they'd never have had the gumption to move the body or take the car.

Some energetic bloody undergraduate more likely, bursting with initiative and *esprit de corps*, fine officer material, oh yes, showing off to his pallid metaphysical Girtonian girlfriend, driving in at Addenbrooke's, all scarf and dashing self-importance, look, old boy, we've got a stiff in the back, can you cope?

Oh, hell take the whole impossible situation.

Newhouse lit a cigarette, coughed drily, feeling already the cold finger of ostracism pointing, wondering how long he could fend off the awful and inevitable scenes with Sarah and Sanderson, staring into a future of nothingness.

Potts came in and said: 'Well, that's the lot for now. Sorry to have kept you so long.' There was an expression of amused malice on his face, and something else, something Newhouse could not analyse.

He said, bewildered: 'Have they found——?'

'Mrs Sanderson? Oh yes,' Potts said, 'we know where Mrs Sanderson is now.'

'For God's sake, where?'

'That,' Potts said, enjoying his authority, 'is a police matter, and I'm under no obligation to tell you. If I were you, I should go home and get some sleep. You look as though you could do with it. We shall be in touch with you if and when we need you.'

'But the inquest——' Newhouse said.

'Dr Newhouse, I've told you to go home. You've made your statement. To the best of my knowledge you haven't committed an indictable offence, whatever my private opinion of your behaviour may be. We aren't going to lock you up, or even ask for bail. You aren't charged with a single damned thing, and I don't intend,' Potts added, with unexpected insight, 'to shove you in a cell just to satisfy your nasty sense of guilt. Is that clear? Right. On your way.'

It was bitterly cold outside, and Newhouse switched on the heater in the Humber. Market Hill, Sidney Street, Magdalen Bridge, turn left at the traffic lights. Up the Madingley Road, into Grange Road, ghostly now under its intermittent street lights, large comfortable Victorian houses mocking his predicament with their unassailable solidity. Newhouse suddenly remembered a court-martial that had been held on his station in Burma during the war. Every morning the accused—a cocky little ex-fighter pilot turned Equipment Officer—was grilled for three or four hours in a spare Nissen hut behind the hangers. When lunch-time came, he and his tormentors sat down together at the same mess-table, and were studiously polite to each other as protocol required. And that, Newhouse thought, is just about what'll happen in this case.

He garaged the car, carefully locked up, sorted out his front door key, walked through into the kitchen: each familiar movement was invested now with a sense of un- reality, the comforting paraphernalia of domestic life seemed withdrawn and alien. So might a ghost feel, Newhouse thought wrily, when it first came back to the house it knew in life.

Sarah was sitting at the kitchen table, reading. She had on an old yellow blouse and a pair of black slacks, very tight and tapering at the ankles. Her untidy auburn hair was scraped back in a Grecian knot; black-rimmed harlequin glasses gave her long, freckle-sanded face an air of *faux- diablerie*, masking the vulnerablity of her restless eyes. Newhouse had once told her she looked like a Bloomsbury authoress after a week's screwing around the Left Bank, and had watched in huge delight while she made up her mind whether to take this as a compliment or an insult. A half-empty bottle of gin stood beside her, and the moment she spoke Newhouse saw that she was in that mildly slurred state which she called 'adjusting the balance'—normality for her being, as she often said, two gins below par.

She said: 'There's some shepherd's pie in the oven if you'd like it.'

Newhouse went to the dresser and got down a new bottle of whisky from the top shelf. He poured out a tumblerful and drank half of it, neat.

'Yes,' he said. 'I'd like that.'

A pleasant steamy smell filled the kitchen. Newhouse sat down and stared at the concave blue-and-white china face of the Dutch clock on the wall. Its tick sounded unusually loud. He took another gulp of whisky.

Sarah dumped a bubbling casserole dish on the table, took out plate, knife and fork, and left Newhouse to help himself. She said: 'I suppose it's no use asking where you've been all this time.' It was a statement rather than a question.

Newhouse helped himself to shepherd's pie, and began to poke at it aimlessly with his fork. He said: 'Where are the girls?'

'Next door at the Griersons', watching the telly. There was some programme, I don't know——'

'Late for them.'

'Yes. They ought to be back any minute.'

Newhouse put his head in his hands.

'Jack darling—what on earth's the matter? You look terrible.'

She came round the table to him. Newhouse could smell

the gin on her breath. For a moment he held her close; then
he broke away and walked over to the sink, shoulders shaking. ·He turned on the cold tap and splashed his face with
water, postponing the inevitable moment.

He said, harshly: 'You've got to know sooner or later.
I was with Celia this afternoon, you were right.'

'Oh dear,' Sarah said, eyes glinting behind harlequin
frames, 'since when have you developed a conscience about
things like that? It's not in character, darling. And frankly
it's rather a bore. I hope you aren't sickening for something.'

Newhouse stared at her. 'You mean you *know*?' he said,
dully.

'Of course I know. So does half Cambridge, I should
think. Look, your supper's getting cold.'

'And you don't *care*?'

Sarah said, patiently: 'If you want me to play the jealous
wife, Jack, you've picked the wrong girl. I don't give a
damn how many women you sleep with as long as you don't
get bored with me in the process.' She moved towards him,
cat-like, tight and neat in her black slacks. 'And you're not
bored, Jack, are you? You want me. At this very moment
you want me like hell. I know you. You want me, and you
need me. That's all that matters.'

'For Christ's sake,' Newhouse said, 'this is serious. I'm
trying to tell you——'

'Don't say this time you're going to leave me, Jack.
Don't pull the old romantic line after all your cosy discreet
little affairs. I expected better than that. Do you think it
worries *me* if you've got to boost your virility by being
a kind of erotic Walter Mitty? I'm sorry for you, Jack,
God knows I'm sorry for you. I was quite happy for you to

enjoy your little dream-world, why not? But at least keep
the courage of your convictions.'

Newhouse said: 'My God, Sarah. You know. You've
always known, haven't you?'

'Yes,' said Sarah, a singularly sweet smile spreading over
her face, 'I've always known. A nasty surprise, isn't it?
Take the edge off your little peccadilloes in future, I
shouldn't wonder. You're a terribly respectable creature at
heart, Jack. You're like that girl in *Under Milk Wood*—
you know, the one who wanted to sin and sin and sin until
she blew up. Just another *bourgeois* husband worried about
his virility and after a little secret romance. Not very world-
shaking is it? I always think Casanova must have been
rather a feeble bore, too.'

'All right,' Newhouse said, savagely, 'see if you're so
bloody smug and prim and academic when you hear what
I've got to tell you. Nothing really *happens* in your world,
does it? Everything's talk, ideas, blah. You can take the
sting out of any sort of horror by making an intellectual
joke about it——'

Sarah flushed, vulnerable now, suddenly on the defensive.
'There wasn't much else I could do, was there?' she said,
eyes blinking. 'I loved you, Jack. I still love you. You're
my husband, and I'm going to make our marriage stick if
it's the last thing I do, can't you see that? I can't and won't
divorce you. If I leave you the failure's as much mine as
yours.'

'Spoken like a true Catholic wife,' Newhouse said, more
moved than he cared to admit, trembling now on the frantic
edge of hysterical collapse. He sat down again, hands
clutching the edge of the table. 'All right, my God, you'd
better dig into your principles now, because you're going

to need them, Sarah. You're going to need everything you've got.'

She looked at him, eyes steady, arms folded. 'All right, Jack,' she said, quietly. 'Tell me.'

Newhouse swallowed. 'I was with Celia this afternoon,' he said, reaching for breath, the words like stones in his throat. 'We made love. She—she had a heart-attack. I've just been with the police.'

There was a short silence. Then Sarah said: 'You mean she's dead.'

Newhouse nodded.

Sarah said: 'You're sure? They confirmed it at the hospital?' Her voice had a controlled calm about it that was more terrifying than any hysterical accusation could have been.

'No—I—I don't know.'

Sarah drew in her breath. She said: '*You left her there. My God, Jack. You left her there.*'

Newhouse began to sob, horrible, grinding, blubbering sobs that racked his entire body. 'Sarah—don't look at me like that—I was thinking of you—the scandal——'

Sarah hit him twice across the face, forehand and back-hand, with all the strength in her body.

'Oh no, Jack,' she said. 'There was only one thing you were thinking of.' She looked at Newhouse as though she had never seen him before.

Newhouse stared back at her, cheeks wealed an angry red, tears of pain and despair trickling from his eyes. He stretched out his arms in a helpless, appealing gesture and said: 'It's now I need you Sarah. Don't abandon me now. Please. Please. Not now.'

Sarah said: 'You abandoned Celia.'

'She was dead, can't you understand? We're alive.'

For, lambkins, we will live.

'Are we, Jack? Are we?' Sarah grimaced as though she had swallowed a dose of quinine. 'Have we ever been alive?'

'For the love of God, Sarah——'

'You've never cared about the love of God till now, Jack. You've never understood what humiliation means, either. You humiliated me again and again, and never knew you'd done it. That was the worst thing of all.'

Newhouse was crying openly and hopelessly now, like a small abandoned child, face distorted, fists doubled up.

Sarah said: 'I'm leaving you, Jack. I'm taking the children away, and leaving you. You can go through with this on your own.'

Newhouse raised a swollen, tear-stained face. 'But you said——'

'Can't you see *why*?' Sarah exclaimed, violently. 'Can't you *still* see why?'

The telephone bell in the hall cut across their silence like a knife.

Sarah looked at Newhouse, hesitated for a second, shrugged, and walked out of the kitchen. Newhouse heard her say: 'Yes, hullo—*who*?', and her voice was so strange that he got up and followed her, blowing his nose vigorously.

'Fine, thank you,' Sarah was saying, as though in a dream. She glanced at Newhouse, her face drained and blank. 'He's here now,' she said, in the same bright, tinny, social voice. 'Would you like a word with him?' She held out the receiver to Newhouse, who took it mechanically.

'Hullo Jack,' said Celia Sanderson. 'I hope I didn't surprise you.'

Newhouse stared at Sarah, wild-eyed.

'Celia?' The word emerged as a curious strangulated croak.

Celia laughed, nastily.

'Oh dear. You *do* sound upset. Are you sweating, Jack? I hope you're sweating. You bastard,' she added, with sudden fierce venom.

'What—? How——?'

'Just a little experiment, Jack. I never dreamed it'd be quite so successful. Oh yes, I had an attack, that was real enough. A very mild one. Very mild indeed. In fact, to be quite honest, Jack, it was all over in about ten seconds. The merest *twinge*, really, you'll doubtless be glad to hear. And I thought, as it was going off, *Let's see what lover-boy does now, shall we?* The moment of truth, Jack. The kill-or-cure treatment.'

Newhouse said nothing. Sarah never took her eyes from his face.

'Are you listening, Jack?' Celia Sanderson said. 'I'd hate you to miss a minute of this.'

'Yes,' Newhouse said, in a flat whisper. 'I'm listening.'

Celia said: 'You never came close enough to find out if I was still breathing, did you? Not even that. The noble adulterer in a moment of crisis. I ought to be grateful to you in a way, Jack. I'm cured of you. Finally and completely cured.'

There was a long pause.

'Nothing to say for yourself, Jack? How unusual. From all I can gather, you've been talking quite a lot this evening. *Pity you didn't keep quiet a bit longer, isn't it?*' Celia laughed. She sounded genuinely amused. 'I had a delight-ful chat with your Inspector Potts when he rang up. He sounds rather fun. And to judge from poor Sarah's voice just now, you've been busy preparing *her* for the worst, too.'

Newhouse said: 'Have you told——?'

'Colin? Oh no. Not on your sweet life. We're all going to go on living here, Jack, good friends and neighbours. Isn't that a charming, civilised prospect? No melodrama, no horse-whipping, nothing like that at all. This is Cam-bridge, Jack: remember? If you don't tell Colin—not that I think you're likely to—no one will. You'll have to find some other outlet for your beastly sense of guilt.'

Newhouse said: 'I'm sorry, Celia. Oh God, I'm so sorry.'

'You're all right, Jack,' Celia said, with unconscious irony. 'Your precious career's safe, isn't it? Just be a bit more careful in future, that's all. Goodnight.'

The line went dead.

Sarah said: 'I'm still leaving you, Jack.'

'There's no need.' A surge of exhilarated relief spread through Newhouse's body. It's all right, he thought. *It's all right.* 'We'll sleep on it,' he said, blowing his nose again, confident now, the horror fading, the future clear. 'You'll feel different in the morning.'

'I won't, you know,' Sarah said. 'Don't kid yourself, Jack. Not this time.'

Newhouse moved towards her, arms outstretched.

'No,' Sarah said, in a cold, small voice. 'That trick won't work any more. You've played it once too often.'

At the bottom of the stairs she paused. 'I'm going to sleep in the spare room,' she said.

The front door bell rang.

Newhouse said: 'That'll be the girls. Sarah, for God's sake, you can't——'

'Yes,' Sarah said, 'I can and I will.' She went slowly up the stairs.

Newhouse exhaled deeply, putting this tiresome problem out of his mind. It'll be all right tomorrow, he told himself. Everything will look different tomorrow. I'll take the girls to early Mass and by breakfast-time Sarah's bound to have come round. It's just the shock. Sarah's been in worse stews before and got over them. He glanced round at the friendly, familiar bric-a-brac that littered the hall. Things haven't changed, he told himself. Not really. He ran a comb quickly through his hair, rehearsing what he would say to Miriam and Sharon. Mummy's feeling a bit tired, poppets, so she's gone up to bed early. Mustn't make too much noise. No, nothing bad, just a headache. Now if you're good girls you can come and have some shepherd's pie in the kitchen, and then Daddy'll give you your baths as a special treat.

I might read to them for a bit in bed afterwards, he thought, a virtuous glow spreading through him. With a light, cheerful step he went to the front door and opened it.

You have to give old Jack one thing, his friends said when taking his character to pieces: he really is mad about those two girls of his.

PROOF OF IDENTITY

SWEETIE, I'm so glad you could make lunch to day—I do think it's a relief to have a nice meal out just once in a while without a *man* organising the whole thing. It's simply ages since we've had the chance for a good long chat. Two dry martinis, please, Raymond—I know you adore them, darling, and they do them really well here, but *sweating* cold, and no nonsense about three-to-one, Raymond says they just take a bit of lemon and dip it in Martini and rub it round the glass like garlic. Well, cheers, anyway. I know you're not supposed to say *that* these days, ever since that woman started off about mirrors and note-paper and mantel-pieces, but honestly, poppet, I've never fancied being dictated to by weedy little pansy couturiers, let alone *her*, and I wear my skirt what length I like and I'm too old to learn new tricks these days. Well, almost too old.

Darling, I *know* it's our wedding anniversary today—and bless you for that *sweet* piece of silver, Michael and I both adored it, it was nice of you to remember. I mean, quite often I forgot it myself, and after fifteen years I'm beginning to wish I could even when I don't, if you see what I mean. Look, let's have the smoked trout, shall us? And then fillet steak and salad. Have to watch the old figure these days. All right, Raymond, medium rare for *madame*

53

and make mine *bleu*, same as usual. And another round of martinis. Yes, I know they are, but you have to draw the line *somewhere* over this calorie racket.

Anyway, poppet, I know you're just *dying* to hear why we're sitting nattering away in this classy dive today of all days—I mean, anniversary and all that, Darby and bloody Joan ought to be holding hands in the Caprice, getting nostalgic about the Thirties. Yes, all right, that was rather a sick-making idea. *Raymond!* Two more— oh, you have. How clever you are, Raymond. Ducky, it does pay to go to a place regularly, don't you think? Well, no, I suppose you don't often in that teaching job. Remember at school when we both decided to be film-stars? Lot or dirty water under the bridges since then, h'm?

It's all a bit complicated, really. I mean, I've got to lead up to it. You would? You *are* sweet. I couldn't tell just *anyone*. Too blush-making, you've no idea. Here goes, then. It began a year ago last September, when the firm had just made Michael a director—yes, darling, I do remember your letter, it was *sweet* of you. Now where was I? Oh yes. Well, the idea was that dear Michael, as a sort of proof of his elevation, as you might say, should be sent out on a fortnight's tour of the Bordeaux area—poke about in the vineyards and have a spot of sip-and-spit instead of squatting in Leadenhall Street unravelling import-export knots, whatever *they* are. I mean till then they hardly let Michael sniff at a *bung-hole*, dear, just kept him anchored to his desk with reams of bumph-work piling up and a wall-eyed secretary to make sure he didn't nip out to Gow's for a quick dozen of Whitstables when there was an R in the month.

Still, virtue was rewarded at last, and no mistake. To

hear old Conroy going on you'd have thought they'd just filled a vacancy in the bloody French Academy. Michael this and Michael that, and my dear boy you must bring your charming wife round for a spot of, and well Michael I must say Caroline is everything a Director's wife should be, as though Michael was Caesar instead of Conroy's long-suffering Production Manager who once—don't mention this to a *soul*, dear—just contrived to keep the old sod out of clink by the length of his well-groomed short back hairs. No, I don't think he actually *cooked the books*, dear, what a revolting phrase that is, but what I mean is, he'd really earned his place on that Board the hard way. So when he asked if I was covered on this expenses jag Conroy was all smiles and affability. Well, actually, he had sort of rubbed my knee at dinner the week before, nothing really, but it may have made a difference, I don't know. No, sweetie, of course I didn't *encourage* him, he's nearly seventy. But I'll admit I didn't exactly withdraw the hem of my garment, either.

So it was all fixed, and Michael was given special leave of absence, and they agreed to the last fortnight in September because Roger and Jane would both be back at boarding-school by then. Boarding schools are one of the brightest English institutions I know. But the funny thing was, I got the feeling old Mike was a bit put out when Conroy came up with the double-bunk stuff and no objections. Not to mention the fact that his first choice of date was *early* September, when I'd still have had the kiddos around the place. Which set little Caroline thinking, I regret to say. I mean, dear, after fifteen years—well, *you* know. Oh—no, I suppose you don't. Sorry, I forgot. Look, what about a spot of Nuits St Georges with that steak? Good-oh. Can't have been very cosy nights with that socking great dragon around, I shouldn't think. That's right, Raymond, the '53. Number 37 on your delicious little list.

The funny thing was, darling, I really was thrilled to bits by the whole shooting match. I hadn't been abroad often, we couldn't afford it with the children and the car and everything, and I'm no use on my own, or at organising things. Clinging feminine type, that's me. Leave all the work to the lord-and-master, he adores it. Butters his male ego up no end. So when the great day came I was in a fine old tizz and no mistake. We'd got the packing finished the night before, but there were all the last minute tiddly-bits, *you* know—sponge-bags and that sort of stuff. And then I thought—I remember, I was just stirring the scrambled eggs, and Michael was in the bathroom shaving—I thought, Look, ducky, you'd better make sure your passport's O.K., it's the only thing you're responsible for and if you make a nonsense of *that* there'll be no end of a rumpus from his lordship. You've no idea how tidy and precise Michael is. Drives me potty sometimes, but I suppose it's just as well with me the way I am.

So I looked in my bag, and there, as they say, it wasn't. I shot out every damn thing, and it still wasn't. Blast, I thought, it must be up in the bedroom. But I didn't really believe it, even then. I'd got that horrid sinking feeling in the tum that Bovril makes no difference to whatever they say on the advertisement hoardings. I shot upstairs two at a time leaving the scrambled eggs to their fate. I'd just turned out the drawers in my dressing-table for the third time, in that compulsive way you get when it's clear to anyone but a cretin that the thing you want just *isn't there* and why the hell don't you admit it, when there was a howl from the bathroom and Michael shot in dripping blood all over the carpet. The silly old poop had first nicked his Adam's apple, which wasn't surprising when you think of its size, and it's a wonder he doesn't do it more often, and then cut two fingers to the *bone* getting the blade out of his razor—why he wanted to God knows, probably felt he had to give it a good talking-to or something. So I had to set to and patch him up, and then there were those eggs to deal with, pretty far gone they were too by the time we got downstairs, belching smoke all over the kitchen—No, love, we hadn't moved to Chelsea then, we were still in that dreary old Victorian horror on Wimbledon Common.

Well, I couldn't put off telling him any longer—I mean, we were due at London Airport in an hour or so, and it's not exactly an easy drive. So if he was going to blow, he'd just have to do it and get it over with. I remember thinking in a silly way, help, there's that old A.R.P. helmet of mine up in the attic, might come in handy for dodging flying splinters. But the funny thing was, he didn't blow at all. Honestly, I've never been so taken aback in all my life. A bit irritated, and who wouldn't be, but mostly, believe it or not, *sorry* for me. Well, that made me think pretty furiously too, later, but at the time I was so relieved I just didn't register. I said to him hopefully, Oh well darling, maybe there's some form or other the passport control chaps can give me at the airport, and Michael said, not so hopefully, We can *try*, anyway, and after that we bundled our gubbins into the boot of the old Alvis, and locked up the house, and pootled off in the general direction of Twickenham. Another thing about Michael, he can take short cuts in London without ever getting lost. It nearly sends me out of my mind, but we always seem to get there on time. Sorry about that steak, darling. Sure it isn't your knife needs sharpening?

Honestly, London Airport is enough to give you the twitches at the best of times—miles from anywhere, and all those tannoys and escalators and *guichets*, if that's the word I want, and people scurrying around like *mice*, dear, and voices intoning about Flight number XYZ one-eight-five being about to depart and will passengers for Pernambuco go to departure door fourteen-B and can Frau Wiener Schnitzel see the immigration officials in Room 101, just like something out of Kafka or *1984*, and Have all Your Documents Ready for Inspection. You can imagine what it was like when my documents *weren't*. The curious thing was, they were all *much* more polite to me when they found out. A nice character in something rather like a chauffeur's uniform said Come in here, please, and Do take a seat, Mrs Barlow, and Let's see if we can sort this out and I thought it was going to be all right, especially when they laid on coffee, but of course it wasn't. Nothing for it, I'm afraid, Mrs Barlow, says this character cheerfully, you'll just have to get another passport. Shouldn't take you all that long. And then the tannoy went with all that blah-blah-blah about passengers for Bordeaux and I realised it was our plane.

Look, darling, Michael says, in a reasonable, man-of-the-world way, we can't let *both* reservations go, the best thing is for me to catch this plane and you to follow on afterwards, isn't it? And before I can open my mouth the official chap is gathering up Michael's bag and overcoat and hooshing him out of the door and saying Yes, yes, quite agree, best line you can take, Mr Barlow, and Michael blows me a fine old thank-God-I-have-done-my-duty sort of farewell kiss,

and that's that. As a special treat the official tells me there's
a waiting list for this Bordeaux plane so I needn't pay for
my seat twice over, just have the reservation transferred.
Well, I thought, rather dazed, I suppose that's one con-
solation. Then Michael's plane was airborne and there
was I sitting on my poop in this mad great place that looks
like something out of *Things to Come* and wondering what
to do next.

I think it was at this point that I began to enjoy myself.
I mean, the kids were at school, and Michael was very
effectively out of reach for the time being, and I was
really on my own for once. It made me realise how seldom I
was, in the normal way of things. And damn it, I thought,
I'm not a schoolgirl, I'm Caroline Barlow, aged, let's face
it, thirty-nine, with two teen-age children and a mind of
my own. And the first thing, I told myself, is to beat all
these bogeys about *not being able to cope with practical
details*. Well, honestly, when I got down to it it was a
pushover. Complicated, but no harder than making a
bombe surprise, say. First of all there was the business of
booking another flight. This was Friday morning, and it
turned out there wasn't another direct flight till the following Monday. You mean to say, I told the booking clerk,
that all the resources of this latter-day Crystal Palace can't
get me to Bordeaux before then? I listened to my voice
admiringly, it sounded like someone else talking. I'm afraid
not, madam, he says. You think again, sonny, says this
deutero-Caroline. Do a little homework, pronto. So he
scrabbles in some time-tables and finally comes up with a
makeshift scheme that just about fits the bill. It seems there's
a late afternoon flight to Paris, six o'clock or thereabouts,
that'll give me time to pick up a train to Bordeaux at the

Gare d'Austerlitz. Right, I tell him, you fix me for that flight or I'll fix you. And I want a refund on the train-fare.

So that was that, and off I went to get a new passport. First of all I had to persuade the chap at the garage that I was me, because he obviously wasn't used to people parking their car for a fortnight and then digging it out of cold storage again an hour later. But by now there was nothing could stop me, but nothing. I talked a blue streak at the poor little man and was nosing the Alvis through the main gates five minutes later, feeling I could take on Monroe, Bardot and the rest of that sleazy old gang with one hand tied behind me. I drove back into London, and found somewhere to park in Petty France, where the Passport Office is. That was no mean feat in itself, come to think of it. Then I thought, aha, the photograph, they're not going to catch me on that one, so I trotted round to a little man in Victoria. He had nasty breath and, to judge by the look of him, a nasty mind to match. But he did his stuff, and back I shot to Petty France, clutching the usual packet of wanted-for-murder portraits, and beginning to feel I could do with a spot of lunch. There was a queue inside about fifty yards long. It didn't seem to be moving much. When it finally disgorged me at the *guichet* I made it close on one o'clock. And then, dear heaven, the first thing the chap wanted to see was my birth certificate. *Well, I ask you.* I waved my brand new photos at him rather feebly, but that only made things worse. I suppose, he said, not at all sympathetic, I suppose you know you've got to get those vouched for as a genuine likeness by some responsible person?

He rattled this little speech off as though he'd made it quite a few times that morning, and then I was elbowed aside by a Lithuanian dwarf, or something, *et voilà*, as they say. Try the *meringue Chantilly*, darling; they make it out of real cream and eggs here. I wonder how many of the dear G.B.P. know that the things they get in Old Englysshe tea-shoppes under the name of meringues are mainly rendered-down fish-glue? Not that I suppose many of them would mind much if they *did* know. Honestly, the way people in this country treat their stomachs appals me sometimes.

So there I was, out on the pavement again. I nipped across the road into a pub obviously designed to cater for this sort of emergency, and treated myself to two double whiskys and a Scotch egg. The whiskys did wonders for my morale and the Scotch egg played absolute hell with my digestion. Everyone in the bar looked at me for just a weeny bit too long, if you get me, and I thought: Blimey, how long is it since I've been in a pub on my own? Then I worked it out just for the hell of it, and got depressed again.

But by now it was rising two o'clock. Back I went to bloody Wimbledon Common, having shaken its dreary dust off my feet for two whole weeks, *I* thought, and merry hell the trip was too, with all that urgent lunch-time traffic weaving and snorting around the place. My birth certificate turned up all right, after a bit of prodding around, sandwiched between a Stratford Festival programme dated 1938 and a pamphlet printed in a sort of Anglo-Japanese telling you just how to calculate your safe period, not that I ever understood a word of it, and later I wished I had. *That's* done, anyhow, I said, and had another double Scotch out of our special reserve stock, just for luck.

Now then, Caroline my girl, I said into the drawing-room mirror (a long gilt-framed thing, rather fly-blown, a present from Michael's mum, and it looked like it), now : can you honestly claim to know anyone *responsible*? My reflection shook its head, and giggled. I looked at my watch. Two-forty-five. Banks shut at three—Why, of course. My dear, dear bank manager. Friend of my bosom and my overdraft. Harry Milman, I told my reflection, you may be bald and pot-bellied and spend your spare time sexing chicks or cross-pollinating azaleas or something equally Freudian, but oh my God no one could say you weren't respectable. So. But there, sweetie, was where I had another of my little illusions shattered, because when I nipped into the old bank just before closing time friend Harry wasn't back yet. After a little pressure the Chief Cashier, who's got a soft spot for me, opined that I *might* just catch Mr Milman at the Pink Cockatoo, which is one of those cosy little expense-account clip-joints that tries to be Chelsea and can't quite make it. And sure enough, there the old rip was, together with a gorgeous little number done up in real zombie *à la mode* style, like a death-mask crowned with a bloody bee-hive. Well of course, they *might* have been discussing the relative methods of computer automation and double-column ledger-work, you never can tell these days, can you?

Why hullo Mr Milman I beamed at him, long time no see! Honestly, I just couldn't restrain myself. I suppose it must have been the Scotch, or something. Really, I was scared his eyes were going to pop out of his head right on to the plate with the bill, and in the Pink Cockatoo he'd never have got them back, either, they'd have served them up to some half-wit American as *Escargots de Boulogne*. But when I told him I wasn't going to stay more than a *second* and would he scribble something to the effect that these jail-house snaps were truly *me*, and, flutter-flutter of eyelashes, we could always trust each other, couldn't we? then the old penny dropped and he whipped out his Parker and got to work right away. Signed and sealed with a loving double brandy, too, bless him. The bee-hive, whose name I gathered was Miss Ponce-Ascot or something, I suppose it *couldn't* have been, but that's what it sounded like, just sat and gawped. She opened her mouth precisely twice, to say Hullo and Goodbye, which emerged from those bloodless lips as Haugh and Baugh. Poor Harry. I suppose he knew what he was doing.

The brandy settled down quite nicely with the Scotch, and the trip back to Petty France seemed to pass in a *flash*, dear, with everyone being *terribly* helpful, and all the lights in my favour. And what do you know, the queue had practically melted away, and all my papers were in order, and I got my lovely precious new passport in half an hour dead. I beamed at the chap who handed it over, I beamed at the commissionaire, I'd even have hugged Selwyn Lloyd if he'd been within range for saying nice things about me inside the front cover. Fancy a member of Her Britannic Majesty's Honourable Privy Council requesting all those whom it might concern to allow me to pass freely without let and hindrance, and all that gun-boat hoo-ha! Anyway, there it was: proof of identity. As far as the little men in peaked caps were concerned, I *existed* again. And I felt it, too. I'd never felt so gloriously *me* in all my life.

I lost some of this first careless rapture on the second run out to London Airport—I mean, no one can be expected to do *that* trip more than once a day—but by the time I'd garaged the old Alvis again and gone swaggering through Customs and Passport Control (ha!) without a care in the world, and been weighed in and rigged out with all those little bits of bumph, I was pretty well back on form again. Besides which I'd managed to fit in another brandy from that gorgeous bar they've got there. And talking of brandy, poppet, what about a spot of Armagnac to go with your coffee?

So I trotted off to the loo and fixed my face, and out I came ready for my plunge into the Unknown, my twenty-four hours escapade into furrin parts, solo and fancy-free. I remembered Michael had told me once, If you're ever going by plane, queue early, then you can be sure of a rear seat. There were only three chaps who'd had the same idea so far. The one in front of me was a shortish character, very broad and dark. I noticed him first of all because of his shiny white mac. It really was something, that garment. All belts and buttons and pockets, with a kind of scolloped cape effect under the shoulder-blades. Brand-new, too; you could almost smell the tissue paper. And shine, my God, I reckon he was luminous in the dark, like a decaying kipper. I stared at the back of this chap's neck, and caught a nice whiff of aftershave lotion. I remember thinking: You're Italian or Spanish, and you need a haircut, my lad. He didn't turn round, but the funny thing was, I could feel him sizing *me* up too, God knows how. Maybe he had a pocket periscope. Anyway, a moment later he ducked out of the queue to ask one of the gold-braid boys something. I just caught a glimpse of a brown, chunky face and thick black eyebrows before the loudspeaker began its usual unintelligible blare—have you ever noticed how a chap talking on one of those things seems to lose all his consonants in some mysterious way?—and the queue started to surge forward, bleating faintly as it was shepherded and corralled.

Well, there I was, almost the first aboard, and remembering Michael's advice I made smartly for the furthest back seat I could find. I slung my little bag into the rack and plunked myself down by the porthole thing, and thought in a rather unpatriotic way, Well, this is about the best view of London I can imagine at the moment, especially when you remember what that particular chunk of ribbon-suburbia looks like. Then someone dumped a book in the empty seat next to mine. Funnily enough I looked at the title before I noticed the owner. It was a collection of historical essays by that chap who didn't quite find Hitler at the end of the war, and collected a very sizable load of lolly by reconstructing *Der Führer's* final moments on this earth. Someone told me they've made him a Professor of History at Oxford, which only goes to show you, doesn't it, dear? I mean, who says those old dreaming spires don't move with the times?

Of course, the next thing I spotted was the shiny white mac, and then there was that square brown face bending down over me, very gallant and respectful, and another whiff of aftershave lotion, and a voice, with only a faint trace of accent, saying Would the *Signora* very kindly permit? Whereupon the *Signora*, being caught off-balance if ever a girl was, smiled graciously—as he knew bloody well she would—and said, Of course, please do, and then turned away very hurriedly and stared hard out of the porthole thing for a bit, and had a rather flustered think.

You see, on the one hand there was a wicked little voice rampaging away in the back of my head, I suppose being left in charge of myself for once and tearing round about the place and knocking back a lot of alc and not all that much food must have sort of let it out of its kennel, and this voice was whispering awful all-too-persuasive nothings at me, such as Nice face, and No moustache thank God, and Anyway what harm could there possibly be in it, *that* sort of line. And Mrs Michael Barlow was answering, in a serious, stuffy sort of way, Look here, I'm an old married woman with two strapping great children and I've always been faithful to my husband and this is the first time anything like this has happened and I'm not sure I like it, in fact I definitely *don't*. And the voice answered, more insidious than ever, Well, you may be an Old Faithful, but are you so sure about Michael? And that one was a facer, dear, because you see I *wasn't*, not by a long chalk. There'd been far too many little bits of evidence all pointing in the same direction. So the Mrs Barlow voice said, rather less certainly, Look, anyway, I don't *know* anything, and I'm damned well not doing anything myself till I do. Oh, says the other voice, quick as a flash, so you do *want* to do something, eh? You're getting me all muddled, the Mrs Barlow voice protested. On the contrary, the little voice whispers, I'm getting you nicely straightened out. Tell me, in confidence, when did you last really enjoy a spot of you-know-what with Michael? *Really*, the Mrs B. voice said, I hardly think—Well, the other voice chips in, that's a pretty fair answer, isn't it? And you've got to admit, this white-mac character has a certain virile charm. Look, girl, get wise to yourself. Why do you think you're so excited about this little escapade of yours? Because you were all set for a nice, harmless, ships-that-pass-in-the-night flirtation. Now weren't you? Be honest. And the Mrs B. voice said, Well, actually, yes, and giggled. And the other voice said, Right, you dope, get on with it.

And at that moment the engines started up, one after an-

other, and that little notice was flashed on saying PLEASE
FASTEN YOUR SAFETY BELTS, and I began to
wrestle rather feebly with mine, wondering why on earth
they had to make the buckle thingummy so outlandishly
complicated. At which point, sweetie, as no doubt you'll
have guessed, a voice, outside my head this time, murmured
Scusi and two very brown hands flipped that safety belt
together in a way that suggested their owner made a
regular habit of air travel. There was a big gold signet
ring on the appropriate finger of the left hand, too, which
somehow appeased the Mrs B. in me, though looking
back I can't really see why; morally I suppose it made things
twice as bad, but then puritan housewives always want to
have their cake and eat it, dear, which doesn't make for
logical thought, does it?

So he said, with great charm, but in a way that made
certain I wouldn't wriggle off the hook again, Allow me
to introduce myself: I am Guido Lazzaroni. And first I
thought, Help, ought I to recognise the name? and then I
said, not having much option about it, I'm Caroline Barlow.
I added, firmly, I'm flying over to join my husband in
Bordeaux, and the way I said it seemed to amuse him. He
beckoned to the stewardess, who came quick as a flash and
said, Yes, Signor Lazzaroni? And he said, Some barley-
sugar for Mrs Barlow, please, she would like it during
take-off, and damn his eyes he was dead right. So I sucked
my barley-sugar as we soared up over London, and then
this Lazzaroni character undid my safety belt again, and
(oh the clever devil) never touched me once while he was
doing it. And when we were settled down for the trip he
said, Allow me to buy you a drink, and without thinking
I said, Yes please, make it a large Scotch, and he really

smiled for the first time, and the corners of his eyes
crinkled up, and something lurched over in the pit of my
tum and I don't mean we hit an air-pocket, either. So there
it was, and we talked like mad all the way to Paris. I've
never met anyone like Guido for winkling information out
of people : I suppose it's because he's a journalist. My dear,
I gave him the whole of my autobiography between Heath
Row and Orly, not that *that* amounts to much. And all
I found out about *him* was that he acted as a sort of roving
Foreign Correspondent for a group of papers in Milan, and
spent most of his time in England or Scandinavia. I didn't
even have the nerve to ask him about his own family. I tried
once, but just couldn't get the words out.

On the other hand, I did tell him all about the day's
doings, as it were, and that was where (from Mrs B.'s
point of view) I made a tactical mistake. You see, he knew
Michael was expecting me in Bordeaux some time before
lunch the next day—I'd sent a wire from the airport—
and so when we landed he really turned on the treatment.
He had a little Fiat 600 of his own waiting for him, and
he bundled me straight into it and drove off, very expertly,
very fast, weaving in and out of the traffic, honking away
like mad the whole time. Very un-English and honestly,
poppet, I'm ashamed to say I rather liked it. We stopped
at the big French Air Terminal near Les Invalides, and
Guido said, Wait here, I've got something to fix up. So
there I sat in this Fiat, bang in the middle of Paris, and
thought : Well, dear, things really are happening to you,
aren't they? And then it occurred to me, as sure as eggs
were eggs, what Guido must be doing, and that was raising
hell with the *bureau de renseignements* to find me a plane-
flight to Bordeaux the next morning, something that would

get me there as soon as this overnight train I was supposed to be catching. Oh-ho and ah-ha, I thought, and did my best to feel virtuous and insulted, but it was a bit of an uphill struggle, especially after all the lovely duty-free Scotch we'd somehow got through during the flight.

Then he came back to the car looking absolutely *livid*, and I knew my chap at London Airport had been telling the truth when he said No flights over the weekend, and to be quite honest, honey, I wasn't sure whether I was more relieved or disappointed. So I said, Bad luck, Guido, there wasn't a plane, was there? and he looked startled for a second and then he roared with laughter and said, Oh Caro, you are full of surprises, aren't you? and took me very firmly by the arm and pulled me out of the car and across the road and into the nearest *bistro*. It was small and noisy and full of bitter cigarette-smoke and there was a metal counter with a jar of lemons on it and I can see it in every little detail, even today.

So we sat and looked at each other, Guido and I, over two glasses of *marc*, and there was a battered old clock on the wall behind Guido's head just like a clock we had in my form-room at boarding-school, and it said half-past eight. Guido said, very seriously: Caro, you are a lovely woman. Don't be silly, I said, and Guido laughed again, looking tender and puzzled at once, and said, Why do English-women always say that when you pay them a compliment? I don't know, I said, feeling this conversation wasn't really taking place, or that the whole thing was a dream. Anyway I'm *not* lovely. And Guido said, Oh darling, you are tall and fair-haired and you have that beautiful complexion with the, what do you say, *freckles*, just a dusting, little ones round your nose, and your eyes are as kind as your mouth, and your mouth is happy and generous and you have the longest legs I have ever seen in nylons and why, why, why do you pretend you are dowdy madam? Perhaps it is a form of English conceit, very subtle, very rare—and he put on the old accent like mad when he said this, and his eyes twinkled. They weren't that opaque black, but a sort of golden hazel, with flecks in them: they reminded me of that odd drink you get in Austria, oh yes, *Alpengold* it's called.

But Guido, I said helplessly, I am married.

Yes, Guido said, and blew a smoke ring.

I am going to join my husband tomorrow.

Guido smiled, and shrugged. Then we cannot waste too much time talking, *carissima*, he observed, as though it were a self-evident fact.

Guido, I said, I am a respectable woman.

Ça se voit, Guido remarked, with obvious sincerity, and an impeccable Parisian accent. But you are also—had you not noticed?—sitting in a *bistro* near Les Invalides with a journalist called Guido Lazzaroni whom you have never met before.

Yes, I said. I could feel myself beginning to blush like mad.

Guido sipped his *marc* with relish. Furthermore, he said, on your own account—do correct me if I'm wrong—this is the first time in what? ten years? that you have been abroad without your husband.

Yes, I said.

It seems to me, Guido said, with that irrefutable Latin logic well to the fore, it seems to me your respectability has much in common with England's so-famous nationalised industries. It needs heavy subsidisation. Remove the brakes, and *pfui*! He grinned, suddenly boyish. Oh, he knew how to switch his moods, did Guido.

I said, rather plaintively, Guido, I'm hungry.

It was his turn to be knocked off his perch, but he was back on it in a flash. He said, Come to my hotel, Caro. Then you can leave your things, and have a wash, and there is a formidable restaurant in the same street—very small, for serious eaters.

Up to that moment I'd vaguely assumed that Guido was like me, a bird of passage, probably on his way back home to *mamma* and the *bambini* in Milan. Now it was clear he had, for the time being at any rate, made himself a nest in Paris. This explained the Fiat, too. The whole situation was getting rapidly out of hand.

Guido, I said, you know what'll happen if I come back to your hotel, don't you?

Of course, he said, primly. Honestly, I might have been trying to teach him his ABC by making up dirty rhymes.

I said, But I don't want to.

His face changed in a flash. I am tactless, he said. You are sick?

No, I said, furious, I've never been healthier in my life, it's just that—And then, of course, I got what he meant, and that made me blush even more.

I said Guido, I think you'd better take me to the Gare d'Austerlitz.

He sighed and shrugged, as at something beyond his comprehension. Then he smiled again. But I shall be charmed, he said. When is your train?

Ten-forty, I said.

Sta bene, Guido murmured, glancing at the clock. It was a quarter to nine. I shall take you to your station, and we will have supper together in one of those egregious restaurants that cluster about all termini, waiting to trap the unwary. You will enjoy the food, and I shall enjoy your company. Then I shall wave to you from the *binario*, sorry, platform, of course, and you will steam away into the night, towards Bordeaux and marital respectability, while I am left looking brave and stricken, like that doctor in your English *Brief Encounter*, making the Great Renunciation. I think, Guido added thoughtfully, that this film explains much which puzzles us about the English character. And there, my poppet, I must say I felt inclined to agree with him.

All right, I said, doubtfully.

Guido promptly sprang to his feet, swept me outside, and whistled for a taxi.

I said, What's wrong with the Fiat?

Guido said, Your concern is touching, my sweet, but the vehicle is correctly parked, its lights are on, and all doors are double-locked.

I didn't mean that, I said.

At this moment a taxi pulled up with a squeal of ancient brakes and Guido had me inside before I could think of any further objections. Gare d'Austerlitz, he told the driver. Then he said, At this particular moment I have a powerful urge to travel by taxi. I see, I said, and that was about the last I said for the next ten minutes, because just then the driver let in his clutch with a bang and a jerk that catapulted me straight into Guido's arms, and my dear, that kiss lasted the whole length of the Rue de Rivoli. I got out feeling like—well, it was as though I'd been swimming in a bath filled with champagne, and had managed to swallow quite a sizable amount of it in the process. Lightheaded, walking on air, all the old clichés—the trouble is, they're dead right. Life is one vast platitude, my poppet, it's only the oddballs who rate original epithets.

So here we are, Guido said, after I'd eaten an absolutely *enormous* supper—*pâté* and steak and *crème brûlé* and goodness knows what else; and there we were indeed, on my departure platform in the Gare d'Austerlitz, with the hands of the station clock pointing to ten thirty-five.

I said, We'd better say goodbye now, Guido. Thank you for a wonderful evening.

Au revoir would be better, Guido said, and held me to him, easily and gently, as though we'd been lovers for years. But all we had done was to walk down to the Seine after supper for a quarter of a hour and sit and kiss and watch the *bâteaux-mouches* go by, and the lights dancing on the water. It was as sloppy-romantic as you like. We sat on the the famous white macintosh, and it got *filthy*. That made me giggle like mad.

Guido said, Give me your address in London. I'm often across on a job.

I bet you are, I thought. Sorry, Guido, I said. There's no point really, is there?

He sighed. I always can be reached through the Press Club, he said. He held me closer.

The guard blew his whistle, and the doors began to slam.

Goodbye, Guido, I said, and kissed him hard, and then I broke away and fled down the platform and threw myself into my compartment without looking back. I collapsed, panting, in the reserved corner-seat, thinking, Well, that's that. And then, when the train was actually moving, Guido poked his brown, chunky face in at the window and said, Darling, you forgot to give me your phone number, and absolutely without thinking I said, Sorry, It's Wimbledon

c*

14278, and then I could have bitten my tongue out. Guido
grinned from ear to ear. Thank you, darling, he said.
Buon viaggio. And was gone.

The funny part of it was, you know, that I turned up
at Michael's hotel in absolutely cracking form, feeling like
a million dollars, and more pro-Mike than I'd been for a
long time. We really got the most out of that fortnight—
or at least, I did; I noticed after a bit that poor old M.
didn't really seem to be *with* me, if you see what I mean.
And then, soon after we got back to London, it all came
out. Michael's always been a great one for what Buchman's
boys refer to as Total Recall—sounds like someone being
sick, doesn't it, and in a way it is, only being sick does less
harm. Anyhow, my vague suspicions turned out to have
been rather more than justified. There was this girl Angela
Thing, honestly I can never remember her other name,
something absolutely colourless—oh yes, Bates, of course.
Not that it matters. The usual story. A little secretary at
the firm, pretty as paint, couldn't have been more than
twenty-two, tucked away in a cosy little flat off the Bayswater Road. A flat, I hardly need tell you, to which Michael
had the key.

You know, it really was a shock. I suppose we all
imagine something like that happening sometime, I mean,
you can hardly get away from the idea with all these films
and plays and books nowadays, you'd think the whole
economy hung on hopping into other people's beds, but
still, when it *does* happen, believe me, you feel it. Look
darling, Michael said, we always agreed it'd be much better
to have everything open and above board, didn't we? Oh
go to hell, I said, and I was all the more furious because
underneath I was feeling, Dear God, there was I holding

back because of a load of silly bloody scruples when all the time—Well, no, it just didn't bear thinking about. The whole thing was a bad joke. And the fact that I was carrying an outsize in puritan guilt-complexes didn't help one little bit. Thank God the children were at school through the worst of the arguments and recriminations and emotional hangovers. It got to the point where I said, All right, carry on, *but for Christ's sake don't tell me about it.* And Michael said, You know I'd never break up the family, Caroline, I'm too fond of you and the children, and anyway I don't believe in all this balls about getting a divorce every time you have an affair, they know about these things on the Continent. So that was how it was when Roger and Jane came home, and as Roger said, rather sharpish, over dinner the first evening, Honestly, Mum, the frost's getting cruel a bit early this year, isn't it?

And then, on the afternoon before Christmas Eve, Guido rang up. I suppose I'd always known he would. He said, Hullo darling, happy Christmas, and I said, Guido, oh God, and Michael took one look at me, and dropped the bit of decoration he was pinning up and walked out of the room, and I heard the click on the line as he picked up the extension phone.

Guido said, I've just flown in from Oslo. It was snowing there.

Was it? I said. I could hear Michael breathing.

Guido said, Darling, can you come out?

When? I asked.

Now. This evening.

Oh Guido, for heaven's sake, don't be silly—it's nearly Christmas, and there are people coming in tonight, and——

All right, Guido said, tomorrow, then.

I thought of Angela Bates, and I said, Yes, Guido, yes, I will. Tomorrow. Where?

He named a very well-known pub in Chelsea. Half-past twelve he said. We'll go to a Chinese place for lunch.

But *Guido*, I wailed. It was no use. Half-past twelve, *carissima*, he said firmly, and put the receiver down. I went and poured myself a whisky. I felt I needed it. A moment later I heard the front-door slam. That, I guessed, was Michael off to seek solace for his bruised ego in the little flat off the Bayswater Road. Oh God, I thought, as I swirled the whisky round the glass, and stared out at the grey miserable London sky, what *has* happened to us all?

Honestly, ducky, I was all set for a real good howl when young Jane came in. Jane is fourteen, and blonde like me, and wears jeans. She is also very precocious and an inspired cook. I looked at her and thought, Bless you, darling, you're a professional situation-saver if ever I saw one. And she said, Golly, Mummy, you drinking Scotch *now*? And I said, Yes, now, so what? And she said, Ah well, I saw Daddy charging off a minute ago like a Bull of Bashan, so I thought you might need moral support. And I said, Jane, poppet, can you manage lunch tomorrow on your own? It's a pleasure, she said, and what about supper? I said: I hadn't thought about supper, and Jane giggled and said, No, Mummy but *he* will, and I said, Oh hell, I give up, my whole family's getting totally out of hand and you're an impertinent little baggage. Don't call me names, Jane said, or I won't cook your lunch and *then* what'll you do? She had something there. All right, I said, you win. She grinned, and flounced out, and a few seconds later I heard the immortal notes of Count Basie floating down from her room. A real, old-fashioned, home-loving miss is our Jane.

Michael didn't come home till nearly midnight. He got into bed, coughed and wheezed a bit in a tentative sort of way, and said, I think I've got 'flu. Take some aspirin, I said, and fell asleep. The next morning he was whooping it up in fine style—sneezing like mad, a barking cough that reminded me of a fox after chickens, and a most impressive cold sweat. I packed him up with hot-water bottles and fed him coddled eggs. I said, Let me take your temperature, darling. Ah bugger off, he said. All right, I said, I will. He tried to look pathetic, which wasn't really very easy for him with rumpled hair and grubby pyjamas and masses of five o'clock shadow, and said, snuffling, Sorry, Caroline, I get a bit tetchy sometimes but honestly I do feel bloody rotten, and it's a bit much your going out on top of everything else—And then he sneezed like a *volcano*, sweetie, and lay back in a sort of Saint Sebastian pose that made me want to kick him. I said, Michael, I'm going to give you the benefit of the doubt and assume that you're not putting this on. He shot me a sad, injured look, and sniffed. I said, Ten to one it's psychosomatic. I'd just found a book all about that, and was dying to try it out on someone. Michael said, What the hell does *psychosomatic* mean? Are you trying to tell me I'm bonkers? No, I said, tucking him up and fluffing out his pillows, I'm telling you *I'm going out to lunch*, and if you want a ministering angel you'll jolly well have to make do with Jane. If you think you're dying she can ring up for an ambulance and have you carted off to one of those nice public wards where you get a really jolly Christmas, senior obstetricians dancing the Charleston in paper hats, that kind of jag, never a dull moment. *All right?* I said, and slammed out before he could say anything.

I got to the pub dead on half-past twelve. Guido was

there already. Sweetie, I felt such a fool. My heart was pounding away nineteen to the dozen, I was blushing like mad, and my hands were trembling. I might have been a seventeen-year-old schoolgirl going to keep a date with her first big crush. Guido took both my hands in his and said, Well, Caro? And I smiled and said, Well, Guido? and then he kissed me, long, close, utterly intimate kiss, bang in the middle of the saloon bar. I felt the other occupants would begin to cheer at any moment. Come and sit down, he said, and oh was I thankful; I felt my legs were going to give way under me at any moment.

But when I'd come round from the anaesthetic, as you might say, I realised that it wasn't going to be the same as that night in Paris. I had changed, and so had Guido. He looked somehow both cheaper and flashier in London, more brash, less sure of himself. But we chattered on happily enough, postponing—well, what *were* we postponing? He took me to lunch in his promised Chinese restaurant, and the food was awful. Then he said, and this really took me aback, Look, darling, someone gave me two complimentary tickets for *Ben-Hur*, have you ever seen it? And like a fool I said No, not telling him that the reason for *that* was that I hate Biblical wideys anyhow and this one went on for nearly four hours which would inevitably give me a migraine. So Guido said, wonderful, we must go now or we shall miss the beginning, and I burped slightly, what with the shock and that frightful Chinese food, and said humbly, That'll be lovely, Guido, thinking that if God had wanted to think up a penance for my particular infidelity He couldn't have chosen anything more diabolically appropriate. So there we sat in all that air-conditioning, in front of a screen that looked about a hundred yards wide, and watched this epic, colossal, etcetera etcetera piece of film-making. At least, Guido watched it, but after a while I shut my eyes for fear of migraine and concentrated on the dialogue instead and fell to wondering which bits of it were by Mr Christopher Fry and how much lolly they'd paid him to write like that. I also thought, rather more seriously, about Michael and Jane and Roger and Angela and what a bloody mess life was if you insisted on making a fuss about it the whole time.

I suppose I ought to have guessed that the main object of this *Ben Hur* episode was to bridge the awkward gap that yawned between lunch and after supper, B.H. being the only film in the whole metropolis long enough to do it. But at the time I didn't. I was bemused and besotted, darling, you've no idea. If Guido had said, let's go down to Trafalgar Square and climb Nelson's column, I'd have had a go at it. Oh, I know there was that horrid little bubble of doubt at the back of my mind, but I kept it well out of sight. But it did just strike me we were on the old see-saw, I mean, that maybe Guido wasn't the one who was making the running now. But he wanted me all right. There was no doubt about that. Indeed there wasn't.

When we finally staggered out into Leicester Square Guido said, This time I will give you a really wonderful meal, very Latin and imperious his tone was, no arguments, follow the great white male Chief. So I perked up, with visions of the Epicure or somewhere like that on Guido's expense account, but oh Lord it turned out to be *Indian* this time, and even greasier and more frightful than the last lot. God, ducky, how my digestion suffered in the cause of true passion. Presumably poor old Guido had some idea that hot curry made a good aphrodisiac.

So we champed our way through toughish chicken legs dunked in a filthy yellow sauce that flayed, but *flayed* the inside of my mouth—honestly, I'm not sure some of those poor old long-suffering taste-buds have come off strike to this day. And there were great flabby chappattis and *mounds* of rather over-cooked rice, and, oh misery, *Bombay Duck*. Lovey, have you ever *smelt* Bombay Duck being cooked? It's indescribable. Michael once said it was like someone frying a tramp's jockstrap, and that was an understatement. And there we were, with a table almost bang over the service hatch, inhaling all the odours that came floating up the lift-shaft. Like those tatty old gods on Olympus, and I bet *they* got pretty sick of the smell of burnt fat, too. So I said to Guido, Guido, let's get a bottle of wine in, because that would help to keep the smell at bay and because suddenly I wanted to get myself well and truly stewed, way out beyond the point of thought or conscience or doubt. And because I wanted to forget how Guido was being, which was very brisk and masterful and laconic, not at all the suave voluble charmer. That horrid little voice in my head whispered: Well, what have you got to bitch about? It's logical, isn't it? *You don't feed a gaffed salmon with bait.* And all the time the street outside echoed to the noise of Christmas carols relayed over God knows how many radios, and the cars swished by in the rain, and I remembered that *bistro* by Les Invalides and I thought, Oh sweet, darling Guido, I want you so much, and I wish, how I wish, it could be now as it was then. But I had rejected that moment, and I couldn't expect to pluck it back from time.

So there it was. And when we had finished our coffee Guido looked at me with a sort of fierce, dog-like impatience and said, Caro, it's all right, I've—borrowed a flat. I nodded, wondering why he hesitated over this proposition, and took an enormous gulp of Chianti. Then he said, Come back and have a Christmas drink with me, and I nearly fell off my chair with surprise at this unexpected descent into the well-worn conventions of *l'affaire anglaise*. I suppose old Guido was a bit of a chameleon really, most journalists are. Adapting himself to the background and local customs. When in Rome, I thought, and wished we were. So I said, very near to tears, Yes, Guido, that would be lovely, acting up the Celia Johnson character that I suppose I am really and wanted, then, so badly to forget. And Guido tipped one of the Indian waiters ten bob to go out in the rain and get us a taxi, and I hastily finished the last of the Chianti, and the dregs tasted absolutely foul.

I couldn't hear the address Guido gave the driver, but it turned out to be—yes, ducky, I thought you'd guess—somewhere in the Bayswater Road area, and I said to myself, Heigh-ho, all we need now is to run into Michael and Angela Whatsit and the old cornucopia will be full to overflowing. And all the way in the taxi Guido sat very stiff and remote and impatient, staring out of the window, and I didn't dare touch him for fear of a rebuff. You stupid romantic cuckoo, my nasty little voice said, isn't this what you wanted? Not exactly, I said, Hard to please, aren't we? the voice said. Milady is hypocritical. Milady must have the parcel wrapped up in lovely tissue paper and Christmas tape—hand-kissings, flowery compliments, protestations of undying love. Why all the fuss? When you get down to it. a—*Shut up,* I told the voice. It *does* make a difference. Don't ask me why, but it does. Without affection we might as well be a couple of dogs. Well, then, says the voice, silkily reasonable, tell him to stop the cab and let you off.

And my dear, I've never felt so ashamed and humiliated in my life, because I was so worked up by now that I couldn't even do that. And anyway, we were there.

It was a peeling, damp, miserable sort of house, tall and narrow, thousands like it all over London. Guido rang the bell, and an old bag with 'landlady' written all over her answered it almost at once, and *that* surprised me, because I thought Guido would at least have borrowed a front-door key. He muttered something, and she nodded, and we marched in past her through a dung-coloured hall with an aspidistra and one of those ghastly great coat-stands, and up a steep narrow flight of stairs with coconut matting instead of a carpet, and I could feel the old bag's eyes appraising me the whole bloody way, dear, and then I realised that is wasn't only 'landlady' that was written all over her but 'madam' as well. Clever Guido had asked around in the Press Club or El Vino's or somewhere else where his nice male journalist chums congregated, and someone had come up with the address of a discreet, out-of-the-way *maison de passe*. Or maybe Guido made a habit of this. Maybe he ran a monthly account for the exclusive use of a room. Maybe—Oh what was the use? Be thankful for what you get in this life, girl, my father used to say. Don't complain because you can't have the moon. I don't suppose he ever envisaged his fine old platitudes giving me comfort in *this* sort of situation. After all, poppet, he *did* end up as a Rural Dean.

When Guido had said a flat, he'd been indulging in slight exaggeration, as I suspected. It was a middling-sized bedsitter, mostly filled by *the* most gigantic bed you've ever seen—honestly, it could have held half-a-dozen, and in that place I shouldn't wonder if it occasionally did, some people really do have *weird* habits at night I've heard, and I remember thinking with a sort of giggle when I saw it, Well, thank God I'm normal, anyway. There was an old-fashioned washstand with a marble top, and a striped water-jug, and—of all things—a framed sepia print over the bedhead of that picture by Holman Hunt, *The Light of the World* I think it's called, and that shook me more than anything. Well, Guido? I said, and then he kissed me, *really* kissed me, and we both undressed as fast as though we were going swimming in hot weather and I thought, Glory be, it's going to be all right after all. And as far as the essentials went, dear, I suppose it was.

It was afterwards that things began to go wrong. That's always the real test, isn't it? I mean, Guido had certainly been an expert lover, all right. There I lay, feeling wonderful—warm, glowing, relaxed, exhausted and absolutely *bursting* with love and tenderness. And curry of course, but I didn't care about that any more. But Guido was fidgeting about with a sort of well-now-*that's*-over-let's-get-on-with-the-next-thing sort of air, and I just couldn't or wouldn't accept it, and I held him tight and nibbled his ears and called him special names and nuzzled my nose into all that gorgeous hair on his chest, and all the time I could feel his toes twitching impatiently and his whole mind sort of detached and floating off somewhere different. And finally he sat up in bed and stretched, and then I did an absolutely mad thing, God knows why, sort of Lady Chatterley impulse I suppose. You know that lovely pearl necklace I wear sometimes, absolutely *yards* long? Well, there it was on the bedside table, and I grabbed it, and draped it round Guido's neck, but round and round, like a choker, and then I took one of his ears in each hand and rocked his head very tenderly from side to side and said, Oh my Guido, my pretty little poppet.

And my God, he was livid. He tore my hands away and fairly ripped the pearls off his neck, and the string broke and those pearls went scattering about every which way, all over the floor. And he said, Caro, if you ever, *ever* do a thing like that again, I swear I will beat you unconscious. All affronted male ego was Guido in that moment, and *Italian* male ego, which is far worse, proud squawmaster with whip, only one jump ahead of the harem mentality, a strutting rooster with cruel claws. Maybe, looking back, my mad impulse had a pretty sane motive behind it, I don't know. But the worst part was to come, because he said, Pick up those damned pearls, and, oh God, I did. I hunted about that bloody bedroom for them on my hands and knees, stark naked, poking under the bed and scratching in corners, while his lordship sat there in bed and smoked a cigarette and watched me. I missed one of them too, which wasn't surprising in the circumstances, and I suppose the old bitch kept it as a souvenir. And when I'd got them all stowed away in my bag, and was about to get back into bed Guido yawned and said, We had better get dressed now.

I said, Is the next client expected?

Guido said, That was a vulgar remark.

Yes, I said, but then the whole situation is ineffably vulgar. I fastened my bra and got my briefs on somehow, and all the time he watched me.

I don't understand, Guido said, out of bed now, knotting his tie with brisk sharp movements. You did not achieve satisfaction? He sounded like a factory P.R.O., my dear, dealing with a customer complaining about faulty goods.

We just don't speak the same language, Guido, I said, zipping up my skirt, and I don't mean Italian and English, either. I'd better go, I think.

You mean back to Wimbledon? Guido said. He somehow made the name sound at once obscene and comic.

Of course, I said, with my back to him. Very carefully I ran a lipstick round my upper lip, squinting in the wardrobe mirror.

I am sorry, Guido said, in that unmistakable prim tone which denotes social, rather than personal, disappointment. I had hoped that you would accompany me to Midnight Mass.

What? I said, and my lipstick dropped to the ground and rolled across the floor. This Guido was incredible beyond my wildest dreams.

It is, after all, Christmas Eve, Guido explained.

I said, feebly, But I'm not a Catholic, am I? As a retort it left something to be desired, but by now I was practically past rational thought.

Guido said, I understand that many Protestants attend Midnight Mass at Christmas?

Not this one, I said.

Guido fired his last shot. I am told, he said, that nowadays it is, what do you say, the *done thing*.

I gaped at him. Then I said: Guido, I am going home now. Please don't come with me, or try to follow me. I don't want to see you again.

He shrugged his shoulders. As you wish, he said, with a slight inclination of the head. He looked faintly relieved. I walked quickly out of the bedroom, closing the door behind me, and down the coconut matting stairs, and through the hall, and out into the drizzling blackness of

Westbourne Grove. The old madam peered round her door at me as I went. She snuffled a bit, but didn't actually say anything. For one ghastly moment I thought she was going to shove her withered paw under my nose for a *pourboire*, ducky, like those terrible old crones in French public loos. Then there I was on the pavement, with no umbrella, at half-past eleven of a dirty wet Christmas Eve, and a trip to Wimbledon ahead of me. This was the gay Bohemian life and no mistake.

I hardly need tell you, do I, sweetie, that I missed the last train? I actually saw its tail light disappearing into the blasted tunnel. And with all this Christmas Eve lark going on it took me another half-hour to find a taxi. By this time I was soaked to the *skin*, and if you think that's a figure of speech just you think again. The taxi-driver spent the whole trip grumbling about being kept out on a night like this, just as though he did it for *fun*, and then socked me double fare and a whacking tip at the end of it all, which just about cleaned me out. By this time the rain was coming down in *torrents*, and my hair was all plastered to my skull in the way those prim little misses in Jane Austen used to wear it. One o'clock on Wimbledon Common, heigh-ho, and not a *glimmer* of light from the *maison* Barlow. Oh no. Mum was out on the razzle-dazzle, and everyone else had hung up their Christmas stockings without a care in the world and were now, no doubt, snoring like so many pigs. Catch them staying up. I didn't know whether to be flattered at their opinion of my survival power, or hurt because they just didn't care. Up to the front door I marched, fumbling in my bag for my key, and determined to make a fine old clatter when I got inside that would be guaranteed to wake the dead.

There was only one little snag about all this; I had whizzed out of the house before lunch in such a tearing hurry that I'd left that blasted front-door key sitting on my dressing-table. So I said several words that I don't suppose Michael thought I knew, and went round to the back door, which, of course, was locked and bolted. Further investigation, as they say in the *Police Gazette*, revealed that for once—*for once*, mark you—some hyper-efficient bastard had gone round last thing shooting every bloody bolt and catch in the place, as though the World Convention of Master Burglars was being held on Wimbledon Common and the Law had agreed to turn a blind eye to the boys keeping their hand in as long as the jamboree lasted. Finally I did what I suppose I ought to have done in the first place, and that was to fling handfuls of gravel at Jane's window.

My God, that girl took some waking. I must have scooped up about half a ton of wet gravel before the sash went up and Jane's head appeared. What the hell do you want, she said, just about audible through the pouring rain, and if that doesn't take the biscuit as the silliest question of all time I'd like to hear the one that beat it. *Come down and let me in, you half-wit,* I roared. I suppose you've forgotten your key again, Jane said, and pulled down the window before I could hurl the last of the gravel at it. After what seemed like about ten minutes the bolts of the front door were yanked back, and Jane appeared, in her old nursery dressing-gown with a rabbit on the pocket. It reached about to her knees, and believe it or not, the first thought that entered my head was, Why on earth haven't I replaced that damned thing years ago, I must pop up to Harrods after the New Year and get her something decent in a sale. Mrs Barlow was back to her treadmill.

It was a wonderful Christmas, ducky, I'll never forget it. Both Michael and I were in bed with streaming colds, and the same bed at that, and not speaking to each other, can you imagine it? I suppose if this had been one of those moral little fables you read under the dryer the result would have been a Grand Reconciliation, and Michael would have dropped Angela Bates, and all that. As it was, Michael got better like bloody lightning when he saw I was stealing his psychosomatic thunder, in fact he was off to the Bayswater Road for a nice quiet Boxing Day supper, and that's where he is at this moment, I shouldn't be surprised. No, of course we're not getting a divorce, those unnatural children of ours are enjoying the whole thing *far* too much, and anyway Michael's firm wouldn't allow it, they're so old-fashioned, don't believe in a director of Conroy and Gilson soiling his feet with the dust of the old law-courts. So there, as you might say, it is, and Guido's never rung up again, and the last time I tried the Press Club they said he was in Saigon. *Et voilà.* No, darling of *course* we're not going Dutch over this lunch, Michael's got an expense account here and in the circumstances I don't see why the hell we shouldn't use it, do you? Wonderful things, expense accounts.

Oh yes; one little detail I forgot—after all this 'flu business was over I decided to turn out the medicine chest, hadn't done it for years, and what do you think I found there, carefully tucked away down at the bottom? That's right, ducky; my passport. Out of date, of course. Rather like me, I suppose. Never mind, *nil carburundum*. Come on we've still got half an hour before that hairdressing appointment. Let's go and look at some new hats, shall us? So good for the old morale.

V.I.P. TREATMENT

THE trouble is, thought Lepage, there's really bugger-all reason for our being here at all.

He shifted his sweating backside on the hard cane chair, opened another button of his faded jungle-green tunic, and began to scratch in the thick damp hair matted across his chest. The only other occupant of the control-tower was a pale, tow-headed airman at the switchboard. The airman's name was Saunders; he wore khaki drill, which in a nominally forward area annoyed Lepage's sense of the proprieties; he suffered distressingly from acne; and he was liable, as now, to pass the time by whistling through his teeth.

'Jesus, Saunders,' Lepage said, in a thick French-Canadian accent, 'do you have to make that filthy Goddam row, huh?'

'Sorry, sir.' The whistling was replaced by a resentful, mutinous silence.

Lepage stared round his small, tawdry domain. *Dans le pays des aveugles,* he thought, *le borgne est roi.* Here am I, the cock-eyed king of an unnecessary country. What do I own? One Aldis signalling lamp with a rusty shutter. One Very pistol, and I rather think the cartridges suffered during last monsoon. One hundred goose-neck kerosene flares. A clapped-out ground-control R.T. set. A log-book, a code-

89

book, a pile of signal-pads, and no end of obsolete bumph.

He heaved himself up out of his chair and walked to the window. Saunders eyed him with dull malevolence, noting the dark, coppery skin, the heavy muscles, the too-quick smile, the pilot's wings and the faded D.F.C. ribbon. Lepage shaded his eyes against the glare, scrabbling in his breast-pocket for dark glasses. Outside, heat bounced skyward off the pierced-steel-planking runway: air shimmered in angry fluidity. Lepage glanced at his wristwatch. Just after three.

God, he thought, what a dump.

For a few weeks, while the war swept forward down the Arakan, Myitchaung had been a key airfield, a vital advance post south of Akyab. American bulldozers had been shipped in to level scrub and jungle; a control tower, this control tower, had been built; three squadrons of Spitfires had flown strike after strike from that single thousand-yard strip beside the Bay of Bengal. But now, barely three months later, Myitchaung was forgotten. Rangoon had fallen, the war was drawing to its close; and Myitchaung, stripped of its fighter squadrons, had become a mere convenience for Transport Command planes flying south from Calcutta or Chittagong—a refuelling and repair depot, a supplier of weather reports and navigational aids.

A bloody fine Flying Control Officer I am, thought Flight Lieutenant Lepage. Two Daks a day and no home-based aircraft. He wiped a hand across his mouth, conscious of the flat silver flask jammed tight against his left buttock, wondering whether it was worth waiting till Saunders went out for a slash. *Discipline, shit,* he thought, and tugged the flask out. The whisky was brackish and volatile: its fumes filled the control-tower. Lepage drank, paused, drank again.

He stared out at the cluster of Nissen huts, the whitewashed H.Q. block, the servicing hangars. In the glare of the afternoon nothing stirred except one mangy pi-dog, nosing about in the refuse behind the cook-house, and a kite that soared and circled, high against the burning sky. Somewhere to the south, there was still a war. Here, all was stagnation, Lepage thought, his eye following the course of the shallow, stinking *chaung* that wound its way inland from the sea to the jungle-choked heart of Burma.

Far away down the runway a figure appeared, pedalling along despondently on a large square Service bicycle. Lepage grinned, stepped out on to the balcony, and picked up the Aldis lamp. Hot metal seared his fingers as he worked the shutter. The figure gave a curious stiff gesture, half wave, half salute, and bent manfully over its handlebars again. Presently there was a clatter at the bottom of the tower, and heavy ironshod boots came clumping up the ladder. In eighteen years' service Flight Sergeant Staines had never, even in the Far East, demeaned himself by wearing shoes.

'Come in, Flight,' Lepage said cheerfully, and then: 'Christ, man, you look hot.'

Staines came to attention and flicked one hand up to his greasy forage-cap, with the continuous, compulsive action of a chain-smoker lighting a cigarette. Then he brought out a large khaki handkerchief and mopped his streaming face.

'Saw your green light, sir,' he said, grinning. 'Pedalled like buggery, but I couldn't get airborne.'

Flight Sergeant Staines had the fiercely vacuous features of an old sheep at bay. His balding cranium was haloed with an incongruous fringe of auburn curls and his complexion did not take kindly to the Eastern sun: it gave him the appearance of having been momentarily submerged in boiling water.

Lepage saw his nostrils twitch faintly: Staines could smell out whisky like a vulture scenting a corpse.

'Well, Flight,' he said, 'what gives? Don't tell me you came over here just to pass the time of day. Not in this heat.'

'No sir.' Staines fumbled in his breast pocket. 'Coded signal in from Group.'

'Oh sod it,' Lepage said. 'Saunders!'

'Sir?'

'Get me the code book. Here's the key to the safe.'

Lepage settled down with the heavy volume, frowning in concentration. He had hardly deciphered the first few words when the switchboard buzzed.

'R.A.F. Myitchaung heah,' Saunders said, in his genteel operator's voice. Like an adenoidal bloody shopwalker, Lepage thought. 'Yes . . . oh, yes, sir. Yes, he is—' Saunders looked up from the switchboard and said: 'For you, sir. Squadron Leader Weller calling from Calcutta.'

Lepage grabbed the receiver. 'Tim, you old devil. Good to hear from you—' Good to hear from anyone, here. Even Tim Weller. Queer as a coot and fat as a barrel. Group Entertainment Officer. Now there was a laugh, if you like.

'Hello there, Jacques.' The voice came faint and crackling over the line, a suave purr. Lepage could almost smell Weller's famous after-shave lotion. 'Listen, ducky, we're giving you a little treat—at rather short notice, I'm afraid.'

'Anything for a change, Tim.' Lepage grinned expansively, as though Weller could see him, flipped a Player in his mouth, snapped his lighter, and exhaled beatific clouds of smoke.

Weller said: 'I take it you've heard of Sandra Black out there in the backwoods?'

'Jesus, who hasn't? The Singing Darling of the Services, all that crap. Not bad, either. Saw her knock them cold at the Palladium——'

'You clever little Canuck, you. Well, you're going to see her again, in about an hour from now.'

'Uh-huh. And I suppose you've laid on Noel Coward and the whole Windmill chorus too, that right?'

'Sarcasm, my dear Jacques, sits ill on the muscle-bound. No, I'm perfectly serious. You ought to have had a signal by now——'

'Yeah. I was just decoding it——'

'Well you can spare yourself the trouble, ducky. Uncle Tim will tell all in words of one syllable. Decoding is such a *bore*. Very simple, really—La Black was scheduled to give a show in Rangoon tonight. *But,* as I have no doubt your devoted weather boys will have informed you, there is a positively *enormous* electric storm moving in from the Bay of Bengal, just north of Mingaladon. Frantic signals from her pilot—such a dear boy, you'd love him, but *not* the cool-headed type. What to do? Turn back? Carry on? Of course, in the end we decided to *compromise*, as usual. The weather's all clear as far as *your* little nest, dear boy, so Myitchaung is going to have the privilege and pleasure, etcetera, etcetera. And now you'd better drag that gorgeous body of yours into action and lay on a suitable *reception committee,* Jacques my lad. Miss Black is *most* fussy.'

Lepage brightened visibly at this. Saunders, who had been listening in at the switchboard, had the glazed expression of a cod on its slab. Flight Sergeant Staines scratched himself with discreet abandon.

Lepage said: 'Who's coming with her?'

'Her *accompanist*, dear. Such a gay little thing, you'll adore him. And he sticks to La Black like a *leech*, so if any of you great peasants want to try the old gin-and-tickle line, you'll have to provide for dear Adrian first. *Malum?*'

'*Tikh hai*, Tim,' Lepage said. 'We'll cope.'

'There's a good boy,' said Weller, and rang off.

Lepage put down the receiver, tilted his chair back to an angle of about forty-five degrees, plunked a pair of suede-shoe-shod feet on his desk ('Bloody brothel-creepers,' thought Staines) and lit a slim black Burmese cheroot from the box beside him. He was already seeing himself in the role of Great Impresario, the Tycoon with the Casting Couch.

'Well, Flight,' he said briskly, 'seems we're having distinguished company tonight.'

'Oh yes, sir?' said Staines, warily. The F.C.O. was looking too cocky by half, trouble in the air somewhere; never did trust these bleeding Canucks, any road. He said: 'Is that what the signal's about then, sir?'

'Ah yes, that signal.' Lepage swung off the desk, and for several moments worked assiduously. The control-tower was silent except for some heavy breathing and the occasional squeak of Lepage's pencil.

'All right, here's the dope,' he said at last. 'Listen: "Flight LX 657—" we've got her scheduled to go through at 1610 hours—"will land Myitchaung stop accommodation requested ENSA party two only stop party will give troop concert stop all facilities requested stop ETA 1615 ETD 0900 stop request refuelling servicing full weather sitrep stop VIP treatment must repeat must be observed." Well now, how d'you like that?'

Flight Sergeant Staines digested this. 'They say there's a war on,' he remarked at length, scratching his auburn fringe. 'I'll believe it when I see it.'

Lepage said: 'Have you ever heard of Sandra Black, Flight?'

'Oh, she's on this do, is she?' Staines said. He didn't seem noticeably impressed. 'If you don't mind my saying so, sir, whoever drafted that signal at Group didn't know 'is arse from 'is elbow, as the saying goes. Lucky you 'ad that phone-call, or we might have bedded 'er ladyship down with you and Mr Summers, mightn't we?'

He looked at Lepage from those guileless, faded-blue sheeps'-eyes, his face deadpan, his point made. Flight Sergeant Staines had seen quite a lot, one way and another, in eighteen years' service.

Lepage either missed the implications of this remark or chose to ignore them. He blew smoke from his cheroot and said: 'Well, seeing as how I'm acting C.O. I suppose I'll have to organise this lot. You'd better put Miss Black in the Old Man's room, for a start——'

Flight Sergeant Staines said: 'The C.O. locked up 'is room before 'e went on leave, sir.'

'Oh, did he? Then you'd better unlock it again.'

''E took the key with 'im, sir.'

Lepage looked coolly at Staines and said: 'Then you'd better use the other one, hadn't you?'

Staines decided to let that one go. 'Right, sir. What about the other party?'

'The other party, Flight, you will be relieved to hear, is male. Technically, anyhow. Get one of your boys to fix him up a *charpoy* in Mr Summers's room.'

'Excuse me asking, sir, but 'adn't we better put it to Mr Summers first?'

'You can take it from me, Flight, Mr Summers won't have any objections.'

The two men's eyes met again. 'No, I don't suppose 'e will, sir,' Staines said. 'That wasn't what was on me mind, exactly.'

A warning flicker of anger came into Lepage's black eyes, and then was gone; but not before Staines had seen it. Then the French-Canadian gave that hearty, insincere laugh of his ('like a bloody buck nigger pissing in a cracked po', Staines had once described it in the sergeants' mess) and said: 'You ought to lay off cycling about in this heat, Flight. We can't afford to have you going round the bend.'

'I'll watch it, sir,' Staines said. 'Now, sir, if I may— about these arrangements.' He glanced at his watch. 'We'll 'ave to move nippy; plane's due in in about forty minutes. Bit short notice for a guard of honour——'

'*Guard of honour?*' Lepage said. 'You'll be lucky if you can find six bods on this camp who know which way up how to hold a bloody rifle, let alone how to present arms. No, we'll have to do without the trimmings.'

'What about a spontaneous demonstration, sir?' Staines said, with the ghost of a wink.

'That's much more like it. Fine. And get Sergeant Rogers down in the cookhouse to lay on a decent meal. Proper local stuff, no bloody corned beef, get it?'

'Sir,' Staines said.

'And someone'll have to organise the canteen for Miss Whatsit's show—flowers, all that crap——'

Staines said, his face expressionless: 'Sounds like a nice job for Sergeant Chubb-Whittington, doesn't it, sir?' He enunciated the name with chumping relish, as though his mouth were full of underdone steak.

'The long-haired type in Signals? Yeah, you've got a point there, Flight. Providing Mr Summers can spare him,' he added, ambiguously.

'Right, sir,' Staines said, without commenting on the last remark. 'If there's nothing else, I'd better get cracking.'

'O.K., Flight. I'll leave the details to you. We'll have the concert straight after supper.' He paused, then added: 'Better break out the beer ration for the men. We want them to give the lady a big hand, don't we?'

'Sir,' Staines said, and saluted. He clumped off down the stairs, sheep-faced and imperturbable, and Lepage heard his bicycle grinding away across to Dispersal. He leant back in his chair again and said to Saunders: 'Get me Mr Summers on the blower.' With Staines out of the way he felt more self-assured. For all his thickheadedness Staines could be disconcertingly shrewd on occasion. He slid out his flask and took another long, comforting pull. The combined smell of whisky and cheroot made Saunders feel decidedly sick.

The switchboard buzzed and clicked. Lepage picked up his receiver with a flourish. 'Hi, Tony . . . Yeah, you've heard, have you? Sure thing, Staines travels fast in the jungle, ha-ha! Bet he didn't tell you about Adrian . . . uh-huh, the accompanist . . . very *gay*, Tim Weller said . . . yeah, well, he should know, shouldn't he? . . . Look, Tony, could you spare that sergeant of yours, man with the siphon in his name . . . yeah, yeah, Chubb-Whittington, that's it. . . . Well, someone's got to tart the canteen up. . . . You can? Fine, fine. Send him right over, will you? . . . Yeah, large pink gin on me, Tony, sure.' Lepage

D

rolled his eyes ceilingwards for the benefit of an imaginary audience and added: 'Oh, Tony, I've billeted dear Adrian on you . . . just for the one night, yeah. That's my boy. I knew you'd co-operate. See you later, then.' And put the receiver down.

Now Lepage picked up an old signals pad and began, with the flashy stereotyped technique that betrayed the former commercial artist, to draw a naked girl. The most peculiar feature about this girl was her hair. It was drawn in far greater detail than the rest of the sketch, and rippled in thick folds nearly to her ankles. Lepage drew this picture at least once a day. Just as he was putting the final touches to it, the long, undulating figure of Michael Chubb-Whittington drifted noiselessly through the open door, and sketched a lackadaisical salute. Then he coughed very gently, like a superior stage butler, and said: 'I was told you wanted me, sir. I do hope I'm not—interrupting anything.'

Lepage looked up with a start, and dropped his pencil on the floor. Bloody little rubber-soled creep, he thought. Then, unable to account for his action, he tore off the top sheet from the signal pad, screwed it into a ball, and shied it at the wastepaper basket. Michael Chubb-Whittington raised one eyebrow.

Lepage felt at once angry and defensive. Christ, he thought, what a turn-out: khaki stockings rucked halfway down his legs, those ridiculous flapping K.D. shorts, shirt buttoned all anyhow. And yet the bastard made him feel awkward just by standing there.

'Sergeant,' he said, 'you look a god-awful mess.'

With a smile of singular sweetness Chubb-Whittington replied: 'I know, sir; this issue stuff is frightful, isn't it?'

Lepage opened his mouth to bark, thought better of it (after all, the plane would be here in not much more than half an hour) and instead told Chubb-Whittington, in his most breezy joss-the-chaps-along voice, exactly what he wanted done in the canteen.

Chubb-Whittington, who had been reading psychology at a provincial university before his call-up, went away feeling obscurely disturbed.

Lepage, having rung up everyone from the M.T. sergeant to the Adjutant and bewildered them with a fusillade of brisk but unintelligible instructions, decided that the time had come to attend to more personal matters. So his Airfield Control Sergeant was hauled, swearing, out of a well-merited siesta and left to preside blearily in the tower, while Lepage walked back to his billet through the blinding afternoon sunlight. Away to the south there were dark piled clouds and the faint rumble of thunder: Lepage kissed his fingers gratefully in their direction.

He spent a long time washing and scraping away with his razor, and dabbing talcum powder and aftershave lotion round his obstinately blue jowls. He changed into fresh jungle-green tunic and slacks, starch-stiff, crackling, with knife-edged creases. He neatly rolled up the sleeves of the tunic, anxious to show off his dark, muscular, hairy arms to the best advantage. Finally, being a Quebec Catholic, he muttered a quick *Our Father* and *Hail Mary*. In religious as in military matters, Jacques Lepage liked to placate Higher Authority wherever possible.

His toilet now complete, Lepage got out a bottle of Canadian Club Whisky and took a long swallow from it before refilling the silver hip-flask. He cranked up the battered portable gramophone that stood beside his bed, and put on a record. *I can't give you anything but le-erv, ba-bee,* the nasal American voice announced. Lepage nodded, as though in agreement, and sat down to draw yet another Rapunzel girl. It was just after four o'clock.

Despite the height at which they were flying, the air inside the Dakota was decidedly stuffy. Adrian Mesurier, whose real name happened to be Solly Steinbaum, yawned and stretched. He was not in the best of moods. Being a short, rotund, well-larded creature, he suffered agonies from prickly heat. He also, at this moment, had a very sizable hang-over. ENSA uniform made him itch, he had been torn away from a very promising friendship in Calcutta, and he was scared to death of being shot up by a stray Japanese Zero. To his friends in the Mandrake he had gone on at length about anything being better than joining up; now he had his doubts.

Adrian shifted in his hard bucket seat, and stared down at the jungle-quilted hills of the Arakan far below him. Like bloody boiled spinach, he thought. He yawned again. The aircraft lurched in an air-pocket, and he felt the first cold fingers of nausea caress his diaphragm. His copy of *Penguin New Writing* slipped to the floor. He remembered the delightfully coarse phrase he had first heard from that Marine—Stan was it?—in Malta. 'Roll on bleeding death.' he said aloud.

Across the aisle Adrian's *raison d'être*, the Singing Darling of the Services, sat writing a letter to her youngest son, who was in his last term at Marlborough. Her broad-nibbed Parker raced in easy, flourishing loops across the thin airmail paper. Adrian's unseemly expletive broke up her train of thought: two worlds which she normally

managed to keep in watertight compartments of her mind
now, momentarily, collided. She said nothing (she had
learnt better than to do that; as Adrian himself was wont
to remark, ' I've got the old cow's number, and she knows
it '), but a tiny frown pleated her forehead, and her lips
compressed themselves in mute censure.

She shook her neat, expensive blonde hair and glanced
over what she had written.

' Darling Dickie—It's been a wonderful trip so far, and
everyone's been too kind for words. Dear Lady Haughley
asked to be remembered to you last week—you probably
won't remember, but she came down to the Manor with
the Governor five years ago when they were on leave. This
is a strange and wonderful country—a bit hot, but such
fun, darling, honestly! The boys have been so appreciative,
too,—I've never had better audiences, or bigger. There's a
grand spirit sustaining them, and when I think of the
gallant show they're putting up, I feel that anything *I* can
do for them is *absurdly* inadequate!! They're so big, and
brown, and simple—I love them, I'd do *anything* for
them——'

It suddenly struck her how someone like Adrian Mesurier
might interpret that final remark. Blushing, she scratched
it out. How I stand that filthy little Yid I can't *think*, she
reflected, and then blushed even more furiously, remembering that anti-Semitism, however justified, was now
unpatriotic and against the War Effort.

Still, we all have to make sacrifices, she told herself
severely, fiddling with the big, chunky diamond on her
engagement finger. After all, Nigel's slaving himself to
death on Government contracts, and we did have all the
boys' education to fork out for, and God knows what it'll

cost to keep the Manor going with inflation and hardly any servants to be had. Anyway, the boys *need* me. I can't let them down.

She crossed her legs carefully, appraising them with a critical eye. Not so good as Marlene's maybe, she thought, but a damn sight better than most, and sheer nylon helps a lot. That article in *Stage* had given her a jolt, though, coupling Marlene's name with hers—*Two Theatrical Grandmothers,* the headline ran, and, lower down, *The Ageless Sandra Black.* Oh why, why, why had Philip got married as soon as he was commissioned? And why had that *bloody* demure little wife of his made the front page with *triplets* ten months later? 'Lady Davidson, better know to millions as singing star Sandra Black, said—' Well, it was a good thing the papers didn't know what she'd really said, wasn't it?

The famous cornflower-blue eyes misted over a little, the slim shoulders sagged in self-pity. Adrian, eyeing her with wan malice, thought: Oh *Lord*, we're in for a dose of the weepies. If only some of those simple adoring peasants could see her Ladyship after a real old jag—all that mascara running down, and a complexion like Clapham Junction in a cloudburst.

The aircraft lurched and slithered. Adrian swallowed, and shut his eyes.

The cockpit door banged open, and the co-pilot came down the aisle, balancing himself against the swoop and shock of each thermal current with the easy aplomb of a bus conductor. He saluted and said: 'We'll be landing at Myitchaung in about ten minutes, Miss Black.'

What a nice boy, she thought, taking in his tanned, ingenuous face, the well-manicured hands, the wispy fair moustache, the wings and Flying Officer's bars pinned to his khaki shirt. A decent background. You could tell by his voice. The right class.

'Thank you so much,' she said, and gave him her famous, intimate smile. He smiled back, bending over her in a touching affectation of gallantry. Then, as he did so, she caught the strong male smell of him, and felt dizzy. A sudden horribly vivid picture came into her mind of this young man stark naked, on a bed. She brought down the shutters of convention against this image as fast as any Leica. Feeling a bit tired, she told herself. Bumpy aircraft. Tummy upset. In a moment or two she was back to normal.

The co-pilot hesitated, uncertain whether to start a conversation. Then he saluted again, and strolled back to the cockpit. Adrian, who despite his condition had watched the whole exchange with fascinated interest, now stared hungrily after that elegant retreating back. Nothing, not even the imminent prospect of throwing up, could deter Adrian from his main interest in life for long.

Jesus, Lepage thought, sweating with fury and embarrassment, they gave her the bird. The bloody bird. There wasn't any getting away from it. And you couldn't blame them in a way. All that patriotic stuff, *here*, of all places. To a cheesed off, dead-beat bunch of bloody-minded Air Force technicians. *Keep it for the pongoes, Grandma,* someone had called out at the end. Christ, she'd gone as white as lard. What a beginning to a party.

He slopped the gin into tumblers, generously. The gramophone was about the only thing keeping its end up. *Money is the root of ALL evil, take it way, take it away, take it away*—He glanced over his shoulder. There they all sat, in those ghastly so-called easy chairs that the P.W.D. dug out from God knows where: half an hour of that treatment was enough to put a pattern on your backside for the next week.

'Here you are, Lady Davidson. You did say pink, didn't you?'

'Thank you, Mr Lepage. That's most kind of you.'

Cool as a cucumber now. *Lady Davidson.* Christ, that was one in the eye. That bloody Limey Chubb-Whitting-ton——

They had taken her down to inspect the canteen before the concert, and there was Chubb-Whittington mucking about with the lighting circuits. She gaped at him and said, 'Why, Michael, what on earth are you doing here?' and he'd said, 'Applying elementary psychology to tangled wires, Lady Davidson,' and they'd both laughed like the clappers and gone off into a long spiel about Marlborough and somebody called Lady Haughley and some one else called Sir Nigel who seemed to be La Black's old man. Lepage had stood there, out of the whole thing, feeling (as he put it to himself) like a proper tit. It reminded him of that crummy painting, what was it called? Oh yes: *When did you last see your Father?*

The air in the whitewashed little Mess was heavy with cigarette smoke. La Black was doing her best to make polite conversation with Summers, whose rabbity eyes kept flicker-ing across to Adrian Mesurier and the fair-haired co-pilot. The Adjutant had gone out half an hour before with the obvious intention of being sick, and hadn't come back. The embarrassing memory of the concert hung over them all like a monsoon cloud.

Lepage put on another record and cranked up the gramophone. *As I was going to Strawberry Fair, singing, singing, buttercups and daisies*—Get some booze into them, chum, he thought, it's your only hope. Adrian was sipping daintily at beer, stone cold sober. Sandra Black had had a couple of double gins, and looked as though she could hold them. Summers had a foul rum-and-orange concoction that looked like lasting him all night. The only heavy drinkers were the Adjutant and the captain of the Dakota, a taciturn Flight Lieutenant with a heavy black moustache, who had retired into the corner very early on, taking two bottles of Scotch along for company. Now one bottle was empty, and the Adj. had flaked out. The Flight Lieutenant, a sodden, melancholy Celt, sat on by himself, working his way steadily through the second bottle.

Oh blue her eyes and gold her hair, as I came down to Strawberry Fair—Well yes, Lepage thought, but what about the age of the chassis, eh? What about that? He poured himself another whisky, remembering the shock of that first meeting at close quarters. *Shag-lines.* Old trout in aspic, and her neck-muscles weren't the only things that were sagging, by the look of it. The Singing Darling of the Services. Well, what d'you know about that? Pardon me, ma'am, your retirement pension's showing. I guess she could get away with it at the Palladium—soft lights, sweet music, and the nearest pop-eyed fan about thirty feet clear of the footlights.

Lepage felt fury, frustration, disgust: the urge to hurt and humiliate. He stared at Sandra Black, sitting there exuding class and frigid manners and matronly respectability, and was astonished by the sheer violence of emotion she aroused in him. You posturing, la-di-da, plum-in-the-mouth old bitch, he said silently. You clapped-out pongo's

D*

idol, you *Tatler* remnant, you stuck-up bloody *sow*——

Adrian Mesurier heaved his sweat-stained, roly-poly body out of the chair in which he had been sprawling, and made for the door. Marble-pale and wicked as sin Adrian looked, a toad disturbed. Roll away the biggest stone in sight, Lepage thought, and you find a gink like that. The wicked fairy in person.

Adrian paused opposite Lepage, took out a cigarette from a gold case, and lit it with a gold lighter. His eyes shone black and hard as melanite, with just the same deep flicker of red in them. Adrian considered Lepage, and seemed satisfied with what he saw. His sad, fat, swarthy Jewish face became taut with purpose.

'Cigarette, ducky?' he said.

'Thanks.'

Lepage squinted as the little flame flickered up under his nose. He looked at the lighter, and the white hand, flecked with black hairs, that held it, and wondered how Mesurier had ever contrived to find a rich boy-friend.

'Come outside a minute,' Adrian said. 'I want to talk to you.'

Lepage hesitated.

'Be your age,' Adrian said. 'This isn't a trade proposition. I know you aren't queer—not,' he added thoughtfully, 'that I'd call you exactly *normal*, all the same.'

Their eyes met. Behind him Lepage could hear Sandra Black telling an involved anecdote about the Nizam of Hyderabad. The fair-haried co-pilot was picking out *The Bluebells of Scotland* with one hand on the Mess piano. Summers looked more rabbity than ever, and the Dakota captain had fallen asleep. Lepage and Adrian Mesurier walked out into the moonlight.

'Not much time, have you?' Adrian said.

'No.'

'I could help you.'

'You?' Lepage frowned He was a little drunk.

'This party's dying on its feet. I'm a pianist, remember?'

'Is that all, bud? Stack the chairs and have ourselves a conga? Sweet goodnights and off in the morning?'

Adrian shook his head. 'You can't see what's under your silly Canuck nose, can you? Don't let that lacquered Madam act fool you. One good push and she'll go like a paper bag——'

'What makes you so goddam sure I *do* want her?' said Lepage.

Adrian sighed. 'I could give you the obvious answers to that, ducky,' he said, 'but I won't. Let's just say it's because you hate her bloody guts, shall we? I've always found hate a *much* more effective aphrodisiac than sheeps'-eyes under the moon.'

In the far south the thunder growled softly. The heavy, humid, tropical air wrapped them about, with its sweetly cloying smell of decay.

Lepage said : 'What do *you* get out of this?'

'Not, I fear, the blond sweetie-pie,' Adrian murmured. 'A long campaign there.' Then his casual air dropped away from him, and he seemed anything but epicene as he gripped Jacques Lepage by both shoulders and said : 'Listen, you dumb hunk. Nothing—*nothing*, do you understand?—would give me more exquisite pleasure than to see Lady bloody Davidson put over the wooden horse——'

'And yelling for mercy?' Clever Jacques, sophisticated Jacques, who has bought paper-backed pornography in Calcutta, and knows all about sadism.

'No,' Adrian whispered. 'Oh Jacques, Jacques, how stupid you are! I know my lady D. by now. I know her better than she knows herself. I want to stand there, in that exquisitely squalid little room, and think of Sir Nigel and the public school tradition, and watch dear Sandra being *honest* for once. Not yelling for mercy, Jacques; oh no; *asking for more.*'

Lepage drew in his breath quickly.

'Christ,' he said. 'Tell me how. That's all. Just tell me how.'

Adrian stifled a tremendous yawn. *Really,* he thought, what a bore this creature was! To Adrian's quick, cruel, unforgiving mind stupidity rated as a far worse crime than malice. But the situation was perfect, and might never recur. Lepage it had to be. And in a way, Lepage's very disabilities gave extra edge to his, Adrian's, satisfaction. To have the immaculate Lady Davidson knocked off her hand-carved perch by this hick Casanova from the lumber-camps —*that,* Adrian reflected, would make the rest of the tour sheer bliss, would offer an ample salve for every snub and slight. If you treat me like your bloody butler, *sweetie,* he murmured to the stars in silent apostrophe, you can't blame me if you get cast for a star part in What the Butler Saw.

Aloud he said: 'A little loosening of the inhibitions to begin with, dear boy. Her Ladyship practically takes her bath in Booth's and Gordon's, so you might try *adulterating* it a little—I gather the local brews are *most* efficacious. And then I think a little sing-song, maybe? Sweet background music on that *horrible* Naafi joanna you have in there, with little Adrian, un-spotlit, at the keyboard. . . .'

He took Lepage's arm and led him lovingly back inside, a diminutive priest ascending the Capitol steps with his white and garlanded bull. The swag, butter-yellow Burmese moon shone down impassively, and night-gadding mosquitoes, malaria-laden, coaxed from imaginary fiddles their hysterical, higher-than-top-C note. To the duty sergeant in the control tower there drifted, faintly, the sound of popular rag-time being thumped out on the battered Officers' Mess piano. He grimaced, rubbed his eyes, and brewed himself another mug of rum-and-cocoa.

'Jacques,' Sandra Black gasped, 'you dance wonderfully——'

Lepage grinned, a wolf beribboned, and held her tighter, spinning to the exotic intricacies of *Jealousy*, with Adrian shamelessly exaggerating each rhythmic pattern, slurring and swooping over the notes with that metallic cynicism which is the peculiar hallmark of the second-rate professional accompanist. The furniture had been pushed back into the corners of the room, and the Dakota captain carried to his whiskified bed. Lepage and the young co-pilot—whose name turned out to be Christopher—danced turn and turn about with Sandra Black, while Summers sprawled, bored, in his chair beside the piano, chain-smoking, his eyes on Adrian. The only light in the room now came from one table-lamp, a jury-rigged affair constructed from a Vat 69 bottle.

With a final flourish Adrian brought the tango to its conclusion. Lepage and Sandra Black stood there for a second after the music had stopped, still locked in their conventionally legitimate embrace. Then, laughing, they dropped side by side into the two empty chairs beside Christopher the co-pilot.

Sandra shook out her hair and said: 'Lord, that was hot

work.' She lay straight back, legs slightly spread, and ran her tongue round her lips. 'Give me a cigarette, Christopher, there's a lamb.'

Like a sleep-walker the boy took out his case and opened it. His hand was trembling visibly. Lepage became acutely conscious of the sound of his own breathing. Sandra Black's hand came out, its chunky diamond glowing in the subdued light, and brushed Christopher's fingers. When she had the cigarette in her mouth, Christopher, performing each gesture as though he were under water, struck a match and cupped his hands round the flame. Sandra Black leant forward, blonde hair falling across her face, and put both hands round Christopher's. The atmosphere in the room was suddenly charged with something more than thunder. In the flare of the match Lepage saw her eyes, their blueness mild no longer, but dilated, mad, brilliant.

Adrian crooned, half to himself: '*A bloody deed! almost as bad, good mother, as kill a king, and marry with his brother.*' He leaned over Lepage's chair, one hand still rippling idly up and down the keyboard, and with the other gave the Canadian's ear a gentle tweak. 'Hamlet's mum,' he said, mischievously.

Lepage didn't get it.

Adrian settled back in his chair, hunched over the piano, a cigarette dangling from his mouth. He looked like Hoagy Carmichael in a distorting mirror: a bulbous, globular, malevolent gnome. He began, very quietly, to play Ravel's *Bolero*. Lepage shivered with frustration and excitement. His eyes devoured Sandra Black. She still had hold of Christopher's hands. As the drumming, hypnotic rhythm of the music reached her she pulled herself up, and drew Christopher into the middle of the floor. She wrapped herself round him, both arms clasped behind his neck, swaying to the rhythm in a strange, boneless fashion, like water rippling.

Adrian quickened the tempo a little. Lepage sat straight up in his chair, gripping both arms fiercely. Summers looked more bored than ever. And then, in a deep, strangled voice more like a man's, Sandra Black gasped: 'Oh *God*—', gripped the back of Christopher's head convulsively, turned her face sideways, like a coy hen about to peck, and clamped her mouth on his like some writhing polyp.

'*Her lips suck forth his soul: see where it flies,*' Adrian quoted happily. His knowledge of the Elizabethans was extensive but specialised.

For an instant Christopher seemed to respond with equal passion. Then, with a jerky, abrupt movement he tore himself away. Adrian stopped dead in the middle of an unresolved chord. Dead sober now, his ridiculous little fair moustache smeared with saliva and lipstick, chest heaving as though he would vomit at any moment, Christopher stood there and stared at Sandra Black. His face registered horror, and disbelief, and nauseated disgust. He looked about fifteen. He tried to say something, but the words would not come. Then he shook his head muzzily and dashed out, clapping a handkerchief to his mouth as he went. The door slammed behind him.

Adrian said: 'Even her best friends wouldn't tell her.' His right hand sketched a series of frivolous little arabesques on the high notes. Then he swung round on his chair and stared at the woman standing in the middle of the floor. Not a minute of this did he intend to miss. He was going to have his money's-worth.

Still Lepage did not move.

Sandra Black's body went quite stiff. An ugly, meaning-less rictus shrank her face into a small dead mask, a wire-and-paper maquette. Her flesh in that moment looked leprous, the colour and consistency of a wasp's nest. She staggered across to her chair and dropped into it. She put her hands over her eyes. After a moment she took them away again.

'You see?' she said, in a flat, brittle voice that matched her expression. 'You see? I can't cry. I can't even cry.'

Lepage moved. He took her glass, half-filled it with neat gin, followed this with about a gill of brandy, and topped the mixture off with a perfunctory squirt of soda.

'Drink up,' he said, shortly.

She held the glass and stared at him.

'You bloody bastard,' she said.

Then she drank the whole glassful at one go, and threw the glass across the room.

She said, bitterly: 'Are you sure you've drunk enough not to care, *Flight Lieutenant*? Will I make *you* sick too? Will I? Will I?' Her voice soared to a high edge of hysteria. '*You'd better see what you're getting, hadn't you?*' she screamed, out of control now, body shaking again, mouth frantic, and with one hand she ripped open the flimsy cotton dress from neckline to waist. Buttons flew about the room, and Adrian gave a high, whinnying squirt of laughter as the strap of her brassière parted with a snap like a small pistol shot. His cold homosexual mind thought: *How hilariously comic our moments of high tragedy are to the observer*. For a moment, to his surprise, he found him-self staring with something very like pity at Sandra Black's pathetic, drooping breasts.

Then, at last, Jacques Lepage went in for the kill. His

victim made no resistance, and he said not a word. His animal vindictiveness expressed itself only in grunts, bites, contemptuous violation. Coldly Adrian Mesurier watched his Laocoön-like writhings, unsatisfied still, waiting for the shameful, uncontrollable heifer's moans that would proclaim Sandra Black's ultimate humiliation.

When that moment came, Adrian Mesurier smiled to himself. He got up, glanced at the now sleeping Summers, and quietly walked out of the Mess in search of his billet for the night. Tomorrow, he reflected, would be enjoyable, to say the least of it. Behind him that tortured, ecstatic voice rose higher and higher, shrill, incoherent, the squeal of a doe-rabbit in a trap.

Flight Sergeant Staines and Sergeant Chubb-Whittington, who were up late in their own Mess, heard the noise, and looked at each other.

Michael said: 'We'd better go see what on earth's happening——'

'Maybe,' Flight Sergeant Staines said. 'Maybe. One thing I've learnt in this mob, boy, is never stick your nose into anything you don't have to.' He looked at Michael with his wise, experienced, blinkered sheep's eyes, and added: 'How d'you know she ain't enjoying it, eh?'

Michael flushed. 'For God's sake,' he said, 'she's not that sort of woman.'

Staines said: 'Any woman is that sort of woman given the chance.' He swallowed his beer, grimacing. 'Yankee horse-piss. What sort of booze ever came out of a *tin*?'

The noise stopped. There was a long silence. Michael Chubb-Whittington got up and said: 'You can do what you like. I'm going over.'

Staines sighed. 'Then I'll just have to come and keep

an eye on you,' he said. 'Can't trust you youngsters an inch.'

Together they walked across in the moonlight. There was a light shining from Lepage's room: Staines peered cautiously through the window, and saw the big French-Canadian sprawled across his bed, half undressed.

'Out for the count,' he whispered to Michael.

They turned across the passageway, and paused at the door of the Officers' Mess. From inside there came a faint groan. Staines quickly opened the door.

'Oh my God,' said Michael Chubb-Whittington. '*Lady Davidson!*'

The spreadeagled figure of Sandra Black stirred, groaned again, and rolled over on its side. With a horrible noise which Michael tried in vain not to hear the Singing Darling of the Services was epically sick on the floor.

Staines glanced quickly at Michael. 'What's the matter, chum?' he said. 'Never seen a bint puke before? Come on, give me a hand with her. We don't want to wake the whole bleeding camp.'

Between them they carried Sandra Black, unconscious and near-naked, to her bed in the C.O.'s room. Here Staines, with a practised delicacy that astonished Michael almost more than anything else, removed what was left of her clothes, searched around till he found her black chiffon night-dress, put it on her, and tucked her up, like a child, between clean sheets. Finally he squeezed out a flannel and sponged her face.

'Now then, young feller-me-lad,' said Flight Sergeant Staines, 'you come back with me and we'll put that Mess to rights. First there's Mr Summers to get out of the way, and then a spot of fatigue-work, eh? You know, Sergeant

Chubb-Whatsit, it's surprising how far you can get with a mop and a bucket of 'ot water.' He grinned at the younger man and added, paternally: 'Cheer up, cock. It's not so very dreadful. Everyone'll have forgotten all about it in the morning, I shouldn't wonder.'

Michael shook his head, in a shock of disillusionment.

Staines said: 'There's no doubt about it, you grow up fast in the Services.'

It was a beautiful morning, without a cloud in the sky. Below them the Bay of Bengal crawled and glittered, cobalt-lacquered, sprinkled with golden flakes. The plane droned steadily southwards, riding as smooth as a Daimler. Immured behind the door of their cockpit, pilot and co-pilot nursed sizable hang-overs. In the main body of the plane Adrian Mesurier sat disconsolate, surrounded by a jumble of freight ranging from spare parts to coils of barbed wire, and stared across the aisle with lacklustre eyes.

'For heaven's sake, Adrian,' Lady Davidson said, 'do stop looking like a wet week-end! It's a wonderful day, and I'm *madly* excited about seeing Rangoon—we *must* see if we can get the C.O. to take us out to the Schwe Dagon Pagoda—I've heard so much about it—it's solid gold, you know, and all those delightful little shrines, and you have to take your shoes off at the bottom of a huge porphyry stair-case, or something—*Adrian*, you're not listening to a *word* I say——'

Adrian Mesurier blinked at the daisy-fresh, trim creature opposite him, so svelte in her well-cut green uniform, and shut his eyes, and let the pure vowels wash over him in a well-bred tide. You can't win, he thought. You just can't win. The next moment he was fast asleep.

Lady Davidson unscrewed her Parker, unzipped her writing-case, and set herself to finish her long letter to Dickie. 'It was a jolly little concert,' she wrote, 'such a change from the big stations, much more intimate, if you see what I mean. The C.O. was away, but everyone was *very* kind—I even had the C.O.'s own room! And now the weather's cleared up again, and I'm all set for the next leg of the trip. Take care of yourself darling, and remember—' her pen hesitated for a moment only, it was an old joke between them—'don't do anything I wouldn't do! Take care of yourself, Dickie, and a big hug from your loving Mummy.' She re-read this effort, frowning a little, then added: 'P.S. I do hope you manage to get your 1st XI Colours after all—I know how much it means to you, and it *does* count for something still, doesn't it?' She smiled, folded the sheets of flimsy, put them in an airmail envelope, and addressed the envelope in her firm, confident sprawling hand.

The door of the cockpit opened, and the fair-haired co-pilot called Christopher came out.

In a stiff, official voice he said: 'We shall be landing at Mingaladon Airport in fifteen minutes, Lady Davidson.' He carefully avoided looking at her as he spoke.

Lady Davidson gave him her famous intimate smile. She said: 'Thank you so much. That's kind of you. You've been terribly sweet to me all this trip. I do appreciate it.'

Christopher blushed scarlet, mumbled something, and retreated behind the privacy of the cockpit door. Funny boy, Lady Davidson thought. So shy, rather nice. She yawned and stretched, tingling with well-being. Not a trace of thunder; it looked as though the monsoon would hold off for at least another week. I really get all the luck, she told herself, staring out at the brilliant blue sky. Then she thought: I mustn't waste this last quarter of an hour, there'll be so many other things to do when we get to Rangoon——

She spread the airmail pad out on her knees again, and dashed off a practised and gracious bread-and-butter letter to Flight Lieutenant Jacques Lepage, R.A.F. Station Myitchaung. As the ground tilted up to meet them she sighed with relief, screwed up her Parker, and took a quick look at her face in her compact mirror, wondering, for the umpteenth time, why air travel always tended to make her nose shine. This small problem was still occupying her as she stepped out of the Dakota and saw, with a flush of pleasure, that this time they'd laid on a proper Guard of Honour.

A QUESTION OF DIALECT

I'D lost sight of Selby-Hill for nearly ten years. I know in the academic world everybody's supposed to know everybody else; but to start with, I'm a mathematician and Selby-Hill specialises in late Greek dialects. For another thing, he's an amateur, and only works when he feels like it. His grandfather made a fortune in the days when you could make fortunes—rubber, I think it was—and his father died of hobnailed liver before more than a quarter of the capital was spent.

I don't know what made Selby-Hill take up scholarship. I suppose he found he had a natural talent for languages. Certainly he swept up all the classical prizes at Cambridge. But it probably went deeper than that. He was, I suspect, rather conscious of being a Nabob—even in the third generation—and was yearning for the gentlemanly eighteenth century ideal. At the same time he didn't get on with the genuine quality at all, and resented the fact. He probably got a hell of a kick out of being able to fly to Constantinople for the weekend to verify a doubtful reading in a manuscript.

He was outspoken as only a really rich man can be, and in Cambridge the effect was devastating. It was like dropping large rocks into a goldfish pond. The thing was, Selby-Hill really believed in scholarship, like a religion, and thought that anyone who didn't was not only a fool but a knave. He referred to the Professor of Ceramics, in public, as a damned grocer, all because he took off Sundays to play golf. They couldn't stop him winning a prize Fellowship—that would have required more casuistry than even a Board of Electors could produce—but they took very good care that he wasn't given a staff appointment. Of course, in Selby-Hill's case, this was something of a empty gesture. As he constantly reminded them on High Table, after one of his more than usually devastating remarks, he wasn't dependant on *them* for a living. He celebrated the end of his three years' tenure by getting spectacularly drunk, and then went off to his house in Hampstead—a large, musty place full of rare books and Turkish rugs and Byzantine paintings—and continued happily with his work on Greek dialects. He had a special bee in his bonnet about a hybrid growth called Arcado-Cypriot, which nobody knew very much about, and he was to be seen every day in the British Museum—a tall, rather ungainly figure, with bony hands and a mop of fair hair that kept falling over one eye.

I don't want you to get the idea from this that I knew Selby-Hill well. I didn't. Apart from one rather special occasion that I'll tell you about in a moment, our paths seldom crossed. But one couldn't help hearing stories about him: he was that sort of person. For instance, his correspondence with Heinrich Von Schlesinger.

Von Schlesinger had the distinction of being the only other scholar in Europe (and as far as I know in the world) who knew anything about Arcado-Cypriot. You might think that he and Selby-Hill would have greeted one another like long-lost brothers, pooled their research, and produced a combined *magnum opus*. Which only shows how little you know about the world of scholarship. When Selby-Hill first came across an article by von Schlesinger on the subject—it was published in one of those Prussian periodicals that take three lines of close type to print their title—he was visibly shaken. He retired to the British Museum for a week; and thereafter emerged, pale but triumphant, with the information that von Schlesinger was a charlatan, and his article a tissue of factual inaccuracies and windy Teutonic speculation. He followed up these personal aspersions with an article in the *Journal of Hellenic Studies*, which for controlled acidulity left Housman at the starting-post.

This was the beginning of the Great Correspondence. Selby-Hill, with ill-concealed relish, sent von Schlesinger an off-print of the article, together with a covering letter containing the choicer gems of rudery which the editor of the *J.H.S.* had tactfully omitted. Thereafter the battle was on. Selby-Hill wrote in English and von Schlesinger in German, but as a slight gesture of international good-will Selby-Hill began his letters '*Liebe Herr*', without an exclamation mark, and von Schlesinger 'My Dear Sir', with one. Unbiassed observers told me, after this had been going on for about a year, that the score was deuce, with an occasional Vantage Server in Selby-Hill's favour. What really scared Selby-Hill, apparently, was the possibility that the unspeakable Hun would be elected to the Chair of Hellenistic and Byzantine Greek in Cambridge.

This Chair was Selby-Hill's dream. He had campaigned for years for its establishment, and the opposition had been tremendous. This was, on the face of it, hardly surprising. Selby-Hill, through his devastating outspokenness, had got himself into the position of being about the best-loathed man in Cambridge. As he said to me one evening when he'd asked me round for a drink (I don't think he was on speaking terms with any of his colleagues at the time): 'The bloody fools have got two courses open to them. Either they can refuse to establish the Chair, or—' his face flushed with anger at the very thought '—they can establish it and elect someone else to spite me.'

'But my dear chap, there's no one else with your quali- fications——'

Selby-Hill looked at me, took a long gulp of brandy, and spat out the two words: 'Von Schlesinger.'

'I see,' I said. I did, too. It was the sort of thing Cam- bridge would love.

'There's no honesty in this damned racket,' said Selby- Hill, and poured himself another double brandy. 'There's one thing, though,' he added, brightening. 'Von Schlesinger hasn't done any field-work.'

'Field-work?'

Selby-Hill launched into a long theory about testing the dialect theories he'd formed in Arcadia and Cyprus. He was sure there'd be vestigial remains among the local inhabit- ants. It was on the tip of my tongue to ask him whether he'd considered taking a tape-recorder round the Soho restaurants I didn't understand more than one word in five—the brandy had warmed him and he was well away—but the upshot of it all was that he packed his bags next day and set off for Greece for three months. He came back with a box-full of recordings and crackling with enthusiasm. Von Schle- singer was fixed once and for all, he said.

A week later the war broke out, and the Chair of Hellenistic and Byzantine Greek, along with a lot of other scholarly luxuries, was suspended for the duration. I went into the Navy and spent five fairly uneventful years working on radar. I didn't think much about Cambridge, and I certainly forgot about Selby-Hill and his feud with Von Schlesinger.

I spent V-E day in Cairo, of all places. I'm not a particularly sociable person, and all the junketings depressed me. I found a quiet corner of the Officers' Club, bought a bottle of whisky, and settled down to drink by myself.

About eight in the evening a tall Colonel of Intelligence pushed through the mob and came to a halt by my table. He had cropped blond hair and a sunburnt face and a D.S.O. He looked vaguely familiar. We stared at one another for a moment.

'Selby-Hill,' I said, not really believing it.

His face broke into a smile. 'My dear fellow,' he said, and sat down rather suddenly. He was extremely tight. I poured him a strong whisky. He said what I presume was the equivalent of 'Down the hatch' in some language I didn't know. I looked interrogative.

'Greek,' he said. He obviously hadn't lost his passion for languages. He carried on for ten minutes without stopping about Cretan dialects. In order to stop the flow I said: 'What have you been doing since I saw you last?' I was really curious, too. I just couldn't see Selby-Hill as a colonel.

He was sporting a little tooth-brush moustache, and he gave it a professional wipe before replying. His vocabulary was an odd mixture now of Army slang and academic precision.

'Look,' he said, 'are you in a hurry?'

I said I wasn't.

'Good show. It's a bit of luck meeting you here. I wanted

to tell someone about it, and you're the only person likely to understand.'

I looked suitably sympathetic. War produces some odd situations, but I'd certainly never expected to act as father-confessor to Selby-Hill.

'Well,' he said, 'the War Office got on to me as soon as the balloon went up. Knew all about my languages, and that expedition I made to Greece in '39. Ignorant lot of so-and-so's. Had some idea that Ancient Greek was the same as Modern. So did most of the broken-down ushers they picked.'

I asked if they sent him on a course.

He smiled modestly. 'Yes,' he said, 'they did. After it was over they kept me on as an instructor.'

Out of self-protection, I shouldn't wonder.

'They sent me out to Greece in '40,' said Selby-Hill. 'Nothing much to do but lounge around Athens, so I got on with my dialects. It was bloody annoying when the evacuation came.'

'Where were you at the time?' I asked.

'Crete. Absolute shambles.'

'Was that where you got your D.S.O.?'

Selby-Hill looked faintly ashamed. 'I'd always heard they sent the damn things up with the rations,' he said. 'Now I'm bloody sure of it. I didn't notice what was going on half the time. You know how absent-minded I am.'

I said I understood. A lot of V.C.'s are the same way.

He settled down more firmly in his chair.

'That isn't the important thing,' he said. He lit a cigarette and frowned. 'I got tired of being in England. Couldn't get on with my own work. Stupid war-time restrictions on correspondence.'

I looked at him sharply, remembering Von Schlesinger. It occurred to me that Selby-Hill probably missed his favourite whipping-boy.

'So I volunteered to go back,' he went on placidly.

'Parachute course, and all that?' I asked.

'Yes,' he said. He'd obviously enjoyed the whole thing. I always suspected there was a streak of *Boys Own Paper* in him somewhere.

'Well,' said Selby-Hill, 'I had a pretty good time on the whole. I was on a job in Arcadia because I knew the terrain. Unrivalled opportunity for studying local accents and idiom, too. We had a good bunch of Partisans, on the whole. When they weren't arguing about Communism.

'Trouble was,' said Selby-Hill, 'they were too damned independent. Wouldn't obey orders.' He shook his head heavily.

'We had a good hide-out in the mountains,' he went on. 'Hardly anyone knew where it was. The Germans certainly didn't. We had a wireless transmitter there. Got Cairo easily. We were the nerve centre for the whole area. Only half a dozen Greeks were in the secret, and they kept it. There were a lot of big operations coming off—this was in '43—and it was essential that this place of ours should remain undisturbed. It was only five miles from German H.Q.'

Selby-Hill poured himself a whisky from my bottle.

'Well, one evening I was just settling down for the night after supper when a couple of my Greeks came in, as pleased as Punch. They'd captured a German officer. They dumped him in a corner of the cave, tied up. Obviously they were expecting to be congratulated.

'I cursed them for five minutes. I had,' said Selby-Hill

modestly, 'made a special study of their more—er—florid objurgations.'

I said I could well believe it.

Selby-Hill went on, dreamily: 'The things I said about their mothers, and what they did with their dogs, were quite artistic. But I was really furious. I asked them what the hell they thought we were going to do with this damned man? They said, cheerfully, interrogate him under torture and then shoot him. They thought it was a great game.

'The nasty thing was, they were right. We couldn't keep the fellow as a prisoner. He might escape, and then the whole show would go up. I suppose what annoyed me most was being forced into the moral responsibility for the whole thing. But I knew it had to be done. A lot of beastly things have to be done in war-time.'

I was beginning to revise my estimate of Selby-Hill.

'So I got them to bring him out of the corner where they'd dumped him,' said Selby-Hill. 'They put him down on the floor of the cave in front of me, and I had a look at him by the light of the fire. He didn't look much of a soldier. Dark and thin, too intelligent. Obviously a conscript. He was scared to death, as well he might be.

'My German's fairly fluent, so I started off with the usual stuff about name, rank and number.'

Selby-Hill hesitated. I could see the scene clearly: the frightened *Wehrmacht* officer, Selby-Hill cloaking himself in his best lecturing manner, the Greek mountaineers gathered round with their knives to enjoy the baiting, the nightmare atmosphere of the cave.

'It was Von Schlesinger,' said Selby-Hill. 'Of all the damned guerillas in Greece, he had to get captured by me.'

I said yes, coincidences did happen in war-time, but did this one make all that difference?

Selby-Hill snorted impatiently. 'Of course it did, you fool,' he said. 'There aren't many people in the world I'd feel much compunction about shooting. But this was a matter of . . . of professional honesty.'

'*What?*' I said.

Selby-Hill explained patiently. 'After the war,' he said, 'there's no doubt the Chair of Hellenistic and Byzantine Greek will be re-established. Don't you see? Here were the only two possible candidates for it in a Greek cave, captor and prisoner. Supposing I shot Von Schlesinger. How was I to be sure of my motives?'

I didn't point out to Selby-Hill that the prisoner's identity was irrelevant to the situation that made his shooting necessary. I was too fascinated by the realisation that Selby-Hill obviously hadn't been as sure of his Arcado-Cypriot theory as he made out. Scholarly honesty is an odd thing.

'There was only one thing to be done,' said Selby-Hill. 'I told him who I was. I must say, he didn't behave very well. He seemed to think this was a good reason for letting him go free on the spot. Oddly sentimental notions these Germans have.'

I felt there was no adequate comment on this.

'I pointed out to him,' Selby-Hill said, his voice getting more precise with each double whisky, 'that here was an admirable moment for resolving some of the points we had discussed, somewhat fruitlessly, by correspondence. He appeared to imagine I was indulging in what his countrymen so expressively call *Schadenfreude*. But in the end I persuaded him I was being reasonable. Obviously, I didn't tell him the reason underlying my actions.'

'Obviously not,' I said.

'So we got down to details,' Selby-Hill said. 'Luckily we both had good memories. It was nearly dawn before I had fully satisfied myself of the complete validity of my claims, and the utter worthlessness of Von Schlesinger to occupy any such position of trust and responsibility as a Professorship.'

'It must have been a rather macabre scene,' I said. 'And what did you do then?'

Selby-Hill lowered his eyes, as if at something distasteful.

'There was only one thing to be done in the circumstances,' he said. 'I took him outside and shot him. I don't think he felt anything.'

Selby-Hill poured the last whisky from the bottom of the bottle, drank it down at one go, and passed out.

That was ten years ago. Skimming through the *Times* one day last month I noticed, under the heading *University News*, the following item:

'The Electors to the Professorship of Hellenistic and Byzantine Greek in the University of Cambridge have elected Dr J. M. B. Selby-Hill, D.S.O., M.A., F.B.A., into the said Professorship with effect from October next. . . .'

It had taken them nine years to overcome their prejudices; but as I tore out the item and put it carefully away in my wallet, I reflected that they'd certainly got the right man.

Then I sat down to write a note of congratulation to the new Professor. I didn't get an answer.

THE PRISONER

THEY had been on patrol for eight hours, and now it was noon. Through the dark tangled tracery of the trees the Burmese sun struck down, strident as a copper gong, drawing steam from the damp black earth. The air had the humidity of a Kew hot-house; it was this, and not the mere heat, that told on Lieutenant Blake and Sergeant McAndrew. Even the African Askaris were bathed in sweat. On them the beaded drops looked incongruous; it was was as if they were black for nothing. The mosquitoes sang in Blake's ears like a fever.

Blake glanced at his wrist watch and waved his hand for the patrol to halt. A runner went forward, bent double, to pass the word to the leading scout. His boots cracked and squelched in the soggy undergrowth, and Blake watched him with nervous irritation.

These nigs are supposed to be trackers, he thought. Trackers my foot. You can hear them a mile off. He removed his watch, rubbing the red patch where the metal had chafed his sweating wrist. Ought to have got a leather strap in Calcutta. Too late now. He let the Smith & Wesson dangle from its lanyard round his neck, unbuttoned the breast-pocket of his tunic and took out a cigarette-case. The matches were inside, together with a strip of abrasive. Any ordinary box would have been soaked in half an hour.

E

He lit a cigarette. Behind him the Africans squatted, their Stens across their knees, breathing heavily.

Blake remained standing, his eyes wrinkled above his map. He was very young, with an aggressively pink and white complexion. Six months ago he had still been at Sandhurst. The rakish bush-hat he wore made him look like a Boy Scout, and the revolver at the end of its lanyard looked as though it might overbalance his slim body.

He was still staring at the map when Sergeant Mc-Andrew made his way up from the rear of the column. McAndrew presented a striking contrast to Blake. His short craggy body, with its wide shoulders and lumpish strength, gave him an almost simian appearance. His face was craggy, too, with the reddish hair and high cheek-bones of the Scot. With all this he was massively imperturbable: a quiet disciplinarian, a cool head in a crisis, a great singer of ballads in camp.

McAndrew came close to Blake and said: 'Shall I be telling the men to take their tiffin, sir?' His voice was surprisingly gentle.

Blake remained silent for a moment, staring him out, McAndrew had one hand in the shoulder-strap of his pack; with the other he held his Sten. It was as though he were challenging Blake to demand an impossible salute.

Blake said: 'Of course. And they'd better be quick about it. We're moving in ten minutes.'

'Ten minutes, sir?' There was a faint hint of reproof in the words. 'It's been damned heavy going, sir. We'll be all the better for a wee bit breather.'

'Are you questioning my orders, Sergeant?'

'Of course not, sir.' McAndrew ran a hairy paw over his brick-red face. 'But . . .'

'There's no "but".' The nearest Askari looked up curiously, recognising the thin edge of hysteria in the officer's tone. McAndrew remained impassive. 'I'd best give the word, then, sir.'

'Very well. Come back as soon as you've finished. I want to talk to you.'

'Sir.' McAndrew turned and pushed his way through the clinging undergrowth. The baby-faced bastard, he thought. He'll have us all up the creek before he's through. I'd as soon patrol under a Glasgie whoor.

McAndrew had been with Blake for three months now, and it had required all his tact and patience to prevent an open row. He was not much given to mental analysis, and Blake puzzled him. The boy was not inefficient: on the contrary, he drove his men ruthlessly. Yet there was something very wrong with him. McAndrew found it unpleasant to look him in the face; those pale blue eyes and thin lips seemed always on the verge of some appalling transformation, from which they were restrained by sheer force of will only.

He hasna been oot here lang enough to be goin' roond the bend, though McAndrew; but Christ, he shows all the signs. Maybe he's scairt. But it isna of the Japs, I'm thinking.

The Askaris squatted motionless, eating with ruminative absorption, cows chewing the cud. They took no notice of the flies that buzzed round their heads, attracted by the smell of food. McAndrew, staring at them, felt repelled, for the hundredth time, by the pink palms of their hands, their sour musky odour. Yet he was, in his undemonstrative way, attached to them: they were first-rate fighting men. If he had a colour prejudice, he had pushed it resolutely into the back of his mind for the duration.

He found Blake where he had left him. As McAndrew approached, Blake took the cigarette from his mouth and ground it out with his heel. This time McAndrew saluted; a mere flick of the hand to the rim of his battered bush-hat. Blake, who was bare-headed, flushed.

'Come and look at this,' he said sharply. The two men squatted down together. McAndrew's eyes were held by the long-fingered, fine-boned hand that darted nervously over the map. Breeding, he thought, half envious, half contemptuous. Long line of officers and gentlemen. Bit too much breeding if you ask me. Needs some healthy blood. Their unspoken antagonism hung in the humid air.

Blake said: 'We've been moving south-east for five hours.' His fingers traced their route. 'We ought to be near the edge of the jungle.' McAndrew nodded. 'Intelligence reports Jap convoys moving up along this road here. Our job's to find out more about it.'

'I see, sir. Just a recce.'

Blake's eyes turned towards McAndrew for the first time. 'After a soft option, Sergeant?' His thin lips compressed themselves. 'I'm sorry to disappoint you, but if you use your brain you'll see what we're up against.' McAndrew said nothing. Blake went on: 'We've got to get details. You can't get details by sitting on your backside in cover with a pair of field-glasses. Besides, Intelligence want— tangible evidence.'

'Tangible evidence, sir?'

'A prisoner.' McAndrew felt Blake's body trembling. Fever? Excitement? Fear? He said, non-committally. 'I see, sir.'

Blake lit another cigarette. He did not offer the case to

McAndrew. Then he said: 'There's a bridge across the river about a mile clear of the jungle. The Japs have got a small guard detachment on it. We're going to collar one of the sentries. Here. Take a look for yourself.'

McAndrew started. 'It's a mile across open paddy— no cover. We've got a chance in a thousand.' Then he saw the expression on Blake's face, and could have bitten his tongue out.

'Windy, McAndrew?'

'No, sir. But I'm no a bluidy fool. . . .'

'We won't bother about that. I didn't say *you* were going on the job. Two men. Volunteers, of course.' He paused, relishing the situation.

The little swine, thought McAndrew. He's cooked this up on his own. Intelligence can be pretty stupid, but this beats all. Why, though? He looked at the thin pink and white face, frowning. He kens damn fine that one of us two'll have to go. And I ken damn fine which it's going to be. He said: 'Well, sir, if we must do it, we must. I'll have a bash.' The bastard. He knows all about cowardice. He had me fine then. Flicking the bloody nerve.

Blake's lips relaxed slightly. 'Good,' he observed. 'You can choose your own man.' He jerked his head towards the Askaris, then added, almost maliciously, 'There's an M.M. in this if you bring it off.'

'Sir.' McAndrew stood up, puzzled, vaguely aware of an unexplained element in his officer's behaviour. Was Blake trying to bribe him, cover up for his own uncertainty?

'Right. We'll get on the move,' Blake said. 'We ought to be clear of this—' he gestured at the heavy undergrowth '—in about half an hour. I'll give you a final briefing then.'

McAndrew saluted mechanically. Two minutes later the patrol began to move forward again.

It could be worse, Blake thought. Much worse.

Propped on his elbows, he focused his glasses on the high wooden bridge, the lenses filming over with condensation, sweat dripping down his cheeks. On the far side, camouflaged among bushes, he made out two tents. A solitary guard paced to and fro on the parapet.

Damned nerve. I suppose they don't expect any trouble so far back. After all, this is their territory. His spine crawled. Anyway, there must be a big force somewhere near. Wouldn't leave a detachment like that all on their own.

Blake twisted the adjuster till the sentry sprang out sharp and clear. He was shivering with excitement. Tall for a Jap. Nearly six foot. Must be an Imperial Guardsman. Odd job for a crack soldier.

Crack soldier. He licked his lips. If only that clot McAndrew doesn't make a nonsense of it. He swallowed. No, not this time. This time he's got to bring it off. But next time it'll be different. Bloody Scotchman.

His mind travelled back to a dusty form-room, to Archie Stewart with his freckles and big bony hands, the crowd of fifth-formers sniggering, the excruciating pain of a knee in his belly, his arm being slowly twisted up behind his back.

'Ye're a beastly little funk, Blake. Go on say it.'

'I won't. I won't.' Laughter, unbearable laughter.

'Oh yes ye will, ye stinking Sassenach.'

And he had.

Now his eye followed the long irrigation embankment

behind which McAndrew and his Askari were edging towards the bridge. They were out of sight. The thought of McAndrew with his belly in the dirt gave Blake a stab of pleasure. But McAndrew would serve his purpose. Blake trained his glasses hungrily on the Japanese sentry.

Under the cover of the bridge McAndrew and the Askari heard the sharp ring of steel-shod boots on the planking above. McAndrew was sweating, and his green denims were filthy with dust. Inconsequentially, he found himself longing for the overdue monsoon.

The Jap wasn't wearing a steel helmet. That was their first, and probably their only, stroke of luck. He looked at the Askari, and grinned. The round ebony face grinned back, with a flash of white teeth. McAndrew beckoned him and whispered: 'When I go up, keep yon tents covered. If there's any trouble, let go with all ye've got. But for the Lord's sake don't make a sound unless ye have to. Savvy?'

'Yes, Baas.'

'O.K. then. Give me a couple of minutes and then come back behind the embankment. I ought to be there by then. I'll need you to help me drag him. If he gets me, beat it back as fast as ye can.'

'O.K. Baas. Yoh don't want me help you up dere?' The African fingered his knife hopefully.

McAndrew shook his head, and the negro moved silently sideways under the arch of the bridge.

The footsteps rang out crisply: left right, left right. The sentry might have been on a barrack square. When he comes off the bridge this side, thought McAndrew; and bit his lip as a mosquito fastened on his bare arm. His Sten slung over his back, he fingered the wicked little blackjack that was a relic of his boyhood in the Glasgow slums.

It's lunatic, he told himself. Even if we get him, he's bound to be missed. Probably in a few minutes. And the country as bare as a baby's backside. There's always yon embankment, though. He had a sudden overwhelming temptation to call the whole thing off, get away while there was still time, rig up a story for Blake. The nig wouldn't talk. Then he remembered Blake's face and voice, and shook his head. The footsteps at this moment moved off the bridge on to the dusty track. Silently McAndrew moved out from under the bridge, and struck.

Blake, in trembling impatience, saw them crawl out from behind the embankment about two hundred yards away. The Askari was in front, the Japanese sentry's arms twisted round his neck. Behind him McAndrew supported the heavy trailing body. They were moving heavily and clumsily on all fours.

Then, clear in the still afternoon air, came a shout from the bridge, and the stammer of a machine-gun. Bullets ran kicking across the ridged paddy-field, scattering dust. A couple of stray shots whined through the trees over Blake's head. He saw the two figures fall flat on their faces.

Oh damn it, they can't pack in now, he cried to himself And then aloud, in a hoarse scream: 'McAndrew! Get him in! Run for it, you fool!'

McAndrew seemed to hear; with the heavy fire all about him he sprang to his feet, hauling the Jap over his back in a fireman's lift. The Askari half-rose, staggered, and fell back to the ground, a crumpled green blot on the endless brown. Blake shut his eyes, blinking away the sweat.

McAndrew came pounding across the open ground, weaving from side to side. Once he staggered and hesitated; but a moment later he broke through the bushes, panting like some great animal, and flung his burden to the ground. His face was streaked with grime and sweat, and a clotted patch of blood showed on his left sleeve.

Blake signalled to two Africans, who came up at the double, stooping through the undergrowth.

'Tie this bastard up,' he said. 'We're getting out of here. You all right, McAndrew?' He spoke perfunctorily. McAndrew nodded, unable to get a word out. 'Good. Cover the rear, then. Take a couple of scouts.' Across the paddy an ominous silence fell. Revolver in hand, Blake went headlong back to what was now the head of the column. McAndrew stared after him.

Blake said: 'We ought to be out of trouble now.' He pushed his bush-hat to the back of his head and surveyed the small clearing. 'Tell the men to stand easy. Half an hour's rest.'

The sun was dropping down the sky, and the heat slowly ebbing away. High above their heads a macaw screeched harshly. McAndrew's arm was beginning to stiffen.

'Sir,' he said. His face was expressionless.

Blake spun his Smith & Wesson round his finger by the trigger-guard. 'Let's have a look at that Jap,' he said. At the sound of his voice McAndrew drew up short. Then he gave the order, and the sentry was brought forward by two Africans. His wrists and ankles were bound with tough creeper. As Blake had seen, he was taller than most of his countrymen; there was an aristocratic look about his wide face, with its high slanting cheek-bones. He had recovered

E*

consciousness, and now stumbled along as best he could in his bonds, an Askari on each arm. His face was set and blank. Only when he saw Blake did a flicker pass over those stony features; it was as if he had recognised something known long before. For a moment the tableau was fixed, immovable, as the two men watched each other.

Blake was the first to shift his gaze. ' Sergeant McAndrew,' he said, in the same odd voice, ' have the prisoner tied up to that tree.' He gestured with his revolver to a giant gingko that stood on the edge of the clearing.

McAndrew said: ' Pardon me, sir. Is that wise? We ought to get back to camp. Another hour or two and it'll be dark.' He nearly added: And what the hell d'ye think ye're after, anyway?

' You heard me, McAndrew. I'm going to interrogate him.'

The events of the afternoon had made McAndrew reckless. He said, shortly: ' That's for Intelligence to do.' He winced as a stab of pain went through his wounded arm.

Blake's eyes narrowed. ' Your recent exploit doesn't entitle you to insubordination, Sergeant,' he said. ' I'd just as readily have you court-martialled as given a medal.' He spoke as though absorbed by some private joke; yet the hysterical edge to his voice had become suddenly more pronounced. ' Now: have that man tied up.' His eyes measured the girth of the gingko. ' As for crucifixion,' he added; and the words shocked McAndrew more than any obscenity could have done.

While he was being tied to the tree the Japanese made no resistance. But all the time his eyes were fixed meditatively on Blake, as if he knew what to expect. The

Askaris stood round in a circle, silent. They too were watching Blake. McAndrew squatted on his heels, chin in hand, fighting against the waves of fatigue that threatened to swallow him up.

Blake began, in halting Japanese: '*Anoné* . . . Why were you on that bridge?'

The sentry said nothing. One of the Africans looked inquiringly at McAndrew. No one moved. Blake, with a nervous abrupt movement, caught up his revolver from the end of its lanyard and levelled it at the sentry's body. It struck McAndrew then that Blake, for some reason, had put *himself* on trial, and that the sentry knew it. He waited for the next move.

But the revolver had some effect. The Japanese said, in flat precise English: 'I am Japanese soldier. I give you name, rank, number.' The words, in that jungle setting, were startlingly incongruous.

'You speak English, do you?' said Blake. 'Right. That makes it easier. First, I want to know how many troops are behind that bridge, and why. Secondly, I want to know about the convoys. . . .'

McAndrew, listening to the sharp staccato voice, thought: There's something damned queer about this. Blake's not a fool entirely. He kens fine he'll get nothing out of yon laddie. He kens we ought to be back before dark. This interrogation's just a formality, face-saving. But why . . . ? And then McAndrew looked at Blake's flushed face, at the revolver in his hand, at the motionless spreadeagled form of the Japanese, and knew why.

The Japanese was repeating, in the same voice: 'Name, rank, number. I give you. But nothing else.'

Blake said: 'We'll see about that.' He stepped quickly

forward and hit the Japanese with all his strength in the middle of the face. McAndrew, a dose of fever beginning to sing through his veins, stared at the bloody cascade that poured down the man's chin to stain his khaki shirt. Just a nice pink and white mother's boy, he thought. La-di-da manners, tea parties, photograph in the *Tatler* in a monkey-jacket. He felt sick.

The prisoner did not make the slightest sound.

Blake hesitated, shaking. He began to say: 'Will you . . .' and then changed his mind. McAndrew, incredulous, saw him raise the revolver, heard the dry click as the hammer was thumbed back.

Standing close to the prisoner, Blake fired. The shot echoed in the confined space, and birds flew up screaming from the treetops. Then Blake stepped back, as if to survey his work, and McAndrew saw, on the trunk of the gingko, a mess of splintered wood and bloody shreds where the index finger of the sentry's right hand had been.

He sprang to his feet with a hoarse cry. 'Ye bluidy swine!' he said.

Blake swung round, the smoking muzzle levelled at McAndrew.

'Sergeant McAndrew,' he said, 'you can consider yourself under arrest.'

'And supposing I send in a report about this?'

'It's your word against mine. Try it and see.'

The Africans watched the two men with silent curiosity. Against the tree the prisoner's bloody face seemed, unbelievably, to be smiling.

McAndrew felt that he was going to faint. He took a desperate grip on himself and walked close to Blake.

'Ye ken damn fine it's not information ye want,' he

said. 'If yon Jap had talked ye'd have been hopping mad. Now, are ye goin' to lay off, ye murderin' bastard?'

Blake hesitated for a split second. McAndrew said: 'Ye can't put me under arrest here. Ye wouldna dare. Ye wouldna be the first white man to be shot by Africans where there wasna a body to see. And this lot are no over-fond of ye, I'm thinkin'.'

Blake was shaking all over. 'You impertinent swine!' he said. Then he caught his pistol by the barrel and hit McAndrew, hard, on the side of the head. The sergeant collapsed on the ground. Blake, standing over his body, fired again: at the left hand this time.

Oh Christ, though McAndrew, his head splitting, his wounded arm twisted under him, rotting leaves in his mouth. Oh Christ, I've mucked it. Waves of nausea swept over him. He heard, muffled as if with cotton-wool, four more shots at irregular intervals, and dimly realised that Blake must be reloading.

He'll get away with it. That kind always get away with it. They'll all back him up, the whole bloody lot from the colonel downwards. It'll be me who stops a packet if I open my mouth. They all stick together like bloody glue.

It occurred to McAndrew at this point that Blake might well shoot him too; he knew far too much. Or was Blake hoping to stop his mouth with the promise of an M.M.? Teeth clenched, he staggered to his feet, swaying. One of the Africans quietly gripped him by the elbows, support-ing him. McAndrew stared into the honest black face, and what he saw there gave him courage. The nightmare pattern suddenly realigned itself.

The Japanese guardsman had fainted, and now his head lolled forward on his chest. McAndrew took one glance at the bloody pulp of his hands, and turned his eyes away. Blake stood in the same place, eyeing his victim. His bush-shirt was completely sodden with perspiration, and he still held the revolver.

All round the clearing McAndrew could hear the Africans breathing heavily. In the rich afternoon light, stippled through trailing leaves, their bodies glowed like beaten bronze. McAndrew looked at his heavy red arms, then at Blake's slim figure. He felt the supporting arm of the Askari about his waist, and it was for him both symbol and omen at once.

He drew himself up and said: 'He hasna talked, then.'

Blake seemed not to hear the words. He stepped forward, seized the inert head, and shook it violently. Nothing happened. McAndrew saw the eyes of the Africans turning from Blake to himself. The shift of forces: the decision to be made.

He put aside the supporting arm and stepped up to Blake. 'Is the man dead?' he asked harshly.

Dully, like a hypnotised person, Blake said: 'No. Not dead.'

'What are ye goin' to do?'

'Leave him.' Blake had an obscenely drained appearance; the hanging figure meant nothing to him now. McAndrew's stomach turned over. He could find no words to express his horror and disgust. But one thing he could do. With shaking hands he unslung his Sten and fired a long burst into the body of the tortured man.

A sigh broke from the lips of the Africans. Only Blake remained indifferent, his back to McAndrew and his victim. He let his revolver swing loose once more at the end of its lanyard.

McAndrew said: 'Are we returnin' to base now, sir?'

Blake blinked, and pulled himself together. He took off his bush-hat and ran one hand through his fair hair. His face was the face of a spoilt and sleepy child.

'Yes,' he said. 'We'll return to base now.'

He replaced his hat.

'Give the order to march, McAndrew.'

'Sir.'

'And McAndrew.'

'Sir?'

'You're no longer under arrest. I've decided to overlook your—insolence.'

I could get him broken for striking me alone, McAndrew thought. But he knew that he would not.

'I think I shall recommend you for an M.M. after all,' said Blake. Then he turned on his heel and moved off, with the easy grace of a thoroughbred.

McAndrew, sick and feverish, saw the mute reproach in the eyes of the blacks. But it was too late, the decisive moment had passed, and Blake had won. McAndrew knew it, and knew that Blake knew. He felt the hopeless, tangling guilt of the conspirator descend on him: the worst guilt of all, not action but the refusal to act, Peter's guilt of denial. There would be no report and no court-martial. Nothing. Nothing except a man who had died horribly and uselessly; and a medal; and a wound; and a carefully worded patrol report.

McAndrew gave the order to march, and the thin column of tired men stumbled forward. It was quite dark when they reached camp. Away in the east thunder snarled and rolled among the hills; and about midnight the monsoon broke.

THE TEA PARTY

THE house was a large, shabby, rambling place, much overgrown with ivy and creeper. It had an air of apologising for itself, as if ashamed both of its own seedy Edwardianism and the brash red brick modernity that had begun to creep over it on either side. It stood well back from the road, half-concealed by rhododendron and privet. Weeds grew here and there in the circular gravel drive; a maze of uncertain ruts hinted urbanely at the Professor's 1938 Austin Twelve.

Brian Grandison paused uncertainly outside the gate, and glanced at his watch. Five minutes early. Four to quarter past, the Professor had said, flinging the time haphazardly into the middle of a pavement argument on early Athenian ceramics. Then he had swept off towards King's Parade, his tattered greenish gown flying in the wind, his long legs moving with somehow absurd energy.

Grandison was eighteen, and a grammar-school scholar. He was also acutely self-conscious. For five years he had lived a curious double life in the Midland town where he was born; ever since his headmaster, a dour sarcastic man of few words and frightening inflexibility, had said to him, out of the blue: 'You've got the makings of a scholar in you. If you're willing to work—and I mean work—I'll get you to the University. But it's entirely up to you.

You've no call to go getting a swelled head. At the moment you know nothing.'

He had paused then, a curiously hard expression on his long lined face. 'When I say the University, Grandison, do you know what I mean?'

'Oxford or Cambridge, sir.'

'Right. You see: you say that automatically. They talk a lot today about the glories of a place called Redbrick. The very name's an insult.'

Grandison remained silent. He knew (as did most people) that the Head had graduated at Redbrick himself; in this very city. The University had been a struggling University College then. Since that time the pious bequests of a generation of civic-minded businessmen had changed matters considerably; but the memory still rankled.

'When I was a young man you needed money and influence to get to Oxford or Cambridge. I won't talk a lot of nonsense about gilded youth and snobbery, but it was true all the same. Some of us—' at the word 'us' Grandison felt as if drawn into a conspiracy '—some of us managed it. They had a pretty poor time. Their lives were made hell because they had a sense of responsibility, because they worked. Now it's easier. But the old attitude's still there. You can talk about the Welfare State till you're blue in the face. But we're showing them, Grandison; we're showing them. Where are the scholars coming from today? Here, and places like this. The public schools think they can rest on their laurels. They can't. Now d'you see why it's up to you?'

Grandison had said, hesitantly. 'But sir . . . if work's the only thing that matters in the long run . . . why are Oxford and Cambridge so much more important than anywhere else? Does it matter *where* the work's done?'

The Head smiled bitterly. 'Scholars are bigger snobs than anyone,' he said. 'That's where you'll find the best teachers; and that's all there is to it.' He stood up, indicating that the interview was at an end. 'By the way, which of the two august establishments do you favour?'

'Oxford, sir.'

'I thought so. You've got an Oxford mind. I'll put you in for Cambridge.'

And that had been that.

His parents had been doubtful when he had gone home bursting with the great news. His mother was as excited as if he were already accepted; but his father said dampingly: 'Well, it's all very fine, lad. But where's it going to get you?'

Brian paused with his mouth open, at a loss for an answer. Mr Grandison, seeing the almost comical dismay on his face, said more kindly: 'I'm not running down education, mind you. Education's a great thing. But it's hard times we're living in. A chap's got to earn his keep. I never went to a University—nor a grammar school, for the matter of that. In my young days we had other things to think about.'

'But Dad—it'll be a scholarship; it wouldn't cost any-thing——'

'Don't you believe it. I've heard how these students carry on with their drinking and rags and all the rest of it——'

'Not all of them. You only hear about the ones that get themselves in the papers. And—and the Head says a chap with a degree's got a better chance of a good job——'

'Well, maybe, maybe. It's early days yet. You get that scholarship and we'll see. But three years is a long time.

You could be getting ahead in a job. . . .' He shook his head. The supper that Brian had looked forward to as a celebration was a silent, constrained affair; it was as if he were already marked as a sacrificial offering, a person apart, odd and different.

During the three years that followed he had become more and more aware of this sense of separation. The Head drove him relentlessly, pouncing on his inaccuracies, unravelling his stumbling ideas with inexorable logic. Grandison did not resent this astringent treatment; it stimulated him, in the way that one is stimulated by the counterpoint of a fugue. He trusted the Head; and because he trusted him, he let his imagination, so long dormant, open out and try to make sense of this new world.

If there had been someone in whom he could have confided, his troubles might have been resolved. But instead he began to find himself in a frighteningly isolated position. Once or twice he had tried to draw his parents out; but these attempts had been met with indifference or suspicion. Mr Grandison had a healthy contempt for the abstract, and made no bones about saying so. After the first uneasy clash of opinion Grandison retreated more and more into his shell. His family took this as an additional sign of superiority, and relations between them degenerated into an uneasy kind of armistice.

The result was the rapid growth of Grandison's dream-world to a point where it occupied his entire waking life. Classical antiquity after a while began to merge imperceptibly into his private conception of what Cambridge must be: a city not of lost causes and dreaming spires—already his allegiance had shifted, and its images with it—but of the pursuit of truth. The phrase acquired for him an almost religious meaning; everything else hinged round it. He imagined Cambridge peopled with scholar-saints, moving gravely in a timeless world of pure knowledge: a kind of Kantian Elysium, had he heard of Kant, but the recluse of Königsburg was not included in his syllabus. There was quite enough to learn already, the Head would have said: the boy isn't going to Oxford, anyway.

It was a remarkable tribute both to Cambridge and his conception of it that when he went there to sit for his scholarship he preserved his illusions intact. The whole week passed for him in a state of feverish and slightly unreal intensity. The questions on the printed sheet in front of him were the secret door into this world; his answers the Open Sesame which—he had no doubts, there could be no doubts—would swing the door open and let him pass through.

Only when he was summoned for a personal interview with his prospective tutor did his courage waver: here if anywhere the intersection of dream and reality might prove disastrous. He sat nervously in a huge ante-room, lined with books, smelling of leather and waxed wood. The winter light filtered bleakly through the tall windows, a clock ticked in the silence.

He found his gaze fixed on a grotesque Chinese dragon on a side-table; he could not take his eyes off it. After a little while he got up and examined it more closely. The head and neck were hinged; he touched them with one finger and the dragon nodded, leering, its jaws opening and shutting in sleepy rhythmicality. While he was thus engaged the inner door opened, and a small, fragile, white-haired man came out. His air was almost apologetic; he seemed to be regretting the necessity to interrupt what might have been a highly important moment. Grandison's initial confusion was at once soothed and dispelled. The interview, as he realised in the train back to the Midlands, had been a very pleasant one. And—more important—he had at last met and spoken with one of the lucky inhabitants of this new world.

The telegram came one evening when they were sitting down to supper. He heard his mother answer the door, and knew instinctively what had happened, before she came back holding the flimsy yellow envelope gingerly in one hand. 'Brian Grandison, Esq.,' she read wonderingly. 'Well, fancy . . .' There was a moment's silence. His father said gruffly, 'You'd better open it.' Brian took the envelope and opened it quickly, without looking at it. Then he read, aloud, in a high unnatural voice: 'Congratulations award hundred pound scholarship—' and broke off. His father took the crumpled sheet from him, as if not believing what he had heard.

Grandison sat there, dazed and uncomprehending, while the congratulations exploded round the little room like crackers. His eyes took in the dingy wall-paper, the lace curtains, the dark cavernous street through the window, blurred and weeping now with rain. He suddenly felt that he must go back at once, the same night; back to this city that had so suddenly and miraculously extended the hand of friendship to him. It seemed intolerable that he should have to wait through the long summer till October. Then he heard his father's voice again.

'Well, Brian lad, you've done us proud. No mistake about that.' Behind the clipped words there was an almost unbearable affection and pride. 'Wait till we tell folks. This is something to talk about.' Brian wanted to say, Don't, don't; it's not fair. You don't know what I feel—about you, and this house, and everything here. I could bear everything except your kindness. But the the gruff cheerful voice went on. 'We'll have to think about fitting you out, I suppose. Can't have you going up there among all those lords and folk and not looking proper. Tomorrow's Saturday. We'll go into town together and find you something. Why, what's the matter, lad?' For Brian had suddenly put his head on the table and burst into floods of tears.

And now October had come, and another January after it. If he had found Cambridge different from what he had expected, he did not let the fact disturb him. The town itself he loved at first sight. Its leisurely grace was in contrast to anything he had ever known, and the mere fact of contrast was enough to lend it magic in his sight. He spent the short winter afternoons wandering through the streets, trying in an incoherent way to lose his identity among these grey weathered stones.

When it was a matter of the personal contacts his college offered him, however, he was shy and tongue-tied, not through any real native awkwardness but because such approaches seemed an intolerable intrusion into his private world. At first he was visited by the representatives of a dozen or so societies; by rugger enthusiasts, rowing men, and all the multifarious proselytisers who every year work indefatigably among freshmen. Nervously but firmly he put them off; and after a while the word went around that he was an unsociable provincial, interested in nothing but work, and the visits gradually ceased.

This fact gave him a kind of pleasure; it was as if he had

won the first round in his battle against an insidious enemy. Like many dons, when he thought of his fellow-under-graduates at all, it was as a foreign element, to be put up with because inevitable, that attemped to drive a wedge between him and his purpose in life. He was an indefatig-able lecture-goer. If anyone had told him that a good deal of his time would have been better employed elsewhere, he would have been both incredulous and shocked. But no one troubled to tell him.

In the heart of this closed society, with its fluctuating cliques and coteries, his isolation was complete: he moved among them like Odysseus among the dead. Yet his gods—to pursue the simile—were Olympian, and he served them with the silent devotion of an acolyte. His only attempt at personal contact—which he obscurely felt might break the spell that bound him to his mentors—had been with the Professor, Carmichael, who brought to his lecturing an off-hand air of enthusiasm, an untidy bubbling eccentricity that broke down the barrier between lecturer and audience without suggesting any more intimate relationship.

One day, greatly daring, Grandison had taken the plunge and accosted the Professor in the hall outside the lecture-rooms. Stammering and blushing, he brought out the point he had been nursing for the last hour. Carmichael listened to him, tall and vague, twisting the bands of his gown between his fingers. He took the occurrence as a matter of course; he had had the air of one who would have im-mersed himself in textual criticism at the top of a mountain, and seemed happily oblivious of Grandison's confusion. Encouraged, the boy plunged in more deeply. Carmichael listened while the milling students poured round them. Occasionally he put in a sharp question. Grandison suddenly

realised he was being talked to as an equal. At length—
'That was interesting, very interesting,' said the Professor.
His glasses had slipped down his long bony nose, and he
pushed them back into place with a rather helpless gesture.
'Now if you'll excuse me . . .' He walked towards the
door. 'We must have another talk soon,' he said, and was
gone. Outside Grandison could hear the Austin coughing
and backfiring. He felt suddenly deflated.

Four o'clock. Grandison pushed open the gate. It had
warped in the heat, and screeched protestingly over the
gravel. Green mould stained his fingers, and as he wiped it
off he realised that his palms were sweating. He ran over in
his mind the topics he would produce—the Cicero emenda-
tion, that awkward passage in the *Agamemnon*. Tea would
be served in the library, by some discreetly self-effacing
servant: the mere ritual accompaniment to discussion.

Suddenly, for the first time, he found himself wondering
if the Professor might be married. He stopped dead in
the middle of the drive, scanning the sombre interior of
the house for any tell-tale signs of domesticity. Nothing
stirred. Then, far away in the depths of the house, a dog
began to bark. Panic seized him; for an instant he felt like
taking to his heels. Then, with an effort, he pulled himself
together. After all, he had been invited. If he failed to
appear it would be, at the least, grossly impolite. He found
himself worried by the seemingly irrelevant intrusion of
this social qualm. But supposing the Professor *was* married?
His mind tried to reconcile this aloof scholar with the kind
of tea-time scene he was accustomed to in his own home,
and failed miserably.

With a pounding heart he walked up to the ivy-grown

porch and stood there a moment, the iron bell-pull in his hand. A pair of women's walking shoes, crusted with mud, stood by the scraper. He stared at them hopelessly; then, with a quick gesture, pulled at the bell. A faint irregular tinkle proclaimed that it was at least working: to save his life he could not have brought himself to knock. A feminine voice said something indistinguishable, and the dog stopped barking. He heard the quick patter of footsteps, and the door was abruptly opened.

Grandison looked at the girl helplessly, and said nothing. She seemed about thirteen; slim and dark, with a bob of black hair and a round plump face. Her complexion was very pale; her eyes, blacker than her hair, regarded him with a strange lack of curiosity. She wore an old tweed suit and sandals. Her legs were bare.

'I haven't seen you before,' she said. Her voice was flat, lacking inflections. Grandison noticed that her eyes did not seem to focus properly.

'I'm—' he was going to say, one of your father's pupils, but then it occurred to him that he didn't know who the girl was, and that anyway he wasn't really one of the Professor's pupils at all.

'I go to Professor Carmichael's lectures,' he got out eventually. 'He very kindly invited me to tea this afternoon.' How ridiculously formal the words sounded. He felt himself blushing. But the girl, after looking him up and down for a moment in a disconcerting way, said abruptly: 'I like you. You're nice. Come in and talk.' Without waiting for a reply she turned a well-tailored back on him and vanished into the hall. Grandison followed her, doubtfully.

The hall was large and dark, and smelt of polish and

waxed wood. Smoky paintings, almost invisible, hung on the panelling. One of them was just askew, maddening Grandison's tidy eye. There was a chest covered with old magazines and a rack full of walking-sticks. Beyond a door the dog began to bark again.

Grandison said. 'Perhaps if you could tell the Professor I'm here. . . ? My name's Grandison . . . He's expecting me . . .'

She took him by the hand and led him to the chest.

'This is where we sit,' she said. Grandison hesitated, biting his lip nervously. 'It's all right. You needn't be afraid. I said I liked you.'

Hypnotised, Grandison obeyed. He realised with a sudden shock that what she had said had been true: he was afraid. But of what? Something was wrong, that was all he could pin down; wrong in the nerve-biting way that the picture was askew. With an effort he got up, walked quickly across the hall, and put it straight. And while he did so he thought: What an extraordinary thing to be doing in someone else's house. The thought echoed faintly in the well of his brain, as if he were under ether; and the girl, when he turned round, looked as if she were at the wrong end of a telescope.

Perhaps I'm ill. I might have fainted in the road and been brought in here. . . . No, that's ridiculous. I remember every moment. The wrong house then? He began to feel the situation slipping out of his control.

'Who—who are you?' he asked. There was a silence. 'I know it's frightfully rude of me . . . but you see it's the first time I've been here. . . .'

'Don't be silly. You know me. I'm Sally.'

'But I've never met you.'

She frowned impatiently. 'Of course you have.'

'When?'

'Lots of times. How old are you?'

'Nineteen. I say, do you think you could ask——'

'You always want me to ask people things. It's so silly. Anyway, you're younger than me. *You* ask.'

'Younger than you?'

'Of course, silly. I'm twenty-six. Do you play chess?'

'No . . . I, that is . . .' He stared at her in frank amazement; then laughed, uncertainly.

'All right. You're twenty-six.' He found that his breath was coming very short, and his hands were sweating again.

She shook her head despondently. 'You're just like everybody else. They all laugh at me. Tell me your name.'

'Brian Grandison. But I thought you knew me?'

'I *do* know you. Don't be so tiresome. What can you do?'

'Do . . . ?'

'Yes, do. You can't do *nothing*.'

'I'm an undergraduate.'

She made a small gesture of impatience. 'I know *that*. Everyone's an undergradute. What *sort*?'

'Well, I read classics—Greek and Latin. You know.'

'Then Daddy must teach you. Why didn't you tell me?'

So she was Carmichael's daughter. Grandison shifted uncomfortably on the chest. The pattern of the afternoon was being twisted into new and alarming shapes. But still he could not move. In the silence a grandfather clock ticked slowly. He was dimly aware of being confronted with a situation that required action. But what the situation was, or how he should deal with it, eluded him.

Sally blinked her black eyes. 'What else do you do?' she asked.

'I don't understand.'

She clasped her hands round her knees and stared at him intensely. The afternoon sunlight swam in dust through the latticed window and lit up her pale face. 'You don't understand . . . You've got all the world to do what you like with. You can walk over the horizon if you want to. And you don't understand . . .'

Bewildered, yet moved by this outburst, Grandison said: 'You talk as if *you* couldn't . . . as if you were a prisoner, or something . . .' The Midland accent was suddenly noticeable in his voice. It was as if he had been shaken out of a trance. He felt himself making contact with this strange creature, and was aware of a sharp exhilaration.

Sally lowered her voice and whispered: 'That's what I am.' The words tumbled out over each other; the round face became contorted, as if it were a reflection in a pool where a stone has been thrown. 'They won't let me go out. They're afraid I might run away and never come back. I would, too. Don't you see how lucky you are? You can walk out of that door and no one would stop you. But if I—' she broke off, grimacing, as if at some horrible memory. 'What's the time?' she asked abruptly.

Grandison looked at his wristwatch. 'Nearly half-past four. I say . . . your father'll be waiting for me . . .'

'I should have had them two hours ago.'

'What?'

'What they make me take . . . so that I can't go away . . . They always know. They're clever . . .' She pulled herself close, a hedgehog turning its prickles outwards against the world. 'Little white tablets. Three of them. Every six hours. Ever since I can remember.'

'I'm terribly sorry . . . Are you ill? Is that it?'

'That's what they all ask. Of course I'm not ill. They'd like to make me think I was ill. I know all about it.' She moved closer to him. He remained still, his heart beating violently. 'But there's a way out,' she said. She looked round, as if fearing she might be overheard. Involuntarily Grandison leant forward, assuming the rôle of fellow-conspirator. 'Books,' she breathed. It was as if the word were a magic talisman. 'If they were really clever, they wouldn't let me read. I know more than they do. Soon I'll know everything. I know Latin and Greek and French. There must be an answer, somewhere.'

'An answer?' Grandison's mind gave a leap of under-standing. The girl was voicing his own secret faith. 'You really believe that?'

'Of course. I'm learning Chinese now. Do you like Chinese?'

'I've never read any . . . Isn't it awfully hard?'

'Yes. That's why it must be good.' she laughed to her-self. Then a worried look came over her face. 'You won't tell them . . . will you? It's a secret.'

'Of course not.' The atmosphere of secrecy grew, en-veloping them both. And in any case, Grandison thought, what could I say? A single ugly word rose in his mind, refused to be put out of sight. He remembered the furtive whisper in which his mother had said of someone, 'She's not quite right in the head,' and then had stopped talking abruptly as he approached. Panic returned. He hardly heard what Sally was saying, till the words forced themselves upon him.

'. . . besides, it's not fair. Especially when she takes things too. I don't see why I shouldn't have secrets.'

'Take things? Who takes things?'

'Mummy, of course. Weren't you listening? She said she'd kill me if I told anyone. You see, I found her out. No one likes being found out, I suppose.' The remark came out flatly, almost as if she were bored: bored with herself, with Grandison, with the unpredictable actions of a shadowy world, indifferent when it was not actively hostile. 'She cried. She's always crying. Sometimes she falls down.' Sally laid her hand on Grandison's sleeves. 'And the thing is,' she went on, 'that it's really funny. I know it oughtn't to be, but it is.'

The tick of the clock was suddenly deafening, as if it were the pulse of the house quickening before some incredible revelation. Then it struck the half-hour. The note was ironically civilised; as out of place as an Ashanti in a top-hat.

Grandison said, articulating his secret dread, the words forced from him as if by hypnosis: 'You've got to look behind the books.' And as he uttered the words he closed his eyes for a moment, shutting out what he was forced to accept.

Sally glanced at his white face incredulously. 'Have *you*?' she asked.

'No,' he said, and opened his eyes. He was aware with a lacerating intensity of her physical presence. And not only of her: every object in the dim cluttered hall suddenly took on a sharp, exciting yet painful reality—the polished wood, the pictures, the brass ornaments and the bric-à-brac. He wanted to feel them, outline their shape with his fingers. Through the window he saw the long blue shadows slanting across the road from the plane trees, and had a desire to rush out into the sunlight. Yet like the blinded man who tears the bandage from his eys too soon, this awareness also brought pain. His body and dormant emotions seemed to be assaulted simultaneously.

Then, almost driving out all other emotions, came resentment. He felt his inner self being prised open, the protective barriers he had built being pulled down by crude frontal assault. This indecently intimate situation had been thrust on him; he had not sought it out. Yet it was he who had approached the Professor, he realised: and by this unpremeditated action with its train of human consequences he had made himself responsible for what was now happening.

Trembling, he stood up.

He felt utterly naked and defenceless: his useless knowledge lay scattered like dust among the bric-à-brac of the still hall.

He felt the need for a decision pressing in on him; but the material from which to make it was not there.

They stood facing each other, close together. A cold flame ran down his spine; he felt, rather than saw, that she was going to kiss him. The decision, the decision . . .

But as pat as the *deus ex machina* on which he lectured so scathingly, the Professor appeared, noiselessly, through the heavy oak door at the end of the hall. He looked from one to the other of them, and the tired lines on his face deepened. Then he straightened his shoulders, as if this were a crisis he had met and conquered many times, and would meet and conquer again. Neither of the two motionless figures noticed his approach.

' Sally,' he said. His voice was gentle and friendly. At the sound the girl turned her head, slowly and vacantly, like a diver under great pressure of water. Her eyes blinked quickly.

'It's time for your rest. Go along now. I'll come up and see you soon.'

'I don't want to rest.' Her eyes strayed wistfully through the deep casement to the sunlit road ouside.

'Sorry, Sally. Nothing to be done about it.' He took her arm gently and led her to the stairs. 'Did you have a nice talk with Mr Grandison?'

She made an odd movement of her head, but said nothing. Then, suddenly, she ran up the stairs and out of sight. A door banged. It was Grandison who said, as if in answer, 'I . . . I'm sorry I'm late, sir. But . . . we were talking . . . I didn't notice the time. It was . . . very interesting.'

The Professor stared at Grandison, as if trying to extract an ironic twist from his words. Grandison avoided his gaze, and stared wretchedly at the floor. There was a short silence.

'Come into the study,' said the Professor at last. He was twisting a signet ring nervously round his finger, right hand over left, and only stopped to throw open the door.

So at last Grandison found himself in the room he had so long imagined, among the books, that lined every wall and spilt over on to the floor, the vast untidy desk, the scattered papers. There was a big copper kettle boiling on a gas-ring, and a plate of sandwiches by it that bore unmistable signs of a masculine hand.

Abruptly the Professor said: 'What did Sally tell you?' Grandison choked.

'I just wanted to get things straight,' said the Professor. 'I don't want you to think I'm a sadist at large, that's all.' His eyes never left Grandison's face. Now, incredibly, he grinned. 'I see my guess was right. Look, I should sit down if I were you.'

This remark was prompted by concern as much as polite-

F

ness: Grandison had turned a nasty white. He lowered himself into the big leather armchair, trembling. The Professor said, very gently: 'I'm afraid this has been a bit of a shock for you. It never occurred to me you wouldn't know.' He lit a cigarette, frowning: he seemed to be hiding behind the cloud of blue smoke he produced. 'Most people are . . . forewarned. That's one of the reasons we don't have many guests. When you go back to College you'll be able to hear all about us.'

Grandison tore his eyes from the Professor's hurt, mocking face and looked wildly round the room. There were the books, solid calf, German paper-backs, crumpled off-prints, their dust forming a dry pot-pourri in his nose. For a dreadful moment he waited in a kind of agony, a hopeless worshipper at the deserted oracle, his world standing still for an answer. But no answer came. And then it was as if the entire room dissolved, wrenching his brain apart, and all that remained was the Professor's face wreathed in smoke, and the plateful of pathetically clumsy sandwiches. The Professor watched him steadily, and with understanding.

At last Grandison said, in a thick Midland voice, all affectation stripped away: 'For God's sake tell me the truth.'

'The truth?' Carmichael drew down the corners of his mouth, like one who has swallowed quinine. He drew a light breath and said: 'The truth is very simple. I have a cretinous daughter and my wife drinks. I'm sorry if you came here under a misapprehension.'

And Grandison, his old world in shreds, saw from the heart of his confusion that the Professor was as naked as himself. Do not reject me, cried the stony mask beneath its stone. I understand what you are suffering. But you too have the power to make suffering. The blood ran hot and hammering through his head. Still in a daze, he looked; and the face was the face of his father.

Ashamed, he said: 'On the contrary, sir. I . . . I owe you a great deal . . . more than I can say. . . .'

'And Sally?'

Grandison gulped. 'Sally as well. She showed me——'

'—reality in a mirror?'

'Yes . . .'

'Ah.' The Professor suddenly stretched his arms, as if some huge burden had been lifted from his shoulders. 'I thought as much.' He began to make the tea. 'Grandison, have you read the *Republic*?'

'Yes sir.'

'Do you remember the shadows in the cave?'

Grandison nodded.

'We've all got to come out of that cave some day,' said the Professor. 'Some of us may try to stay there all our lives. We may even convince ourselves for a while that the shadows are the real thing.'

The evening sunlight, shafted through tall leaded windows, laid lozenges of gold across the books. Grandison's eyes followed their patterns.

'It's a hard business losing an ideal. Even if it's the wrong one. Scholarship's so seductive. It appeals to our essential puritanism, and offers us a cloister at the same time. Irresistible. Especially . . . if one has good reason for wanting a cloister.'

Their eyes met. Grandison thought: That's what we both wanted. Only Sally knew the truth. And she can never use her knowledge. He realised the Professor was offering him a cup of tea, and took it automatically. The tension had evaporated completely, leaving them exhausted but calm. The Professor ran his hand through his hair in his usual vague way and said: 'Well, Grandison. I'm sure you've brought some fiendish textual problems to argue out . . . ?' His eyes twinkled. The episode was closed, then. But Grandison said: 'No . . . not this time. Couldn't we just . . . talk?'

The Professor looked at him. 'Tell me something about your home,' he said.

Grandison thought: So this is the beginning. It is like being a child again: clumsy footsteps, clutching at supports, the immensity of the world. He turned his gaze through the window. Among the great trees people were walking together, brightly coloured, absorbed in each other. The hum of their voices drifted through the casement, together with a whiff of summer flowers.

His eyes abstracted in this living picture, his tea growing cold beside him, Grandison talked. hesitantly at first, and then with growing confidence.

Listening in his chair, the Professor smiled.

THE HOUSE-HUNTERS

IT was raining on the day we set out to Mareshill. Not a decent downpour, but that grey, defeated smirr which seems endemic to the Cambridgeshire landscape, and might have been specially designed to confound all normal windscreen-wipers. Simon was driving. His temper had been simmering on a low burner all morning, and now, after a rather heavy lunch, showed signs of coming to the boil. The smeared windscreen—how well I knew the signs by now—would merely act as a final precipitate.

Sure enough, soon after we had got on the Haverhill road, Simon said: 'I wish to Christ it'd either rain properly or stop.'

I carefully avoided looking at him or making any reply. I had the Ordnance Survey map spread out over my lap—a rather difficult business in the confined space of a Morris Minor, especially if you happen to be six months' pregnant —and began to check over our route with a pencil.

Simon snorted through his nose: an ominous sign. I didn't like the way he was driving, either. You can tell a lot about Simon from his habits at the wheel. Now he was pushing the needle up well over seventy, the tyres hissing on the wet road, the engine labouring from excess of throttle. He changed down sharply as we approached a roundabout, without braking: the gears meshed and screamed in angry protest, reducing speed, straining every moving part of the car.

We swerved round the corner in a flurry of spray, and instinctively I jammed my feet against the floorboards to counteract the centrifugal force of the turn. It was, I thought, a sick twinge shooting coldly through me, as though Simon had put out an invisible hand to thrust me out, outside, out into the rain. I stared down at the map, and the lines, red, black, blue, danced in a blurred pattern. Something obscene about them. As though alive. Arteries, that was it. Veins and arteries. Arterial roads. Cut the veins, blood on the chart——

Steady, I told myself. Steady, for God's sake. This is what he wants. Simon the Tiger smells blood, licks lips, is reasonable, argues logically. *No.* I swallowed, conscious of the cold prickle of sweat on my forehead, breathed deeply. But it was no use.

'Simon,' I said, in a ridiculous, strangulated voice, 'if you don't drive slower I'm going to be sick.' There, now. There's a nice meaty bone for you to get hold of, sod you. Sod you, sod you, sod you. Go on. Make something of it.

But for the moment Simon said nothing. He twitched one eyebrow, slackened speed a little, leant over and opened my window. Then he withdrew himself again and sat, hunched, cold, efficient, eyes on the grey road ahead of him, mind God knows where. His heavy, dead personality was stamped all over the car. All over me, too, come to think of it. Probably more than I knew.

Simon began to whistle tunelessly through his teeth: some complicated theme, probably from a Brahms quartet. When in doubt with Simon's whistling, try Brahms. Irritation mounted in me, thrust up the private steam-gauge at the back of my head towards the red horizontal division labelled 'hysteria'. Let's get this straight, the voice in my head said, with shattering reasonableness. You don't object to Simon enjoying music, do you? No. Even though you're tone-deaf yourself? Certainly not. Well, then —All right, *well then*. What gets me is turning this music thing into a weapon, a sort of knobkerry in the Simon-Lavinia World Title Fight. If I don't like music Simon is deprived. If I don't like music I'm uncultured, moronic, there's something wrong with me. I'm just doing it to annoy Simon——

At this point Simon suddenly broke silence to say: 'For God's sake, what the hell are you moping about?'

'Because you're a stupid egocentric bastard, that's why, and I don't see why I should have to trot along behind your bloody interests all the time like a baa-lamb—' And as I said *baa-lamb*, my voice scooped skyward in a way that would have made me giggle if I hadn't been so furious and miserable, and I burst into loud, undignified sobs.

Simon, still belting down the road, put on his special for-any-witnesses-that-may-be-present-and-I-only-wish-there-were-more-of-them Saint Sebastian face; it made him look like a T.V. executive hunting for the bismuth after lunch, and looking back I rather wish I'd told him so. Make Simon laugh at himself and you get no trouble for the next twenty-four hours. The trouble is, I'm never quite sure what'll do the trick, and if it doesn't come off, you're landed with a Force Ten hurricane instead.

This time, damn his eyes, he had a case. I'm not always quite sure when I'm saying something or just thinking it —who is, anyway?—and when I blew off, I somehow assumed that we'd been arguing about music. Well, so we had, but not actually *then*. Which of course, made me more irritable than ever.

Simon said, wearily: 'Oh for God's sake, Vinny, do pull yourself together. You don't want the Reverend Whatsit to think you're a case of the vapours, do you?'

What you mean is, I thought, seething, *you* don't want him to. Regrettable behaviour of don's wife in public. Gossip. Chances of promotion. The public decencies. Oh God, I groaned to myself, in some black, scarcely acknowledged corner of my soul, what in Heaven's name *is* this creature I've married? It's all so unfair, unfair, damnably unfair. I want to shout and scream. But he's got all the answers. He won't make a decent row of it, oh no. He'll treat me like a delinquent child moron, with great forbearance.

Look, you fool, you've got to see this house. You've got to get him there in a reasonably good mood. Try again.

'Simon, I think we're near the turn now. Better look out for it. One of those triangle turns—and there should be a pub on the right-hand side. As far as I can make out the Rectory's about a quarter of a mile up on the left.' Efficiency, that's the line. If there's one thing Simon is nuts on, it's efficiency. For this all, or nearly all, will be forgiven. Unfortunately I'm not very good at it. Like being at school again. Your locker's a *mess*, Lavinia. Report to Miss Bates after prayers, Lavinia. Lavinia, show me those hands. This isn't the sort of behaviour we expect at a decent school, an *English* school, Lavinia——

And I wanted to claw their eyes out, to shake them for their smug, stupid, English self-complacency, to shout: 'I'm Irish, Irish, Irish, nothing to do with you at all.

Foreign. I hate you.' But I didn't. On one occasion some atavistic urge from my childhood (could old Madge the cook have dropped it in my ear?) made me shout 'Bloody Protestant!' at one more than usually infuriating and tweedy headmistress. But as I wasn't a Catholic then, this was taken as pure impertinence, and treated accordingly.

Now there was Simon, so un-English by this own account, so original, so anti-Establishment, and yet under the surface just another suburban conformist like anyone else. It took me a long time to find that one out. Too long. And here we were in the pouring rain in the middle of Cambridgeshire (of all Christ-forsaken, dead counties) with an accidental child on the way, and a lease-expired flat to get out of, and an Assistant Lecturer's salary to kick around for the fun of it. Which, incidentally, was subject to revision in a year or so—the Lectureship, I mean, not the salary. The nasty little phrase 'non-renewal of contract' haunted my dreams at night, and I'm pretty certain it haunted Simon's too, though he never admitted it.

Simon changed down with rather less viciousness, and brought the Morris to a halt at the corner of an unbelievably decayed-looking village green. The rain was sluicing down in great torrents now, and the squeegee wipers were creaking and sloshing away across the windscreen like a pair of skinny and garrulous charwomen. I thought of telling Simon this, but then decided against it: he has an absolute genius for killing that sort of fancy stone dead with one acidulous little phrase.

'This should be it,' he said, in his special damp, God-what-a-bore-all-this-is voice.

I waited for him to drive up the lane to where the Rectory must be, but he didn't; he sat there absolutely

F*

motionless, like a sack, staring miserably at the rain outside. The drumming on the roof was absolutely deafening.

'Well, come on,' I said, rather louder than I had meant; but after all, there was the rain to contend with.

'Oh don't be so bloody peevish—of all the miserable, cross-grained, neurotic *cows* I've ever met—' Simon pulled a packet of Players out of one pocket, flipped a cigarette into his mouth, flicked his lighter (a rather cheap and nasty one, which I'd been vainly trying to make him get rid of for years) and exhaled a long feather of smoke. All this was done in one quick, compulsive sequence of actions: straight out of the psychological rule-book.

Try telling Simon something about his inner motives and tics, and watch the result. Light blue fuse paper and retire, rapidly. I don't think I've ever met a man with Simon's brain-capacity who was so completely extrovert, so utterly incurious about his own mental make-up.

'Look, Simon,' I said, desperately, 'we've *got* to find a house soon——'

'Yes, so you've said before.' Puff, puff.

I *hate* the smell of those cigarettes. I detest the way Simon lets them stain his fingers the colour of fumed oak. Not to mention his utterly revolting habit of stubbing them out in any handy plate, usually in the middle of some left-over food.

'Well, can't you face the facts, Simon, *please*? *I've* had to do all the ringing up of agents. *I've* had to make appointments, and argue with the bank manager, and——'

'Look, Vinny, there are only twenty-four hours in a day. God knows when you think I get my work done. And if I don't get this book finished and accepted, you know what'll happen when my lectureship comes up for renewal.

Can't you hear that old bastard Raynor on the Faculty Board—"H'm, yes, Mannering—hasn't *published* anything, has he? Nothing against that, of course, still——"'

Simon twisted round savagely in his seat, eyes flickering over me with barely-concealed disgust. He was well away now.

'Honestly, Vinny, what sort of dream-world do you live in? Yak-yak-yak about my domestic duties all night long. Where do you suppose the money comes from?'

'I *know*, Simon, I'm grateful, really I am, but——'

'But, but, but,' he mimicked, the cigarette wagging up and down in his mouth at each repeated monosyllable. '*But,* Miss oh-so-landed-gentry Killonen—my God, what a name!—doesn't think it *nice* to talk about money. Money's something that grows on trees, that's just *there*. Well why the hell didn't you marry some boozy rich Galway squireen if that's what you wanted? Why pick on me?'

'I didn't pick on you, you oaf, you wouldn't take no, and now I'm going to have this baby and I wish I wasn't and I hate you, I hate you, *I hate you* and I wish you were dead.'

Simon breathed heavily through his nose again, shut his eyes, and said nothing. Our cooped-up anger was actually producing condensation on the inside of the car.

'Why don't you leave me?' I said.

'Oh don't be so *stupid*, Lavinia. How could I?'

'Very easily. Catch the next train to London. I presume you're capable of packing a bag for yourself.'

Simon swore, very coarsely indeed. He had spent most of the war as an infantry sergeant, and it still showed on occasion, rather disconcertingly, through the top-dressing of Cambridge academicism.

'Look, Lady Whatsit,' he said, 'will you do me the favour of getting your feet on the deck for a moment? To begin with there's the child——'

'I'd manage a child far better without you around the house,' I yelled, 'with your foul temper and sulks and selfishness——'

'And what do you propose to live on? *Daddy,* I suppose.' He made the word *Daddy* sound like some unprintably taboo obscenity. 'Anyhow, I can't leave Cambridge like this right in the middle of the year—there are obliga-tions——'

'Obligations, is it?' I said, and regretted the Irishry the instant it was out, watching Simon's left eyebrow flick up in that maddeningly superior way he had, cool, ready to pounce on this messy, jellified, tear-stained creature and beat it to a logical pulp.

Oh Simon, Simon, I thought why can't you stop worrying for one instant about what will people think and can we afford and is it reasonable? And with that thought, oddly, came a perverse flood of affection, and despite myself I laid one hand on his tweed sleeve and said: 'I'm sorry, Simon. I do get stupidly worked up sometimes in this state. I take it back, honestly I do——'

But this time the formula didn't work, the cruel, hurting, half-true accusations lay between us like a cold fog. He jerked his arm away and said, in a voice of dead despair: 'I suppose we might as well look at this bloody place now we're here.'

'Yes,' I said hopelessly, 'I suppose so.'

Simon tugged irritably at the starter. The rain was easing off now, pattering down in windy gusts. Greyness soaked into the grass and trees, ran miserably through the choked gutters. The air was full of multifoliate dripping noises. What on earth would it be like living here? I wondered. Too much laurel and yew, too many dank reminders of mortality. Through the open window I smelt the rich, depressing odour of rotten leaf-mould.

It could have been such fun, I thought, tears brimming in my eyes again, my mind snatching at the wretched rags of that small, vulnerable dream. Rain or no rain—an adventure, something to add to our shared experience. Better not to think about it like that. Nostalgia, the great corrosive.

Suddenly, the child kicked, once, like an uneasy sleeper— which I suppose it was. A great weight of futility pressed down on me. All right, I told myself, let us consider this thing in a practical way. Here are Mr and Mrs Simon Mannering, and *there* is a large white elephant of a house going cheap. Let us restrict ourselves to that. If we can.

Simon flicked the butt of his cigarette through the window, and braked sharply. I stared at the heavy crumbling wall, of moss-mouldered red brick. Above it there lowered a dense bank of foliage—rhododendrons, laurel, yew, and a couple of huge pine-trees. Through this dark barrier the drive tunnelled its way. Weeds sprouted in the gravel, the gate sagged despondently on its hinges. I looked at Simon. He was examining this dismal façade with meticulous attention. There was an unexpected expression on his face, as though he were, well, *listening* for something.

And in that instant the atmosphere changed, as precisely and unmistakably as a car changing gear. Why or how I didn't know; and I was by no means sure it would be a change for the better.

'Well,' Simon said, 'this is it, I suppose.' He spun the

wheel and nosed the Morris cautiously up the drive. We came out in what I can only describe as a quintessentially Church of England front garden. Behind all the laurels and trees there was a big, civilised, but decidedly down-at-heels lawn, that hinted shamefacedly at long-vanished croquet parties in the Victorian hey-day of cheap gardeners and parlour-maids. The house itself was all of a piece with this: a patched and peeling façade, part stucco, part brick, its paintwork cracked and peeling, some of its slates visibly askew.

We stood there for moment, saying nothing, glad to be out of the car. The rain had now stopped altogether. I glanced at my watch. Five o'clock. We'd have to drive back in the dark. Already the harsh February light was draining slowly away. A small scintilla of fear sparked into existence, somewhere behind the last door of my mind; and as I resolutely put it away, bringing to bear on this unreasonable, not-to-be-admitted adversary the whole weight of my training, my oh so carefully instilled scientific background, the problem of Simon receded, went abruptly out of focus. It didn't vanish entirely; the shadow was still there. But I had to deal with a sudden shift of perspective. It was only later that I appreciated just what this implied.

Simon had made no attempt to ring the bell. He was prowling up and down the front of the house like a cat, treading a very careful, zig-zag course, as though avoiding invisible obstacles. I began to say something, then stopped myself. No, I thought. I've got him here, and I'm not going to spoil it now. I kept quiet.

'The Fall of the House of Usher,' Simon said, squinting up at the eaves. There was certainly a bleak look about Mareshill Rectory; it was very like one of those nineteenth century steel engravings that Simon had collected as an undergraduate, and which now lay gathering dust in the tin trunk under our bed. But his voice had changed; the duel was, for the time being at any rate, concluded.

Then he chuckled, in a way he had when he was about to say something particularly unpleasant, and added: 'Do you remember that M. R. James story—"The Mezzotint", wasn't it—?' and left the rest of the sentence hanging in mid-air. I looked at the house again, and the feeling I had tried to stifle ever since we stopped came flooding into my throat like bile. For no good reason that I could name. I was horribly, humiliatingly scared.

You hysterical, stupid, pregnant bitch, I told myself, picking Simon's favourite insults with silent care. A light snapped on in the room next to the hall, and at once it seemed darker outside. Something rustled in the laurels: rain still dripped steadily from a thousand leaves.

'Look, Simon,' I said, thickly, 'let's give this a miss. It's obviously not the sort of thing we want——'

Instantly he was bristling again. 'I've given up half a day for this damn-fool errand, so we might as well go through with it now we're here.' He hunched his shoulders inside his overcoat, and began to move stubbornly towards the house. He had given me a quick, interested glance when I spoke, but that was all. Probably pure irritation. I was too tired and scared even to feel resentment.

'*Please*, Simon——'

'Oh, come on, Vinny.' He marched up to the front porch and, with only the slightest hesitation, pressed the bell. I wiped cold, sweaty palms on my skirt and followed him.

There were shuffling steps inside. First there was the

unmistakable rattle of the door being taken off its chain; then two heavy bolts were shot back. Simon and I looked at each other. Finally, with much creaking, the door swung open. The Rector stood there, silhouetted against the light from the hall: a small, wrinkled, dried-up tortoise of a man.

'Mr and Mrs Mannering?' he said, and barely waited for Simon's assent before hustling us inside. He then, somewhat alarmingly, went through his whole rigmarole again in reverse, even to the chain. An unpleasant, highly irrational thought floated like scum to the top of my mind, and refused to be dislodged. It's for all the world, I thought, as though he were trying to stop someone—or something—else getting in with us. I swallowed uneasily.

'Well now,' said the Rector, rubbing his hands, 'you'll be wanting to see round, I expect.' His voice echoed through the big, bare hall with a sort of cracked bonhomie. I looked more carefully at him, noting the carpet slippers and rumpled alpaca jacket, the inevitable stained waistcoat, the nutcracker jaw and the wiry halo of brindled hair. With an awful certainty it struck home to me, in that moment, that the Rector was considerably more frightened than I was.

Simon—and I wasn't sure whether this comforted or infuriated me more—seemed quite oblivious to the atmosphere of the place. He had the Order to View out, and now began to fire brisk, practical questions at the Rector. How old was the house? What was its previous history? Who had been responsible for the upkeep? The Rector blinked a little at all this, and cleared his throat in the frantic way of someone stalling for time. Then, as though in response to some telepathic S.O.S. he had tapped out through the uneasy air, there came the sound of shuffling footsteps down the corridor, and a woman appeared.

'Hilda,' the Rector said, with evident relief, 'this is Mr Mannering——'

'Delighted to meet you,' Simon said, and took her hand firmly. He was putting on—oh God, how well I knew it—his special charm act for elderly women: the warm intimate glance, the boyish frankness of voice, the faint flutter of eyelashes. They always fell for it. I think at the time he always believed in it himself.

The Rector's wife was as large and shapeless as a badly stuffed bolster. She wore thick beige stockings and a thick beige dress, and her hair reminded me of the White Queen's. Her face was large and white and faintly wrinkled; it had that unpleasant texture that your hands get when you leave them too long in water. She was (and I found a twinge of Simon-engendered embarrassment nagging at me as I made this private judgement) quite evidently a lady; while the Rector was—well—a Rector. Her eyes were pale blue, and never rested long in any one spot; like a bad actress, she found her hands a problem.

'Well, Mrs Mannering,' she cried, in a quick, fluting, breathy voice, 'I expect you'd like me to show you the more *domestic* details wouldn't you? I mean, we might leave the men to *explore*, don't you think, and then we could pop down to my little cubby-hole in the kitchen and have a good chat about anything you want to know—it's very kind of you to come out all this way,' she went on, with practically no change of verbal gear, 'I mean, we're so off the beaten track and I can't think why anyone should want—well no, ha-ha, I don't mean *that*, you know, it's just that most people nowadays always want *company*—all these building

estates and bungalows and Development Corporations, so
vulgar I always think, but there, there's no accounting for
taste, is there, Mrs Mannering——'

'No, of course not, I said, reflecting to myself that if
there was one thing the Rector's wife needed at this moment
it was company, lots of it, preferably in a whacking great
block of flats where the lights were never turned off day or
night and no single object in the place was old enough to
have acquired associations of any sort. But clearly she was
not expecting an answer to her question, because she was
off again almost before the first word was out of my mouth,
eyes flickering from side to side, occasionally injecting a
tinny little laugh between phrases to show how bright and
relaxed and unnervous she was. Well, one problem was
solved anyway, I thought: no need to ask why they want to
move.

Simon had been observing this little scene with an air of
grave and detached charm. I could have kicked his stupid
insensitive face in. The air was thick with fear and evil and
hysteria; I could feel my nerves, already taut enough,
being screwed up, notch by notch. It only needed Simon to
put out a long, probing finger and twang them. Honestly.
I thought, it's like living with—with a cripple, or a para-
lytic, or something: there are great areas of sensitivity and
awareness in Simon that are just, I don't know what,
anaesthetised seems the only word.

The Rector's wife's eyes suddenly met mine, in a quick
but agonised appeal. *For God's sake don't leave me alone,*
they said.

'Simon,' I said, as casually as I could, 'perhaps you and
Mr—er—' I suddenly realised I'd never been told the
Rector's name.

'Venables,' the Rector said, caressing the syllables with proprietory relish. Venables. No one called Venables could fail to be a clergyman, I thought wildly. Venables should have been an archdeacon at the very least.

'—Mr Venables would like to go over the house first? I'm sure Mrs Venables could tell me a lot I'd like to know——'

Simon said: 'But look, Lavinia, I thought you wanted——'

'Not just yet,' I said.

The Rector said, eyes blinking like mad: 'Hilda, wouldn't *you* like to take Mr Mannering round——?'

'Oh, of course,' cried Mrs Venables, with an air of desperately skittish gaiety (like an old whore on a rainy night, as Simon said afterwards), 'but really, dear, I'm sure there are things Mrs Mannering and I have to discuss which you don't know about——'

Oh heavens, I thought, are we going to have a nice gynaecological heart-to-heart about babies and periods? She looks just the sort.

'Yes, yes, my dear; I suppose so.' The Rector sighed. 'Well, now, Mr Mannering, if you'll just come with me——'

He and Simon stepped out of the lobby and moved down a dark, shabby corridor to the left. 'Now this,' I heard his dry, cracked voice enunciating, 'is my study—' and then there was the click of a door and silence.

Hilda Venables slipped an arm through mine, fingers clutching, talking away as though her life depended on it.

'Well now, we'll just go down *this* way—mind the step, Mrs Mannering, we mustn't have you falling about in your condition must we? and when's it due, May I suppose, I always think that's a nice month for babies, not that I've any of my own, mind you, a great disappointment that was to us both, and of course I always say I'd have made a really good mother, but I suppose you can't tell——'

It was true; she would have made an infuriatingly good mother. Unlike me, I thought. I was nervous, awkward, rational, inhibited, full of theories; Hilda Venables' troubles were very different, the neurosis of a basically uncomplicated woman whose life has run into a frightening blind alley. She envied me my fertility; I, to my surprise, found myself envying her those rich maternal gifts that had been so pitifully wasted.

'You know, Mrs Mannering, it hasn't been all that much fun as a parson's wife—not that Edward isn't the soul of kindliness, but somehow it's the atmosphere of the whole thing, you know—they make all those jokes about the odour of sanctity but there's something in it, polished brass and old ladies' dresses and oak pews and dust, not *incense*, of course, one thing I will say for Edward, he isn't *high* like some of them round here, oh dear, I'm getting off the point, well what I mean is, I think it's just the faintest bit *morbid*——'

Now we're getting to it, I thought, realising that Mrs Venables' apparently aimless torrent of speech formed, as it were, the camouflage behind which she sidled up towards a predetermined objective.

'You know,' she went on, letting go my arm and wrestling with the kitchen door-handle, 'it's always being on top of the *graveyard*, unhygienic it seemed to me at the beginning, I suppose because I'd trained as a nurse, but of course on a curate's stipend you have to take the accommodation you're offered, don't you, and that always meant some

gigantic vicarage you couldn't afford to keep up, most of
them look as though they were built to house about twenty
children——'

Poor Mrs Venables, I thought; oh, poor Hilda. The con-
stant cold reminder of barrenness. Mouldering crosses
glimpsed by moonlight through an ivy-encrusted window.
The aching, empty, unfulfilled heart. But Nature abhors a
vacuum, isn't that so? Therefore something had moved in
to fill the emptiness. Something? If not love, then fear.
Fear was a difficult tenant, casual with the rent and almost
impossible to evict.

Mrs Venables got the door open at last, and began to
snap on light after light, with feverish relief. The kitchen
seemed like an oasis of sanity in that mad, deprived, un-
friendly house: a room where the fog of evil had not
penetrated. It was bright and modern, with a gay tiled
floor and a Welsh dresser from which copper pans winked
redly in the electric glow, and chintz curtains and a cuckoo-
clock and a garish seed-manufacturer's calender and a
surprising number of modern gadgets—infra-red grill, big
refrigerator, spin-drier, washing-up machine. The furniture
was ultra-modern—all formica surfaces and tubular legs.

I remembered my visit, several years before, to a certain
Iron Curtain country, and how after a week in the capital
Simon and I had had an invitation to dinner at the British
Embassy. The relief I had felt on that occasion and the
relief I felt now were exactly identical.

There was a kettle singing away on the stove, a large iron
affair that looked as though it were on twenty-four hour
duty for endless brews of strong tea. How much of the day
—or night—did Hilda Venables spend in here? Glancing
round I noticed piles of paperback novels, mending-bag,

piles of correspondence, the clutter that more rightly belonged to a living room than a kitchen.

'I expect you could do with a cup?' Mrs Venables said, and began to pour out without waiting for an answer. The tea-service was Meissen, the tray Woolworth plastic: I felt this ought to tell me something about Mrs Venables' character, but I wasn't sure what.

For once, too, her flow of conversation seemed to have dried up: perhaps it was the influence of the kitchen. I wondered if she *had* to talk non-stop outside this protected room simply to keep her courage, if not her sanity.

As though reading my thoughts she said, out of the blue: 'I suppose you're wondering why we want to move, aren't you, well of course you would be, you're no fool, anyone can see that—' she bent forward across the table, confidentially, and it occurred to me that with a slight change of accent she would be the very spit of any garrulous charwoman. 'The thing is, you see, I had a complete nervous breakdown about a couple of years ago, and the doctor said when I came out—out of hospital that is,' she added mechanically, as though she'd been taught to attach this qualification every time she told the story, 'well, you see, he said this was a bad *atmosphere* for me to be in, and I needed somewhere with more sunshine and sea-air and company, but of course it wasn't all that easy to move, what with Edward not being on too good terms with his Bishop, and then there was the business of the Church Commissioners having spent a lot on renovations here and not wanting to lose it because there was talk of making it a plural living if Edward did go, and after all it wasn't a living for years at the end of last century——'

This time I managed to get my question in, though hardly

more than sideways, but it seemed suddenly of vital importance that I should ask it.

I said: 'What was the place used for all that time—who lived here?' And then, because I couldn't help myself and I knew that she knew that I knew: '*What happened*, for God's sake?'

For the first time, Mrs Venables looked straight at me and said, in a quiet voice, as different as could be from her usual febrile chatter: 'It was—it was a home for delinquent boys, I suppose you'd call it——'

'A Remand Home, you mean?'

'Oh no, something different—a private venture—I know it sounds fantastic in these days, but that sort of thing did happen. There was a City businessman, a bachelor I believe, with a great deal of money—Hampton his name was. It seems he determined to set up some kind of philanthropic institution, a lot of them did in those days, of course there wasn't anything like this Welfare State then——'

Homes for Fallen Women. The Age of the Orphanage Trustee, with Dotheboys Hall a not-too-remote memory. I shivered, and goose-pimples rose gently along my arms.

Mrs Venables went on, the words tumbling out: 'This man Hampton did a lot of voluntary welfare work. I think he was a J.P. too, I wouldn't be certain. Anyhow, he bought the Rectory, and had some sort of arrangement with the Courts in London to take on a lot of these boys—I don't know the details. But he was here, and they were here, that's certain.'

'When did all this happen?' I asked.

'Well, it must have been going on for about ten years before 1887, I suppose,' Mrs Venables said, pouring me out another cup of tea.

'How can you be so sure of the date?'

She blinked nervously at me. 'That was the year of the scandal,' she said, and then, perfunctorily: 'I shouldn't really be telling you all this.'

'*What happened?*'

'Well—I don't understand the details, but it seems there was something very queer about this Mr Hampton——'

For a split second I wondered if Mrs Venables could have been using the adjective in its modern, specialised sense, but decided immediately against it.

'You see when they got the police in they found some very odd things—leg-irons and whips and birches, he must have been horribly cruel, I mean, whatever those boys had done——'

'How did the police come into it?'

'Oh, it was too horrible, Mrs Mannering, you don't want to hear such things in your state——'

'I shall feel a damned sight worse if you *don't* tell me,' I said, and meant it.

'Well, there had been a lot of gossip in the village, but nothing for certain, you know—and then one dark night, just about this time of year, too, there was a knocking at a house down the road, I don't know which exactly, and there was one of the boys. His back was a mess of blood, and he'd gone a bit turned in his wits; but the mere sight of him was enough to send them off for the police.'

Mrs Venables paused, and in the silence the cuckoo suddenly lunged out of his ornate clock six times, in noisy and rapid succession.

She said: 'They found three of the boys dead of starvation, another one dying from his beatings, and Hampton lying upstairs with a pistol in his hand and his brains blown out. There'd been a couple who helped him—an ex-gamekeeper and his wife—and they'd vanished. No one ever saw them again.'

'So that's the story,' I said.

Mrs Venables nodded.

I said: 'Look, Mrs Venables, do *you* believe this house is haunted?'

She said: 'I don't know what to think. I've heard—whimperings, noises like blows, scufflings, that sort of thing. Tapping on the window-panes. Of course, you do hear noises in big old houses, and I knew about the story, so I might have imagined it all, mightn't I?'

I said: 'What does your husband think?'

Mrs Venables' face crumpled queerly. 'He *refuses* to admit there's anything—anything at all. He says it's against all his principles. You see, Edward's very modern, very advanced—you may think clergymen are silly, but Edward knows all about modern science—someone who came here wanted Edward to *exorcise* the Rectory, of all silly outdated superstitious nonsense, but Edward soon put *him* in his place.'

You miserable, unhappy, loyal woman, I thought. You'd give your very soul to have this place exorcised, and I don't blame you.

I said: 'But your husband is frightened.' I stated it as a fact.

'Yes,' she said helplessly. 'But he won't admit it. He says there's no *reason* for it. Just, oh what did he call it? auto-suggestion working on perfectly normal and natural phenomena.'

'And you agree with him?'

'What else can I do?' It was a cry from the heart. 'And

now I've told you all this there's not a chance of your buying the place——'

I said: 'You'd never have let us, would you?'

She shook her head, blinking the tears away. Then she
said something that really shook me. Her voice was hesitant,
searching for the right words. 'Sometimes,' she whispered,
'I feel that it's only Edward who's frightened, not me. I
feel that—that they *need* me. Those cries, those scratching, searching, lost, desperate fingers—They were only
children, really, you know, just unhappy children. Orphans,
most of them. Broken homes. They weren't wicked. They
needed love, that was all. Love, not punishment. Sometimes
I think all wickedness comes from the loss of love.'

I looked at her, feeling I had never seen her till this
moment, stripping away all my glib preconceptions, beginning again from the beginning.

'So you see, Mrs Mannering,' she said softly, 'you see, I
can never leave this place. Not while I am needed.'

In my mind I could hear Simon, jeeringly rational, saying: My dear Vinny, what a set-up: the old boy's gaga, and
the old girl's right round the bend. Playing Mummy to a
bunch of delinquent spooks: that's a new one for the case-
book.

I said: 'Mrs Venables, I think you told me something
just now that wasn't quite true. You said you weren't
frightened. I don't believe you.'

She dabbed hopelessly at her eyes with a small handkerchief. In so large a woman the gesture was incongruous
beyond belief.

'I want you to know,' I said, hearing my own voice
utter the words as though it were another person, 'that I
think you are the bravest creature I have ever met.'

Mrs Venables did not make any self-deprecatory fuss at this. She said: 'Thank you, my dear,' with great dignity; and then suggested, diffidently, that we ought perhaps to go and find the others.

As we walked back down the shabby corridor I said: 'Where are they?'

Mrs Venables, misunderstanding me, replied: 'In the attics and cellars it's worst. They used the attics as their dormitories, you see, and it was down in the cellar that Hampton used to do—the things he wanted to do.'

I shivered. The small life curled within me—produced one thoughtless night after a little too much whisky, unpremeditated and perhaps unwanted—stirred tentatively, as though seeking comfort. Or reassurance. Once again Mrs Venables slipped her arm through mine; but this time I felt she was giving comfort, not soliciting it.

We heard Simon and the Rector coming down the stairs. The Rector was saying: 'I do assure you, my dear chap, that our surveyor told me there would be no difficulty, no difficulty whatsoever about that damp patch in the drawing-room. Just a matter of lifting some bricks and inserting an—ah—damp-course, I gather. No trouble at all. And of course, ha-ha, absolutely no dry-rot, that I can assure you——'

Round the angle of the wall I heard Simon say: 'I'd like to have a look round the cellars, if I may.'

'Do you think that's really necessary, Mr Mannering?'

'If you please, Rector.' Simon had on his High Table voice: it was polite, but brooked no contradiction.

There was a jingle of keys, and the sound of a door being unlocked.

The Rector said, querulously: 'Please forgive me if I

don't come down with you, Mr Mannering—a touch of arthritis, you know, and at my age those cellar steps are a bit steep, ha-ha. You'll find the light switch down there on the left——'

A pause. Then Simon's voice, muffled, from below ground: 'I'm afraid the light isn't working, Rector. But I have a pocket torch, so don't worry.'

He would have remembered a torch. And a steel rule, and a probe for dry-rot, and probably a handy little manual entitled ' 101 Things to Remember When Buying a House'.

Mrs Venables and I looked at each other. Then we went round the bend in the corridor and joined the Rector, who by now had retreated to the old oak settle in the lobby, about as far as he could get in all politeness from the open cellar door. He was fussing busily with his pipe.

'Ah,' he said, in that bright, false, cracked voice, 'the ladies are back I see.' He breathed out fragrant clouds, the very brand-image of a wise old clergyman in some slick tobacco advertisement. 'Well, Mrs Mannering, I hope you found out all you wanted to know.'

'Yes, Mr Venables,' I said. 'I did.' The air crawled with damp evil; a cold, sour draught seemed to come eddying up from the cellar.

The Rector glanced at his wife, with—it seemed to me—an air of ill-suppressed annoyance. Then he called out: 'Mr Mannering—have you quite finished down there?'

In the same instant Simon appeared, still holding his torch. There was a smear of dirt—or perhaps a dislodged cobweb—on one cheek, and in the artificial light his naturally pallid complexion had a dead quality about it, like tallow. I noticed a faint beading of sweat on his forehead.

'Hullo Vinney,' he said, and his voice was as cool as ever. Then he glanced at his wristwatch. 'Well, if you've seen all you want to see in the domestic quarters, I think we'd better be making tracks. We mustn't trespass on the Rector's time for too long.'

'I'm ready,' I said.

With outstretched hand, his voice a little too eager and anxious, the Rector said: 'It's been a great pleausre, Mr Mannering, a very great pleasure. I hope to hear from you very soon——'

'We'll let you know our decision, naturally,' Simon said.

'And about that damp patch, I can assure you——'

'You've made yourself quite clear, Mr Venables,' Simon said. 'Don't give it another thought.' He shook hands with brisk efficiency. 'Goodbye, Mrs Venables.'

'Goodbye,' she said, but she was looking at me as she said it.

Somehow we negotiated the front door. It was now quite dark. The Venables, both of them, stood framed in the oblong of light till we had gone.

The rain had stopped altogether, and a few stars were shining as we drove back along the Haverhill Road towards Cambridge. Simon said nothing for about ten minutes. In front of his face the cigarette-tip glowed, even and red, momentarily lighting up his face in a faint glow each time he inhaled. I thought: We might as well be on separate desert islands. There is no point of contact at all. And at that thought, silently, I began to cry, the tears trickling down my cheeks, a tight knot of pain and loss drawn taut inside me.

Suddenly Simon said: 'My God, I'm glad to be clear of that dump.'

Faintly I said: 'Why? Why are you glad Simon?'

'Didn't you feel it? You must have felt it. I nearly vomited down in that cellar——'

He knew. He had known all the time. Suddenly it struck me, with a jolting shock, how much I had been trained to judge people by their faces: what they said, looked, professed. The rational interpretation of evidence. Now, twice in one day, I had had my assumptions challenged. I have been married to Simon for eight years, I thought, wonderingly, and I have never really looked at him.

'Oh Simon,' I whispered through my tears, 'Simon darling—' Simon took his left hand off the steering-wheel and put it round my shoulders, holding me close. Explanations could come later, if at all. The tyres drummed on the damp road; and behind us, from Mareshill Rectory, long black tentacles of evil reached out in pursuit of us, stretched, broke, faded, and were gone.

DEVONSHIRE SPLITS
WITH CREAM

THE dunes lay powdered and shimmering in the white-hot sunlight of a mid-July afternoon. Mark Crompton, fresh from the sea, salt crusting in his hair and across his shoulders, gazed out across the level blue dancing-floor of the Atlantic to where Lundy crouched like an old dog, haze-faint on the fluid horizon. Below him stretched the three-mile expanse of beach (its perspectives vulgarised in countless station travel posters) upon which, in slow and dignified succession, great glassy combers exploded one by one, leaving a long line of surf along the tide-line, brown and sticky as the head on a pint of stout. At either end of the bay long naked headlands, lizard-green, rock-encumbered, dwindled westwards towards America. Nestling under the shelf of the dunes, out of the wind, sat the squat white bathing-huts, roofs dabbed with bright spots of colour where costumes were spread out to dry. In the middle distance a game of beach cricket was in progress: small brown figures darted to and fro, bright and eager as fish in a tropical aquarium. Here and there a lazy sun-bather sprawled. But for the greater part of its length the beach was deserted, wrapped in drowsy somnolence, enjoying siesta-time. From high overhead came the faint, bee-like drone of an aeroplane, forming a remote descant to the warm humming silence that was like a giant shell held to one's ear in dreams.

Mark yawned and stretched like a cat, narrowing his
eyes against the dazzle of sky and sea, swinging the wicker
picnic basket that bulged comfortably with towels and
thermos and sandwich-tins, sun-tan lotion, dark glasses, the
books stuffed in at the last moment as a gesture and doomed,
inevitably, never to be read. He had on nothing but open-
work sandals and a pair of neat dark-blue swimming
trunks; after three weeks' unbroken fine weather his body
was toasted to a light, even tan, without a hint of peeling
or sunburn. The sand, blown dry and burning between
hussocks of coarse couch-grass, silted between his toes as he
stood there, absorbed in the view, feeling the sun soak into
his skin, euphoric and relaxed.

'Penny for them, Mark,' said Brenda Page, smiling.

'Oh, I don't know—all this—' he waved his free arm in
an expansive gesture that embraced the whole of the bay.
'*You* know.'

Brenda nodded. 'I know.'

'I wish it could go on for ever,' Mark said.

'Do you, Mark?'

Their eyes met and lingered.

Mark said: 'Nothing to worry about. All the time in
the world. Just sun and sea and sky. And——'

He broke off, hesitant, looking away from Brenda.

'And——?' she insisted, softly.

Mark scuffed one foot in the sand, but said nothing.

'You're a sweet boy, Mark,' Brenda Page said. 'I'm going
to miss you when you're gone.'

Mark's face clouded. He said: 'I don't want to think
about going.'

'Never mind: we've still got two days. Let's make the
most of them. Come on.'

Brenda turned and set off along the dunes, rich coppery hair gleaming in the sunlight, fiery-dark against the pale lemon ribbon at her neck. Mark, walking close behind her, mouth dry, heart pounding, sea and sun forgotten now, saw only the smooth fair expanse of her bare shoulders, lightly dusted with freckles, saw her body's easy, effortless movements, broad hips turning slightly at each stride in the black latex costume that fitted her like a second skin. Brenda Page was a big, heavily-built girl; she looked better out of her clothes than in them.

For over a mile they continued thus, between the sea and the soft Devon hills, feet slithering in hot sand that no tide ever reached, backs baked by the relentless sun. They knew where they were going. Far beyond the bathing-huts and the games of beach-cricket they walked, the hollow roar of the Atlantic breakers in their ears, till they reached the deep wind-sheltered hollow they had found a week before, where the sand lay cool and shadowed, facing inland, untouched by the burning heat of the afternoon.

With a sigh of relief Mark put down the picnic basket and spread out the big striped bathing towel. All around them the heat-haze quivered and danced, draining colour from coombe and headland, mirage-like, eliding distance, playing odd impressionistic tricks with the landscape. There was not a soul in sight; even the parched golf-links were deserted, and the rusty flag at the thirteenth green fluttered despondently, a distress signal from some invisible island.

Mark and Brenda knelt facing each other on the towel. Neither of them said a word: there was a slow, grave, ritual precision about their movements. Each wore the same concentrated, serious expression. With unhurried care Mark untied the lemon ribbon, and a cascade of copper

G

hair streamed down Brenda's back. He stroked it with light fingers for a little; then he began to trace the outlines of Brenda's features—broad freckled cheek-bones, snub nose, warm unpainted lips—barely touching them, silent still, all the time watching her grey eyes that never left his own face. Presently, with equal gentleness, she stretched out her arms and set about exploring the hollows and curves of Mark's bare torso as though she were blind: lingering on a shoulder-blade, sketching the line of the pectoral muscles, running lightly up and down the central spinal ridge.

Still they did not kiss, though their lips were only a matter of inches apart.

At last, as though on some invisible signal, Mark's right hand sought and found the small metal tag between Brenda's shoulders. He zipped it downwards, in one long decisive moment, as a hunter might skin a shot deer; and the black sheath loosened, crumpling down and away as Brenda rose to her feet, exposing heavy white breasts, freckles fading into a network of fine blue veins, nipples as pink and innocent as a baby's smile. Mark, rising too, tugged at the latex with both hands, peeling its blackness down over wide white hips, kneeling again as Brenda stepped out of it, unable to take his eyes from the flaming wedge-shaped maquis of hair that lay so neatly between those marbled and resplendent thighs. He clasped his arms round Brenda's back, pressed his burning face into the soft warmth of her. Half in a dream he felt her strip him naked, too: floating, he was aware of the soft sand pressing up into his shoulder-blades through the towel, and the un-imaginable body of Brenda Page arched lightly over him, elbows resting in the sand, breasts brushing downwards across the line of his rib-cage, skin and hair barely touching,

moving away again, burning with the naked shock of ex-
posed wires, to and fro, softly, urgently, and then, then,
then the scalding furnace descended and drew him in, and
Brenda's open mouth was on his, everywhere the never-
before-known, out-of-this-world fire licking and consuming
him, flaking the flesh, white-hot now—now, now, *now*, and
when the pale sky stopped spinning Mark woke to Brenda
Page's heavy, relaxed body lying soft on his, and the last
echoes of those weird, terrifying, scarcely human moans
still sounding in his ears.

Lazily now he held Brenda close to him, hands exploring
with wonder the soft fullness of her buttocks, her strongly-
muscled back, her rich, fiery hair. She sighed and stirred,
mouth at his ear, and whispered: 'Oh Mark. Oh my
darling.'

Mark, mind running with wonder and delight on the
small battered volume he had picked up in Bideford, the
poet (a name only hitherto) who miraculously, centuries
ago, had mapped the world he himself was now discovering,
murmured: ' " O my America! my new-found-land——" '
and blinked sensuously, eyes closed, lulled by the muted
thunder of the sea behind the dunes.

Brenda giggled. 'I'm not sure that's a compliment,' she
said. 'America's a big place.'

' I like you big.'

Brenda sat up in a kneeling position, balancing on her
heels, still astride Mark's recumbent body, and shook out
her hair. 'Do you, Mark?' she said. 'Do you really like
me?' She was smiling now, grey eyes soft and happy,
luxuriating in her nakedness and Mark's eager gaze.

He stretched out one hand to caress her breasts.

' Try me and see.'

'Greedy boy.'

'Please, Brenda.'

'No, Mark *really*——' But she was beginning to breathe faster again already.

'That's how you like it, isn't it, Brenda? Like that? And that?'

'Oh God. Please. *Please*, Mark——'

Mark laughed happily, jack-knifed upright, and bore Brenda down in a flurry of flailing limbs, savouring his pleasure now, making it last, watching with conscious delight and power the onset of Brenda's frenzy.

Afterwards Brenda grinned, a little lopsidedly, and said: 'My God. They ought to keep you on a chain.'

Mark said: 'I suppose they do, in a way.'

They both laughed. Brenda stretched and lay back on the towel. Tiny beads of sweat gleamed along her upper lip. Mark rummaged in the picnic basket till he found a battered packet of Players and a box of matches. He put a cigarette in Brenda's mouth and lit it.

'Thanks, darling.' Brenda inhaled deeply, and blew a long feather of smoke from each nostril. 'Give me my dark glasses, will you? I can't stand this glare.'

Mark put them on for her, fingers lingering in the thick hair above her ears. He said, hopefully: 'Shall I rub some sun-tan lotion in for you? You know how easily you burn.'

'*No*, darling. Decidedly not. You know perfectly well what would happen.'

'M'm,' said Mark, nodding. 'Nice.' He giggled, and then added, inconsequentially: 'Gosh, I'm ravenous.'

Brenda sat up, amused. 'For heaven's sake, Mark! No one could call you *complicated*, could they? Here, give me my clothes. I'm going to get dressed. So had you, Rabbit.'

Mark rummaged in the bottom of the big basket, and came up with a crumpled linen skirt, a chequered blouse, a black bra and a pair of briefs.

He said : ' I'm glad you like *Winnie-the-Pooh*. Lots of people think it's soppy. I love it. Can I help you dress? '

' No,' said Brenda Page, ' you most certainly can't. I don't trust you an inch.'

' Good-oh,' Mark observed. He quickly wriggled into a white aertex shirt and a pair of grey shorts, and then sat watching Brenda's every move with fascinated curiosity.

' Don't you ever use lipstick? ' he asked at length.

Brenda shook her head. ' No. Can't stand the stuff. If you were a real gentleman you'd tell me I didn't need it anyway.' She twinkled.

' Well, you don't,' Mark said, hastily. ' Anyway, I think it's horrid, too.'

' Thank you, sir, she said. I suppose it's making a virtue of a necessity, in a way. I can't use any make-up in term-time—the Head'd be down on me like a ton of bricks. Bad influence on the girls, and all that nonsense.'

Mark said : ' It does seem funny, you being a mistress— I just can't get used to the idea.' Then he blushed crimson and added : ' A schoolmistress, I mean,' which made it worse.

' If it comes to that——' Brenda began, and then broke off, biting her lip.

But Mark was still pursuing his own train of thought. ' Most schoolmistresses I've known have been the most awful hags,' he said. ' Buns and pince-nez, that sort of thing.'

Brenda laughed. 'Oh, we've got plenty of *those* around
the place. I'm just a games-mistress—not the genuine article
at all.' She knotted the lemon ribbon and gave her hair a
final pat. 'What about some food, Mark? I thought you
said you were ravenous.'

Mark glanced at his watch. 'Look,' he said, 'I've got a
much better idea. Let's catch the afternoon bus from Puts-
borough and go and have tea in Braunton.'

'What, and waste all the food we've brought?'

'Oh, we can have that later.' Mark stood up, showering
sand all round him. 'I want to buy you a really *enormous*
tea—Devonshire splits with cream, strawberry jam, cakes,
the lot. *Please*, Brenda—it'd be such fun.'

'You are sweet, Mark. All right. But you mustn't spend
your money on me. It'll be my treat.'

Mark frowned. 'It was my idea,' he said, obstinately.
'I'm jolly well paying for it.'

'Sorry, Mark,' Brenda said, softly. 'That was tactless of
me. I'd love to have tea with you, of course I would. Thank
you very much.'

Mark's face cleared at once. He picked up the picnic
basket and slipped his free arm round Brenda's waist. Together they turned inland, leaving the dunes and the sea
behind them, trudging across the coomb-side that sloped
gently up beyond the golf-course. The grass was short and
springy underfoot, dotted with clumps of gorse. A light
breeze ruffled Brenda's hair: once a rabbit shot away in
front of them, its white scut gleaming in the sunlight.

'If anyone had told me a month ago——' Mark said,
wonderingly, and broke off.

Brenda smiled; but her eyes were searching the landscape,
and a faint expression of anxiety had settled on her face.

Mark did not notice: he was glowing, self-contained in his private happiness, more conscious at this moment of the bright afternoon that matched his mood so well than of the girl who had brought it about.

He said, the words coming slowly and with difficulty: 'I shall always think of you *here*, Brenda. This is where you belong for me. With the sun and the sea and the gorse. I can't imagine you teaching girls lacrosse or hockey or whatever you do teach them, and I don't want to.'

'Why ever not, Mark?'

Mark kicked at a hussock of grass, frowning. 'It spoils it, somehow,' he said.

'You *are* a cuckoo, aren't you?' Brenda said, and blinked, as though at some unwelcome thought. 'You can't stop time, Mark, and you can't keep out the world. I've learnt that the hard way, believe me. This fortnight's been wonderful—you'll never know how wonderful—but it can't last for ever. We've got to go on living, Mark.'

Mark said, suddenly: '"The world is too much with us——"'

'You are bright. Always quoting. That's Wordsworth, isn't it?'

'M'm.'

'I remember—I learnt that one at school.'

'So did I,' Mark said. They glanced quickly at each other, and Brenda flushed.

'Oh Mark, this is hopeless, can't you see? It's not just us alone, it's more than a summer afternoon. Do be sensible. People——'

Mark said, with abrupt vehemence: 'I hate people.'

'But you can't get rid of them, Mark. You don't really know much about me, do you? I'm just the girl with red hair you met on holiday. Nothing to do with your world. A fairy-tale girl in the sand-dunes. That's it, isn't it?'

'I wish you wouldn't talk like that, Brenda.'

Brenda said, almost desperately: 'I've got to, Mark. There's so little time left.'

They stopped, and faced one another. Brenda suddenly kissed Mark, with hungry desperation, pressing her body hard against his.

'Oh God,' she whispered.

Somewhere overhead a lark trilled faintly in the summer air, a thin clear rivulet of sound.

Trembling, Brenda pulled away from him and said: 'No, Mark—we must get on. We'll miss that bus if we're not careful.'

Mark looked at her and saw, astonished, the faint glitter of suppressed tears in her eyes.

'Brenda, you're crying.'

Then, like a sudden tidal wave, black misery surged up inside him, overwhelming and irresistible. His mouth twisted and he began to sob, the muscles of his diaphragm contracting in spasms as though he were being sick. Brenda drew him to her, cradling his head against her breast, stroking his rough, fuzzy hair.

'Oh Mark,' she whispered. 'My poor baby. My darling.'

Gradually the storm spent itself. Mark sniffed, gulped, and fished a remarkably dirty handkerchief from the pocket of his shorts, together with a twist of string, a penknife, and an unopened packet of chewing-gum. He blew his nose vigorously, wiped his eyes, sniffed again, gave a rather lop-sided smile, and said: 'Sorry. Made an ass of myself.'

Brenda shook her head, still not trusting herself to speak. They stood there a moment longer, then began to walk on again. Mark kept one arm round her. After a little he began to chatter nervously, filling in the unbearable silence, trying to obliterate his embarrassment.

'I'm going to miss the surf-riding, aren't you?' he said. 'Coming in on top of those huge waves—you feel nothing can stop you, ever. Do you feel like that, Brenda? Remember when we tried to swim out to the point? And the donkeys coming down the steps at Clovelly? And that trip across to Lundy in the fog?'

'The less said about *that* the better, Mark Crompton.' Brenda was in control of herself again: her voice was light and bantering. 'If I remember rightly, you spent most of your time trying to get off with Barbara Randell.'

'I did *not*.' Mark coloured up. 'She was after me.'

Brenda giggled. 'What a very unchivalrous thing to say. Anyway I don't blame you. She's an attractive creature.'

'She's just a kid,' Mark protested.

There was a brief and awful silence. Then Mark went on: 'Besides, that was before——'

'I know it was, silly. I'm only teasing.' Brenda flashed him a quick affectionate grin.

Mark said: 'Girls like that are just stupid.'

Brenda said, tenderly: 'Come on, now, stop giving yourself airs, poppet. Barbara Randell is a very nice girl.'

'She's not like you, anyway.'

'Perhaps that's just as well,' Brenda said.

'Oh shut *up*, Brenda.'

'Sorry.'

Mark thought for a moment and then said: 'If I told you I *did* like Barbara, you wouldn't think she was so nice, would you?'

'Clever boy. You're learning.'

'Brenda——'

'M'm?'

'I've been thinking about what you said.'

Brenda gave him a quick, slightly apprehensive glance.

'You're quite right. I don't really *know* you, Brenda, not properly.' He frowned in concentration, following an unfamiliar train of thought. 'I want to. I do, really. Tell me all about yourself.'

'What, now?'

'Yes.'

Brenda laughed. 'You impatient creature,' she said. 'All right. Where shall I begin?'

'At the beginning, of course, silly.'

'Well,' said Brenda, in a small, flat voice Mark had never heard before, as though she was talking to herself, 'well, I was an only child, for a start.'

'So'm I. That's why we understand each other.'

'There, my sweet,' said Brenda Page, 'you may speak truer than you know.'

'What do you mean?'

'Never mind. Skip it. Let's go on with the exclusive story of my life.'

'Why were you an only child?' Mark asked.

'Very simple. My father went off on a voyage to Hong-Kong and was killed in a waterside brawl there.'

'Oh Brenda. How awful.'

'It wasn't awful at all. From what I can make out he must have been a prize bastard.' She added, as an afterthought: 'So am I, technically speaking.'

'You mean they weren't *married*?'

'Don't sound so horrified, Mark. I suppose illegitimacy

simply doesn't exist in Pinner, does it? They tidy it away with anything else remotely unpleasant.'

Mark said: 'Well, I've never *met* anyone who was, not till now.' He looked at Brenda as though expecting to see some subtle physical peculiarity about her.

'They'd hardly proclaim the fact even if they were, would they?'

'I suppose not. I'd never thought of that.' A pleased expression came over Mark's face. 'Gosh,' he said, and held Brenda closer.

'Mark, you are sweet. Now where was I? Oh yes. Mummy had a little tobacconist's shop, down in Whitechapel, a legacy from her Uncle Harry. Not much of a place, but it just about kept our heads above water.'

'Didn't she ever get married?'

'No. One experience like my father was quite enough. Anyway, she wasn't all that young, even then. Not much of a catch, you see. An unmarried widow with a growing daughter. Oh, quite a few of them tried it on. Dirty old men with pot-bellies and stinking breath.' Cold disgust filled Brenda's voice. 'Mummy used to let me help out behind the counter. They'd come sidling in and ask for a packet of fags, and try to hold my hand when I gave the change. "You're a fine big girlie, aren't you?" they'd say, and titter and leer in that horrible furtive way old men have. "Just like your Mum, eh, dead spit of her, wait till you grow up," they'd say, "you'll have a high old time." I dream about them sometimes, still.'

'How awful, Brenda.'

'"You put in a word for me with your Mum, Brenda," they'd tell me. "I know a little girlie who'll get some chocs if she does what she's told." They'd try to send me out on errands so they could get Mummy on her own. When I went to school it was awful. Mummy complained to the police once.' Brenda blinked. 'They more or less told her she was no better than she should be, and what the hell did she expect? In the end——' She broke off, and then said, harshly: 'I shouldn't be telling you all this.'

'*Please*, Brenda. I want to know.'

'Give me a cigarette. They're in the basket.'

'Here you are.'

'Thanks. Want one?'

Mark shook his head. Brenda inhaled deeply.

'In the end——?' Mark prompted.

'In the end,' Brenda said, in that frightening, neutral voice, 'she settled for Uncle Joe.'

'Uncle Joe?'

'Oh, he wasn't a real uncle.' Brenda gave a short, humour-less laugh. 'But the pretences had to be kept up. "Uncle Joe's going to stay with us for a bit, darling. You don't mind, do you?" There wasn't even a spare room. Poor Mummy. I suppose she thought if she had one of them in residence at least it'd keep the others off.'

'What was he like?' Mark asked.

'Horrible. Tall and thin and bald, with false teeth that didn't fit. You could hear them clicking whenever he talked. He always needed a shave, and he had that ghastly greenish white sort of skin, like a dead fish. He used to sit there after supper, with his feet stretched out in front of him, smoking a filthy old pipe. I can see him to this day. He never wore carpet-slippers, and I don't think he changed his socks from one week to the next. The thing I always remember about him is his adam's-apple. He had one of those long thin necks, and his adam's-apple bobbed up and down every time he swallowed. He'd take off his collar and tie, and stretch, and say, "Nell, get me a bottle of Bass, girl," and Mummy would go off to the local, and leave me staring at that adam's-apple. Up and down, up and down, over his brass front stud.'

Mark said: 'How perfectly beastly for you.'

'Oh, I suppose he was kind enough to Mummy in his way. He was a builder's foreman, a good one I dare say, and he wasn't stingy with his money.' Brenda suddenly giggled.

'What's the joke?'

'He had to have a bowler,' Brenda said. 'All builders' foremen wear bowlers, it's like a sergeant's stripes, but Uncle Joe looked so funny in his, trotting off every morning with his sandwiches and that silly hat stuck on his head.'

Mark smiled uncertainly. 'Was he decent to you?' he asked.

'In a way, yes. To begin with. I was a bright girl at school, and my headmistress wanted me to try for a place at the local Grammar. But that meant money in those days. Not much, but enough. Uncle Joe said he'd pay. Mummy was all over him. So was I. At first.'

'What happened?'

'He was a clever bastard, was Uncle Joe,' Brenda said, as though she hadn't heard. 'He bided his time. He let me get a good taste of the Grammar—a full year, no less—before he tried anything on. I did well, too. Worked myself sick. Homework every evening till all hours. There was nothing I couldn't do, I reckoned. I saw the door opening, Mark—away from that bloody shop and Whitechapel and the dirty old men. Away from Uncle Joe, too, I thought. But that was where I made a big mistake.'

Brenda took a last pull on her cigarette and flicked the fag-end away into the gorse.

'I was twelve by then, rising thirteen, and big for my age. Yes, I know, Mark. Don't interrupt. Let me tell this my way. One afternoon I came home from school and found Uncle Joe alone in the place, just putting up the shutters. "Where's Mummy?" I said. "Gone off to see your Aunt Mabel," Uncle Joe told me. "Seems she's been taken bad." And he gave me a cold, thoughtful sort of up-and-down look that I didn't like one bit. But nothing happened then. We had our supper—I cooked it—and then I settled down to my homework. Uncle Joe just sat in his big arm-chair by the fire and looked at me. After a bit he got up and came over to the table where I was working. "What's all this, then?" he said, breathing beer down my neck. "Algebra, Uncle Joe," I told him, not looking round. "Stone the crows," he said. "Fancy a nice little bit like you wasting your time on that sort of caper." He was breathing through his nose in a funny sort of way. "But that's what you want, isn't it?" "Yes," I said, "that's what I want, Uncle Joe." "More than anything in the world, right?" I just nodded, hoping to God he'd get tired of fooling around, and let me get on with my algebra. "That's what I reckoned, Brenda," he said, "that's what I reckoned, girl," and then he—he——'

Brenda swallowed.

'Go on,' said Mark, in a low voice.

'Then he put out his hand, that great bony hand with the brown patches on the back, and he took hold of mine, and pulled it behind the chair where I couldn't see, and said: "Come on, girlie, feel this." I jumped up as though I'd been scalded, and he must have seen I was going to scream, because he grabbed hold of me and held his hand over my mouth, and then he whispered: "Listen, Brenda, you're not going to come to any harm, I'm not that sort, girl, just a little fun, see, and no one the worse for it." But I still fought and wriggled to get away. I was nearly out of my mind. And then he said, in a different, nastier voice: "You want to stay on at the Grammar, don't you? Right, then. You be nice to me and I'll be nice to you, get it?" And oh God, Mark, that was where the old swine had me, and knew he had.'

'You mean—you *let* him?'

Brenda's cheeks were a fiery crimson. She stared away across the coombe-side and said: 'Yes, Mark. I let him. You've no idea what that grammar-school meant to me; you couldn't have in your position. It was the Open Sesame to a new world, the key that would let me out of prison. *Anything* was worth it for that.'

She shrugged, and lit another cigarette.

'The joke comes now,' she said. 'After six months or so—during which, I may say, I got into a really desperate state—Uncle Joe became a bit careless. So careless, in fact, that one night Mummy came in and found a most interesting little scene going on, the details of which I'll leave to your imagination. Mark, is all this a bit much for you?'

Mark shook his head, but Brenda, glancing at him, saw the pallor under the sunburn, the shocked and desolate expression in his eyes.

'So you see,' she said, 'the great sacrifice was completely wasted. Mummy and Uncle Joe had a most frightful row, and Uncle Joe left that night, and I was taken away from grammar-school at the end of the term.'

Mark said: 'Couldn't your mother have kept you on there, somehow?'

'That,' said Brenda Page, 'was the cream of the joke. Yes. She could have done. She said so, anyway.'

'Then why on earth——?'

'Very simple, Mark. She got it into her head—how shall I put it?—that I was what you might call a willing accomplice. So I was, in a way, you know. In fact, before she was through I think she convinced herself she'd got a sort of infant Jezebel on her hands, who'd actually seduced her bloody meal-ticket from the straight and narrow. So, no more grammar-school. I spent a miserable couple of years at the local Secondary, and then she had me working in the shop.'

'Oh Brenda.'

'Yes. I don't think I've ever been more miserable in my life. I needed love, Mark. Real love. I needed it desperately. I'd loved Mummy, and now all I got was that cold fishy disgusted stare. We didn't exchange two words from one week's end to the next. I think I'd have gone mad if it hadn't been for Eric.'

'Who was Eric?'

'Oh, just a boy. About your age. Rather like you, come to think of it. He lived across the road—his father ran a wireless shop. We got to be good friends. He'd come across and help me behind the counter when he could. We used to go to the flicks together, and talk about what we were going to do when we grew up. All rather silly, really, but it just about kept me sane. He taught me chess, too. He even tried to get me interested in electrical theory—he was going to night school at the time. Very ambitious, was Eric. I suppose I was in love with him, in a way, though we never so much as touched each other. I was grateful for that. But he was kind and gentle and considerate—he made me feel I was a person again, not just a *thing*. Can you understand that, Mark?'

'M'm. I had a master once like that. He meant the earth to me.'

'I suppose it was Eric who got me where I am now,' Brenda said, still half to herself. 'He was nuts on games and gym and swimming, everything like that. He used to make me go in for ping-pong tournaments, and lugged me off to the local baths, and said I ought to join evening P.T. classes—it'd keep my mind off things. It did, too: I really enjoyed myself. Natural co-ordination they said I had. I got a bronze medal for swimming when I'd only been at it a year.'

From the depths of his envy Mark said: 'Eric sounds all right to me.'

'Yes. He was.'

'What happened to him?'

Brenda said: 'One evening I was just going over the road to get him—it was November, and there'd been a lot of rain in the afternoon. I was standing on the pavement, waiting to cross. It was quite dark, and the whole street was a blaze of lights, and the tyres of the traffic were whirring over the wet—buses and cars and heaven knows what. Everyone was on their way home, the drivers tired and slap-happy—you know. Then he came out of the shop, and I waved to him, and he waved back, and he stepped out off the pavement, still looking at me, straight under one of those damned great heavy haulage trucks, all stacked up with cement bags.'

Mark said: 'He was killed, wasn't he?'

'Oh, yes. Instantly. The funny thing was, he hardly had a mark on him that you could see. Just one deep blue bruise over the right temple. But that was the end of Eric, and for a time I thought it was the end of me too. I couldn't get it out of my head that I'd been responsible, you see; that if I hadn't been there it would never have happened. Just as if it hadn't been for me Mum might still have been cosy and happy with Uncle Joe.'

'You can't blame yourself, Brenda,' Mark said. 'It wasn't your fault.'

'I'm not so sure, even now. I was *there*, both times. Seems to me I'm a sort of Jonah.'

'That's silly.'

'Jonah didn't think so. He took ship to Tarshish.'

'Maybe,' Mark said. 'But he survived the whale.'

Brenda laughed. 'True enough. I hadn't thought of that.' They walked on for a little in silence.

'What happened then?' Mark said.

'The war, for a start. I was just leaving school when it broke out, and I could hardly wait till I was old enough to join up. Mummy bitched like hell, but there was nothing she could do about it. I got myself into the W.R.N.S and spent three years as a P.T.I. I'd never expected to get out of England, but they posted me to Colombo for eighteen months. One long holiday. Marvellous. *And* a free training for the job I wanted to do.'

'You deserved some luck after what you'd been through.' Mark frowned thoughtfully. 'It must have been a bit difficult afterwards, though—I mean, coming back to the shop, and all that.'

'A buzz-bomb took care of the shop for me,' Brenda said, without any noticeable emotion. 'Direct hit.'

' And your mother? '

' Was in bed at the time. I'm afraid. With Uncle Joe's successor. Bad luck on her, I've always thought.'

' I'm sorry, Brenda.'

' You needn't be. It was a bit of a shock at the time, of course. But then it gave me a wonderful feeling of release. The past seemed to be wiped out with the house. I was on my own at last, I had some sort of a future before me. What with the compensation and the insurance and my gratuity, I wasn't too badly off, either.'

Mark said, as though working out some private problem: ' Did you ever meet Uncle Joe again? '

Brenda gave him a quick, rather startled glance. ' No,' she said. ' Why do you ask? '

' I don't know. Just a feeling.'

' Mark, what are you getting at? '

' The way you talked about him,' Mark said. ' As though you *missed* him somehow.'

' Oh my God,' Brenda said softly.

' Well, did you? '

' Let's drop this, shall we? '

' I want to know.'

' You wouldn't understand.'

' I see,' Mark said, huffily, and removed his arm from Brenda's waist.

' I'm sorry, Mark—I just don't want to hurt you. And it's so hard to explain.'

' Won't you try? '

Brenda considered for a moment. Then she said: ' You're fond of chocolate, aren't you? '

' Yes, but what on earth——? '

' Eating chocolate can become a habit. You may loathe

the sweet taste of the stuff, and not be in the least hungry, but you just can't keep your fingers away from the box. It's the same with smoking. Do you see what I'm driving at?'

'I think so. I'm not sure.'

'You asked me just now if I'd ever met Uncle Joe again. The answer is no. But he left his legacy behind, Mark. In a way I've never got rid of him. He started something. Something beyond my control.' She drew a deep breath and said: 'Well, there it is. I hope you're satisfied.'

'Oh, I don't think that's so very awful,' Mark said. 'You'll get over it all right. It must have been jolly nasty at the time, but it happened ages ago, didn't it?'

'Mark, you don't—' Brenda began, and then she broke off wearily and said: 'Yes. It happened ages ago. And it's a lovely afternoon, and I want to talk about something more cheerful.'

'Such as Devonshire splits with cream,' Mark said, grinning.

'That's right. Such as Devonshire splits with cream. Oh, what a greedy beast you are, Mark.'

'Not greedy, just hungry.' Mark tucked his arm through hers. 'Funny, I always am when I'm with you. Golly, we'll miss the bus if we don't brace up.'

'Come on, then, lazybones.'

The road was in sight ahead of them, a white dusty line scored across the green slope of the tor, and flanked by a low stone wall beyond which cattle grazed. Through the shimmering air Mark could see a solitary figure plodding along, dwarfed by the immensity of sky and empty landscape. He screwed up his eyes against the glare and said: 'I think that's Major Ferguson.'

'What? Where?' Brenda quickly detached her arm from Mark's.

'Coming along the road.'

Brenda fished in the pocket of her linen skirt, took out her dark glasses, put them on, peered, and said: 'Yes, I believe you're right.'

'I suppose he'll be catching the bus too.' Mark sounded despondent.

'It looks very much like it.' Brenda hesitated a second, then said: 'Mark—you will behave, won't you?'

'Behave? Oh. Yes. I see. Don't worry.'

'I'm sorry, Mark. But we've got to be sensible.'

'*People*,' Mark said, bitterly.

'I'm afraid so.'

'This *would* have to happen. Oh *damn* Major Ferguson. I hate him.'

'Why, Mark? I think he's rather sweet. Didn't he know your father during the war?'

'Yes,' Mark said shortly. 'They were in the same regiment.'

'Aren't you being a bit silly?'

'He makes me sick.' How can I compete with a D.S.O. and M.C., with that intolerable weight of age and glamorous experience? It's so beastly unfair.

'*Please*, Mark.'

'I said don't worry, didn't I?'

Brenda sighed.

When they reached the road Ian Ferguson was waiting there for them, a tall elegant figure in well-cut navy-blue slacks and off-white linen jacket. He raised his Panama as they approached, revealing a head of close-cropped, wiry black hair. His teeth, when he smiled in greeting, showed white but irregular against that seamed, leathery complexion. He stood leaning on a heavy blackthorn stick, his bull-terrier bitch curled up watchfully at his feet. As Mark and Brenda clambered over the stile, this unpleasant beast cocked a baleful pink-rimmed eye at them, and growled garglingly in its throat.

' Quiet, Gina,' the Major said. ' *Sta tranquilla.*' The soft Scottish inflections of his voice were barely discernible through the acquired military briskness. But there was something else too, a lingering feline element which obscurely bothered Mark, and didn't fit in with the public *persona* Major Ferguson presented to the world.

' Good afternoon to you, Miss Page,' the Major said. ' Being a Good Samaritan again, I see. Hullo, young Mark. Thought I recognised you. Going into Braunton? '

Brenda said : ' We thought of treating ourselves to a real Devonshire tea.'

' Capital idea,' said the Major, rubbing his hands. But his dark eyes were cold and watchful, flicking from Brenda to Mark and back again. How old is he? Mark wondered. Must be forty at least. He wriggled uncomfortably under Ferguson's sardonic scrutiny, and tried to concentrate on his moustache, a pencil-thin black line which he found both repellent and ridiculous.

Brenda said : ' What takes *you* into Braunton, Major? '

' The same as you, my dear,' the Major said, and though his voice was light and amused, Mark once more caught that steely feline edge to it. ' I rather fancy a spot of Devonshire tea myself.'

Mark glanced at Brenda, but her face remained impassive behind the dark glasses.

' Well, well,' she said. ' An unexpected sweet tooth.'

'We all have our little weaknesses,' the Major said.

'I thought yours was golf.'

The Major gently caressed the powerful Zeiss binoculars he wore slung by a strap round his neck.

'There are times,' he said, 'when I desert it for bird-watching. A soothing pursuit, don't you find?'

Brenda shrugged. 'Frankly, Major Ferguson, I've never tried it. I doubt whether I've got the observer's temperament.'

'Ah. You prefer the active to the contemplative life.' Malice gleamed openly for an instant in his eye. Gina stirred and growled; from far away down the road came the faint but unmistakable sound of a bus changing gear.

'I take it,' Brenda said, 'that you've been—how shall I put it?—indulging your taste for ornithology this afternoon?'

'*Evidemment.*' The Major smiled thin-lipped and began to draw patterns in the dust with his blackthorn.

Mark glanced uneasily from one to the other. He said: 'Is my father playing golf this afternoon, sir?'

The Major shook his head. 'Too hot even for him. Between you and me, Mark. I rather fancy he's taking slightly more than forty winks. Though I don't doubt his slumbers are enlivened by ghostly professionals telling him just what's wrong with his back-swing.'

Mark giggled. 'He does get rather steamed up about it all, I must say.'

Brenda said: 'Why shouldn't he, poor man? It's a harmless enthusiasm. I like to see people take a real interest in something.'

'There,' said Major Ferguson, 'I couldn't agree with you more, Miss Page. Ah—here come the bus.'

When Gina, and the picnic basket, and the Major's satchel had all been safely stowed away, it somehow turned out that Mark was sitting next to the window with the Major beside him and Brenda on her own in the seat in front. The bus was small, noisy, and half-empty: it smelt pleasantly of old leather.

The Major said: 'Can I join this amiable little bun-fight of yours, Miss Page?'

Brenda was busy lighting a cigarette. When she had finished she turned round, wreathed in smoke, and said: 'It's Mark's party. You'd better ask him.'

'Is it now?' the Major said. '*Quis custodiet*, eh? Well, what about it, young feller-me-lad?'

'Yes, all right,' Mark muttered, and then, remembering what Brenda had told him pulled his face into a stiff smile and said: 'Do join us, sir. We'd be delighted.'

'Excellent,' the Major said, beaming. 'Nice manners you've got, young Mark. Don't you agree, Miss Page?'

Brenda didn't answer. The back of her neck had a stiff, obstinate look about it. Mark suddenly became conscious of perspiration beading his forehead.

He said: 'Could I have a look at those field-glasses, sir?'

The Major obligingly unslung them. Mark squinted, fiddling with the viewfinder.

'No, like this,' Major Ferguson said, and for a second or two his hands rested gently over Mark's.

Mark half-rose in his seat and focused, swaying, through the open bus-window.

'Gosh, they're powerful.'

'Yes. The Germans certainly know their stuff when it comes to optics.'

Mark said, despite himself: 'Did you get these in the war, sir?'

The Major grinned, without amusement. 'You might say they were given to me. Together with an even more remarkable toy. Like to see that too?' He stooped under his seat and fumbled in his satchel. Gina whined, licking his hand noisily. The Major sat up holding a square leather case. From it he produced the most intricate and exotic camera Mark had ever seen.

'Well may you looked pop-eyed, young Mark. This is a very special job, even for Zeiss.'

Mark peered, frowning. 'What's *that*?' he asked.

'Ah,' the Major said, his eyes on Brenda Page, 'I rather thought my little gadget might stump you. That since you ask, is a collapsible telephoto lens attachment. The Germans used it for getting shots of military installations in enemy territory. But it has other possibilities. Bird-watchers, for instance, find it most profitable.'

Brenda sat rigid for a second. 'I see,' she said, in a small, flat voice, and very carefully stubbed out her cigarette. Then she turned round a frozen smile on her face, and said: 'No wonder you did well in the war, Major Ferguson.'

'Attention to detail never comes amiss,' said the Major, amiably. 'Thanks for the compliment.'

'Do you do your own developing, sir?' Mark asked, interested despite himself.

'I'll be most surprised if he doesn't,' Brenda said, before the Major could answer; and the tone in which this remark was made puzzled Mark considerably.

But the Major was not at all put out. 'Quite right, I'm afraid: I do. Chemists, I've found, are both expensive and unreliable.'

'Yes,' Brenda said thoughtfully, 'I can see that one.'

'Would you care to look at some of the shots I've taken with this contraption? Quite extraordinary. Every detail absolutely clear.'

'I'd be fascinated.'

'Fine,' the Major said, briskly. 'We'll have a little session, then, eh? Later this evening, perhaps?'

'Perhaps,' Brenda said.

Well, that's pretty cool, Mark thought, speechless with fury. Right under my nose. He might as well have said 'Come up and see my etchings', and had done with it. I suppose he's so beastly superior it doesn't even *occur* to him that——

Mark caught himself up short, consciously aware for the first time, with horrified clarity, just how the Major—and indeed the world at large—must view him in relation to Brenda. It's like that Father Brown story about the postman, he thought. I'm sort of *invisible*. As far as they're concerned I just don't exist. Not that way. He turned this proposition over in his mind. Presently the first shock wore off, and was replaced by a certain sly delight. *They're not so infallible after all*, he told himself. *In fact, they're plain stupid.* Mark smiled, nursing his secret, luxuriating in this revolutionary discovery concerning his elders and betters.

When the bus pulled up in Braunton Major Ferguson said: 'Right, young Mark. Lead on to the flesh pots.'

They got out in silence. Brenda dropped the picnic basket, and Mark tripped over Gina's lead. Only the Major, limping a little as he strode along, and leaning on his blackthorn, seemed unaffected by the sultry atmosphere. Panama cocked at a rakish angle, linen jacket flapping loose in the breeze, satchel slung from his shoulder, he looked like an advertisement for the Holiday Spirit.

The tea-shop was a dim, untidy, comfortable place, two steps down from street-level. Blackened beams ran across the low ceiling and down the walls. Horse-brasses were much in evidence and a solitary wasp buzzed up and down the window-pane. The Major led the way to a corner table. Mark and Brenda sat down uncertainly. They were the only customers. Apart from the wasp, and a heavy grandfather clock ticking away in one corner, not a sound was to be heard. Silence pressed in on them. The Major found a small ornate hand-bell, and banged it twice, imperiously. Mark stared at his fingers, and Brenda lit another cigarette. She didn't offer one to the Major.

'Damned inefficient service,' the Major said, and banged the hand-bell again, as though it was a personal enemy.

A plump elderly women shuffled in, beaming indiscriminately through steel-rimmed spectacles, and wiping her hands on a tea-cloth. She wore a flowered apron and appeared to be the same thickness all the way down. Mark decided she was rather nice. The Major was obviously not so impressed.

'Was it tea you wanted?' she enquired.

'Tea for three,' said the Major briskly, just as Mark was opening his mouth to reply. 'Splits and cream, the whole shooting-match. Better make it a double ration of cream, too,' he added, with a wolfish twinkle at Mark. 'Schoolboy appetites, you know.'

Mark looked furious, but said nothing. The woman took herself off, hennishly ruffled, and a cross clatter of cutlery and plates began behind the service door. The Major leaned back in his chair, ran a finger along his moustache, and said: 'Haven't seen much of you on the links these last few days, young Mark.'

'Sorry, sir,' Mark mumbled, and then, feeling some excuse was called for, added: 'I've been swimming a lot, you see.'

'Yes,' said the Major thoughtfully. 'I see.' He picked up a knife, twiddled it about, balanced it on his forefinger. 'You could be a good golfer if you practised more. Better than your father. Needs application, though. No use just having a bash when the fancy takes you.'

The ash trembled on Brenda's cigarette, and the Major pushed an ornate pottery ash-tray across the table towards her.

'Concentration,' he went on. 'That's the secret. Don't let yourself be sidetracked. You could have a single-figure handicap if you wanted to. Maybe play in the Junior Open. Wouldn't you like that, young Mark?'

Mark looked up, hot with resentment, and, somewhat to his own surprise, heard himself say: 'Not particularly.'

The Major frowned. 'I don't know what's come over you lately,' he said. 'That's a downright sloppy attitude. You used to be as keen as mustard.'

Mark said: 'Golf isn't the only thing in the world.'

'You'd better not talk like that when you get to Rugby,' the Major said. 'They'll soon put you to rights.'

'Cold showers and the team spirit,' Brenda said, acidly.

'I suppose you're against the public school system, Miss Page?'

'You suppose right, Major Ferguson.'

The Major said, thinly: 'Might one enquire why?'

'One might, but not at tea-time.'

The Major, however, refused to be put off. 'What, for instance, is wrong with the team spirit?'

'Nothing that a little individualism wouldn't put right. And incidentally, how much team spirit is there in golf?'

Mark giggled, saw the look on the Major's face, and rather unsuccessfully tried to turn the noise into a cough. At this moment, much to his relief, the elderly waitress came back, balancing a large and perilously overloaded tea-tray. They all three sat in silence while sugar, milk, jam, cream, cakes, a plateful of splits and a large glazed Devonshire tea-pot (inscribed for no ascertainable reason with a coy motto in Scots dialect) were arranged about the table according to some mad private pattern.

The tea was the colour of sweet British sherry, and smelt faintly like boot-polish.

'Real Army brew,' the Major said, stirring experimentally.

Mark scooped up two enormous spoonfuls of cream and jam, buttered his splits thickly, and set to.

'Gosh,' he said, with an air of mild wonder, 'I'm absolutely *ravenous*.'

'It must be all that swimming,' the Major said, and to Brenda: 'Big boy for his age, isn't he?'

'Yes,' Brenda said, expressionlessly.

'Athletic type. Bags of energy.'

Mark's ears burnt suddenly crimson.

'Sooner he gets to Rugby the better,' the Major said. 'All this hanging around between schools doesn't do any good.'

'I wish you'd stop talking about me as though I wasn't there,' Mark said, through a large mouthful.

'Sorry, I didn't quite catch that,' the Major observed, sipping his tea.

'Nothing. Doesn't matter.'

There was a gritty silence. Mark buttered another split, and with the absorbed air of a master bricklayer proceeded to add thick successive wodges of cream and jam. He bit off about half of this concoction, and grinned cheerfully at Brenda. The Major's left hand, which was resting on the table, clenched into a hard, angry fist.

Brenda said: 'How much longer are you staying here, Major?'

'Another week. You're leaving the day after tomorrow, I believe?'

'That's right.'

The Major watched the remainder of the split disappear into Mark's mouth. He said: 'Perhaps our young friend here will have a little more time for golf when there isn't so much inducement to go swimming.'

'Just what do you mean by that?' Brenda said. Mark looked at her quickly, disturbed by the unpleasant rasp in her voice.

'My dear Miss Page, how touchy you are. It must be the heat. Everyone's very grateful to you for giving up so much of your time to Mark. I hear he's coming on quite remarkably at tennis, too.'

'Brenda's got a really wizard serve,' Mark said. 'I can't touch it.'

The Major grunted. Mark brushed the crumbs from his mouth and began to demolish a large slice of coffee-and-walnut cake. Brenda took off her dark glasses and sat staring at nothing, a sick, defeated expression on her face. Dust motes danced in the sunlight slanting through the window; from outside there came the sound of children's voices, high and excited, and cars changing down as they turned into the narrow street.

Presently the Major wiped his moustache, folded his paper napkin with neat, finical movements, and banged on the handbell. This time the waitress appeared almost instantly, as though she were under starter's orders.

'My bill, please,' the Major said, taking out his wallet.

Mark said, stuttering a little, 'L—look, sir, this was *my* idea. P—please let me——' and fished the battered ten-shilling note from the pocket of his shorts.

The Major raised his eyebrows very slightly, as though confronted with a hitherto docile performing animal that had suddenly developed independent ideas about its act.

'Nonsense, young Mark,' he said, with brisk good humour. 'One of the more enjoyable privileges possessed by the very young—forgive me for reminding you of the fact, but you *are* very young—is that of being stood whacking great blowouts by their elders. Take advantage of it while you can. It won't last for ever.'

Mark sat flushed and speechless, the note still crumpled in his fingers.

'You wait and see,' the Major went on, in his silkiest, most lilting voice. 'Before you've been at Rugby more than a couple of terms, your uncles will think twice before tipping you at the end of the holidays. Give it another year or so after that, and you'll be wanting a razor for Christmas and getting crushes on other chaps' sisters. By the time you're sixteen, young Mark, it'll be beneath your dignity to tuck into a cream tea, and you'll probably be in training anyway. So make the most of what you've got now.'

The waitress shuffled back with the bill on a plate. The

Major peeled a new pound note from the thick sheaf in his pigskin wallet, said 'Keep the change' in an off-hand way, yawned, glanced at his wrist-watch, and levered himself to his feet.

'Well,' he said, 'mustn't lose the best of the afternoon.' He picked up stick, satchel, and binoculars.

'More bird-watching, Major Ferguson?' Brenda asked.

'Perhaps. The Estuary is an interesting place, Miss Page. You should let me take you out there one day when you're not—otherwise occupied.'

'I'm quite sure I should be safe with you,' Brenda said, enigmatically.

The Major flushed in his turn. He said: 'If you are leaving us so soon I fear it will have to wait till another occasion—unless you could spare the time now.'

Brenda said: 'Well, actually——'

'Of course,' the Major said. 'I quite understand. But I do feel it might be a good idea if we had a drink and a chat before you went, don't you?'

Brenda carefully put on her dark glasses again, and lit a cigarette. Then she said: 'I don't think we really have very much in common, Major Ferguson.'

'One thing, perhaps.'

'Perhaps.'

'We should get to know each other better, then.'

Brenda shrugged.

The Major said: 'You're a charming girl, Miss Page. I should hate to see you in any sort of trouble.'

'Naturally.'

'Shall we say about nine this evening? In the hotel bar?'

'Very well.'

'Good,' said the Major. 'I shall look forward to that. Goodbye, young Mark. Enjoy yourself.'

In a cool, polite voice Mark said: 'Thanks for the tea, sir. It was most kind of you.'

For once the Major seemed a little taken aback. Then he said: 'Not at all, my boy. It's Miss Page you really ought to thank. Think of all the time she's spent looking after you.'

'Yes, sir.' Mark's face was expressionless.

'I hope you're properly grateful.'

'Yes, sir.'

'Well, then.' The Major hesitated momentarily, then raised his hand in a curious truncated gesture—half wave, half salute—turned, and went quickly out of the low room, stooping under the beams, Gina following at his heels, his blackthorn tapping on the stone-flagged floor. Mark found himself reminded, for no apparent reason, of Blind Pew's sinister appearance at the 'Admiral Benbow' in *Treasure Island*.

Then he and Brenda turned and looked at each other, desolation in their eyes.

'I'm sorry, Brenda,' Mark said, miserably, features puckering. 'I never meant it to be like this.'

'It wasn't your fault, sweet.'

They sat in silence, the crumby remains of tea lying between them. Brenda's cup was still half full, and a fine film had formed on its contents. The elderly waitress bustled in (perhaps, Mark thought, she had been peering through some secret spy-hole, waiting till the Major left) and began to clear away, with much clattering of crockery. Mark and Brenda got up slowly, and gathered their belongings together.

H

The waitress beamed archly at Brenda through her steel-rimmed glasses and said: 'I hope the little gentleman had enough.'

'It was an excellent tea, thank you,' Mark said, in a chilly voice.

The waitress's smile vanished abruptly.

When she had gone Brenda said: 'That wasn't very nice of you, Mark.'

'Sorry. It was just her saying——'

'Yes. I know.'

'*People*,' Mark said again, with a wealth of expression.

'You can't pretend they're not there.'

'No.'

They walked out into the sunlit street. The door-bell pinged softly behind them.

'They don't understand,' Mark said, shoulders hunched.

'Would you rather they did?'

'Yes. No. Oh what a *mess* life is.'

Brenda said: 'That's something you just have to accept.'

Mark sighed. 'I suppose so. But—but I feel so *silly*.' He paused, struggling with his thoughts. 'It's all right when we're alone, Brenda. I wish we could be alone for always.'

Brenda shook her head. 'But we can't.'

They walked slowly along, side by side.

Mark suddenly burst out: 'I can't help being young. It's not my fault.'

'Poor Mark.'

'Brenda, don't be *sorry* for me.'

'I'm not. Not like that.'

'I wish——' Mark said, and was silent.

'What?'

'You'll laugh at me.'

Brenda said, gently: 'I'd never laugh at you, Mark.'

'I wish I could get it all over, just like that.'

'What?'

'Growing up,' Mark said, half to himself. 'I want to have it all behind me. I want to have a job, and money, and live on my own, and—oh, everything,' he concluded lamely.

'You will.'

'I want it *now*.'

'Because of me, Mark?'

'Yes. But not only because of you. I'm sick of being talked down to, and put in my place, and treated like a— like a——'

'Schoolboy?'

'I knew you'd laugh at me.'

'I'm not laughing, Mark. I know how you feel, all right.'

Mark said: 'I feel like a fish out of water. I don't belong anywhere.'

'You'll get over it. Truly you will.'

'I don't want to get over it. I want to be—I don't know— *accepted*.'

'Don't make things harder for yourself, sweet.'

'Even you,' Mark said.

'What do you mean?'

'You wouldn't walk arm-in-arm with me down this street, would you, Brenda? People might think it was funny.'

'Oh, Mark, do try to understand. You say you want to be grown-up. This is part of it. Facing facts as they are. Not as you'd like them to be.'

Mark was silent for a moment. Then he said: 'Do you like Major Ferguson?'

Brenda said: 'That creep? I loathe his guts.'

'But you're having a drink with him this evening, aren't you? You let him spoil this afternoon.'

'Mark, for heaven's sake——'

'*He's* got it all behind him, hasn't he? *He* doesn't have to do what people tell him.'

'I said he was a creep.'

'Then why are you seeing him this evening?'

Brenda said, hopelessly: 'You wouldn't understand.'

Mark stared at her. 'I see,' he said.

'You *don't*.'

'I suppose I will when I'm a bit older, that's it, isn't it?'

'Oh Mark, you're such a *child*——' she broke off, horrified.

'Yes,' Mark said. 'That's what I thought you meant.'

They stood on the pavement, looking at each other.

'I think I'd better go back on the early bus,' Mark said.

Brenda shook her head hopelessly. 'If that's the way you feel,' she said.

'I want to sort things out a bit. And if we go on like this we're going to have an awful row.'

'Oh hell,' Brenda said. She looked as though she might cry at any moment.

Mark said with vehemence: 'I hate rows. They're so *messy*.'

Brenda repeated, in a dull hopeless voice: 'You don't understand. How could you possibly understand?'

'I understand more than you think.'

'What do you mean?'

'You and Major Ferguson——'

'If you believe that,' Brenda said, 'you'd believe anything.'

Mark said: 'I'm not a complete fool.'

Brenda sighed. 'Oh, what's the use?' she said.

'You see?'

'All right, then, go. I don't like rows any more than you do.'

Mark hesitated, then turned away.

'Mark——'

'What?'

'I'll see you this evening, won't I?'

'I don't know.'

'*Please*, darling.'

'I suppose so,' Mark said, and walked quickly away down the street, his shadow slanting beside him. Brenda stood there, shoulders hunched, sunlight glinting back from the coppery glory of her hair, a motionless watching figure. Mark turned the corner without looking back. Long after he was gone Brenda still remained where he had left her, oblivious to the curious glances of other holidaymakers as they hurried past to the warm afternoon beaches, the exhilarating swell and explosion of the great Atlantic combers.

'The secret of the drive,' Mr Crompton said, 'lies in the back-swing.' He wriggled his feet on the carpet of the hotel lounge, working himself into a comfortable stance, fingers interlocking round the shaft of an imaginary club. 'Head down, so. Weight on the left foot. Don't break the swing at the elbow. Flex the wrists. And then—' his arms descended in a flailing arc—'a clean, straight follow-through.' Several guests glanced up from their magazines, mildly amused. Mr Crompton didn't notice them.

'I've been working along the wrong lines altogether,' he went on. 'The theory was all wrong——'

'But this time,' Mark said, 'you've really got it taped.'

His father looked at him suspiciously.

'That's right,' he said, his voice noticeably less enthusiastic.

'Jolly good,' Mark said, wondering how on earth he could get away without being actively rude.

'I suppose you think all this is damned silly,' Mr Crompton said. '*You* just pick up a club, swing it any old how, and belt the ball into the middle of next week. No science about it at all.'

Mark said: 'I haven't got any time to *think* when I'm playing golf. Anyway, it'd put me off my stroke.'

'You wait till you're a bit older,' his father said, with what Mark felt was rather unpleasant anticipatory relish. 'Something'll go wrong, and you won't have the first idea how to put it right.'

'Well,' Mark said, nettled by yet another reminder of his juvenile status, 'I can beat *you*, anyhow.'

'Don't be pert, Mark.'

The inevitable answer when he's stumped for a good comeback, Mark reflected.

'Sorry,' he said. 'Where's Mummy?'

'Up in her room. She's got a headache.'

That means they've been rowing again, Mark thought. Oh Lord. It's going to be a really smashing evening at this rate.

Mr Crompton adjusted his jacket. He was a neat, slim, dapper man, with crisp iron-grey hair and wary, rather nervous eyes. His superiors in the Treasury, while conceding his worth at his job, made little jokes about him behind his back, and his subordinates went out of their way to treat him with unctuous politeness, which he invariably took at its face-value. Waiters and taxi-drivers despised him on sight, seeing through the rather querulous arrogance to the shrinking ego beneath. His wife, unwisely, had been impressed by his tantrums, and decided very early in their marriage that a policy of conciliation was the best thing for all concerned. She was the only person on whom he could vent his edgy temper with impunity, and he took full advantage of the privilege thus accorded him.

Now he coughed, blinked, and said: 'Mark, I think the time has come for us to have a little man-to-man talk.'

'M'm,' said Mark, cautiously, wondering what on earth was biting the old man now.

Mr Crompton led the way to a deserted corner of the lounge, motioned Mark to an armchair, and sat down himself. Then he took out pipe and tobacco-pouch, and set about the complicated ritual of lighting up. Mark fiddled with a magazine, watching his father's fingers poking and prodding the dark brown strands of shag into a neat compact mass.

'You're getting to be a big boy now,' Mr Crompton said, blowing puffs of blue smoke round a fluctuating match-flame.

Mark felt that comment on this statement was neither possible nor, in fact, desired: his father was simply circling the real subject of discussion like an old sheep-dog compos-ing itself for sleep in its basket.

'You're going to a public school this autumn,' Mr Cromp-ton went on. 'A great public school. You must under-stand that I have made very considerable personal sacrifices to send you there.'

'I did get a scholarship,' Mark said.

Mr Crompton puffed furiously. 'Without that scholar-ship,' he remarked, 'it wouldn't have been possible at all.' He contrived to make this remark sound like a re-proof.

'I only meant that I'd done my bit to help.'

Mr Crompton ignored this.

'In the circumstances, Mark, you have a very particular obligation not to let me down when you get there.'

Mark said: 'I'll do my best, Daddy. I've always done my best.'

'Yes, of course. But—ah—you must realise that a public school is not like a prep school. There are—' puff, puff, puff— 'special temptations for young boys such as yourself.' He peered at Mark to see what effect this remark had on him. Mark merely looked blank.

Mr Crompton tried again. 'You have probably been aware, during the past few months, of—ah—physical changes in yourself.'

Mark repressed a sudden desire to giggle. So *that* was it.

'Yes, I s'pose so.'

'Just so. This is quite natural. Nothing to be worried about. The only danger——' He broke off, sucked on his pipe, and struck another match. 'The only danger is that you may *abuse* your changed condition.'

Mark remembered a prematurely hairy boy in his class who had, with good reason, been nick-named the Toss-Pot.

'Old Waggers told us all about that at the end of last term,' he said.

Mr Crompton looked relieved. 'I'm very glad to hear it,' he said, 'though I would be obliged if you would refer to Mr Wagstaff by his proper name. The fact that you have left Salford House does not entitle you to vulgar familiarities of that sort.'

'Sorry, Daddy.'

'Yes. Well. Did Mr Wagstaff tell you *why* this practice was to be avoided?'

Mark said: 'He burbled something about it making us slack at games.'

'There is a certain degree of truth in what he said. Now Mark, I'm not going to lecture you like an old-fashioned parent. Fifty years ago you'd have heard a lot of nonsense about hell-fire and going blind and heaven knows what else.' Mr Crompton licked his lips and began to get into his stride. It struck Mark that his father, the initial barrier of shyness once past, was positively enjoying himself. 'Let me give you a simple, practical illustration. When you pull a lavatory-chain——'

This time Mark failed to restrain himself. A squirt of laughter burst through his closed lips.

'I fail to see anything funny in what I said,' Mr Crompton snapped, primly.

'Sorry,' Mark gasped. 'I didn't mean to blow a raspberry. It just happened.'

'Kindly control yourself. When you pull a lavatory-chain, the water runs out of the cistern, doesn't it?'

Mark nodded.

'You have to let the cistern refill, don't you?'

'Yes.'

'If you pull the chain again too soon, what happens?'

'No water,' said Mark.

'Exactly. Do you see what I mean?'

Mark frowned in thought for a moment, then said: 'I oughtn't to do it too often.'

'Are you trying to be impertinent?'

'No,' said Mark, with a genuine sense of outrage, 'just answering questions.'

H*

'What I'm trying to tell you,' said Mr Crompton, getting worked up again, 'is that you shouldn't do it *at all*.'

'I don't,' said Mark.

There was a slight pause.

'*Never?*' said Mr Crompton. He sounded almost disappointed.

Mark said: 'Not now,' and smiled secretly to himself. Mr Crompton tapped out some ash from his pipe and struck another match.

'Of course,' he said, rallying, 'there will be other temptations. Older boys——'

'Not interested,' Mark said, promptly.

For the first time that evening Mr Crompton eyed his son with genuine curiosity.

'H'm,' he said, and frowned in a thoughtful, portentous fashion. Mark waited patiently for the next broadside.

'Yes, well, that brings me to, ah, another matter.' Mr Crompton squinted severely at the bowl of his pipe, as though it were an insubordinate Other Rank. 'I mean *girls*.' He coughed and swallowed. It occurred to Mark that his father was much less sure of his ground on this topic. The realisation started an interesting train of thought.

'When I was your age I didn't give them a thought,' Mr Crompton asserted. 'Not a thought. Too much else on my plate. We all thought girls were a bore. Nowadays, well, I don't know, I really don't. Children seem to mature so early. All this rich food and psychology and American teen-age nonsense. Downright unhealthy, if you ask me. But there it is, times change, and you can't blink the fact.'

What the hell's he getting at? Mark wondered, beginning to feel a little uneasy.

'Anyway,' Mr Crompton went on, 'I thought I ought to

have a little chat to you on the subject. Otherwise you may find yourself in deep water before you know where you are.'

Oh Lord, Mark thought. Has he guessed something? Has that bloody Major Ferguson been dropping discreet little hints?

'You're big for your age, Mark.' Mr Crompton's eyes were swivelling rather desperately round the room, as though looking for reinforcements. 'You're bound to find girls, probably not the right type of girl, taking an interest in you soon. With all this cheap sensationalism about in the papers and on T.V., you may well be tempted to respond. You will be flattered by their attentions.'

'Is that a bad thing, Daddy? You make it sound worse than messing about with boys at school.'

'At your age it could have, ah, very unfortunate consequences.'

Mark rubbed moist palms on his trousers. 'Look,' he said, 'have you got any particular reason for telling me all this now?'

'It has not escaped my notice, or, I may say, your mother's, that you have been seeing rather a lot of a certain, ah, young person in this hotel.'

Come to the point, for heaven's sake, Mark thought. If you know, why don't you say so?

'Now, Mark, I'm the last person to be a spoilsport. I hope I always take a broadminded view of things as a parent. But I've been in the world a good deal longer than you have. Take my word for it, you don't want to get serious about anyone at your age. There are as many good fish in the sea as ever came out of it. You'll learn as you get older.'

'I don't understand,' Mark said, puzzled. 'You didn't say anything like this before. You didn't seem to mind at all.'

'Well, I didn't want to spoil your holiday,' Mr Crompton said, smiling magnanimously. 'Mark you, I don't say there was any harm in your—ah—association. The girl seems a well-brought-up young lady, from what I've seen of her. It's just the principle of the thing.'

Mark was speechless.

'Ah,' Mr Crompton said, in a lower voice, 'talk of the devil, eh?'

Barbara Randell came prinking across the lounge, a pert grin on her face.

'Evening, Mr Crompton,' she said. 'Hi, Mark.' She affected a faint American accent; her black hair was scraped back into a pony-tail, which she was constantly tossing. She wore blue jeans, and a boy's T-shirt that was rather too small for her. Mark looked from her to his father, and a huge bubble of laughter began to form somewhere under his diaphragm.

'They're going to roll up the carpet next door and start a spot of jiving,' Barbara announced. 'You interested, Mark? Man, they've got some really hot discs. I mean, the mostest!'

Mr Crompton eyed this prematurely busty fourteen-year-old with dark suspicion.

'Isn't it a little late for you to be up, Barbara?' he enquired. 'I'm sure this, ah, dance is really for grown-ups.'

Barbara beamed at him, and swivelled her neat hips. 'Oo,' she said delightedly, 'just dig the heavy parent act! Why don't you come out on that floor, Mr Crompton? We'd have you right in the groove before you knew where you were.'

'I'm afraid I don't understand modern dancing,' Mr Crompton said stiffly, uncertain how far his adult authority could be extended to include other men's pert daughters. Then, as a concession to foreign idiom, he added: 'I am, I believe, what you would describe as a *square*.'

'Oh Daddy-o,' said Barbara Randell, 'you're telling me! Look, you can't keep Mark locked up like the Crown Jewels. It's positively troglodytic.'

'Mark and I have various matters to discuss,' Mr Crompton said. 'Now, I trust you will excuse us, Barbara.'

'Maybe see you later, Mark,' Barbara said, quite unmoved by this dismissal, and whisked off through the lounge, pony-tail bobbing.

'That's the sort of thing I mean,' Mr Crompton said, the moment she was gone. 'No manners. No respect. And that uncouth jargon they all affect—quite revolting! Impertinent undisciplined little brats. They might be grown men and women, the way they address their elders. I'm not going to have you geting mixed up with—Mark, do you mind telling me what you're laughing at?'

Mark's suppressed hysteria had finally surfaced in a series of vast guffaws.

'Sorry,' he gasped at last, wiping his eyes. 'It was just that you thought *she*—I mean, that Barbara and I—oh Lord!' And he became speechless again.

Mr Crompton said: 'Her bad manners are no excuse for yours. Kindly pull yourself together.'

Mark said at length: 'If only you knew how funny it was.'

'I hope you are not intending to deny having, ah, associated with this girl?'

'I suppose you could call it that,' Mark said, reflecting privately that the Old Man was even dimmer than he'd supposed.

'I can't see what else you could call it. There were several *comments* I overheard during the trip to Lundy.'

'Yes, Daddy,' Mark said, meekly, his mind working overtime.

'Tell me,' Mr Crompton said suddenly, 'have you ever kissed her?'

'Sort of.'

'What do you mean, sort of? Don't prevaricate.'

'Not properly.'

'Oh? And what in your opinion is "properly"?'

Watch it, Mark thought, suddenly panic-stricken.

'Oh, I dunno,' he said vaguely. 'Like they do on the flicks, I suppose.'

Mr Crompton relaxed a little. He said: 'And you have never been led to, ah, *interfere* with her in any way?'

'*Interfere*?'

Mr Crompton coughed. 'Nothing apart from kissing, I mean.'

Mark shook his head and tried to look shocked.

'Well, then,' Mr Crompton said, and was very busy with his pipe for a moment. 'Perhaps I've been doing you an injustice, Mark. But I somehow got the feeling——' He frowned to himself. 'No, it doesn't matter. Just remember that girls aren't to be taken seriously at your age, that's all.'

Mark said, tentatively: 'What about falling in love, though?'

'Most of it's sentimental rubbish,' said his father, and a faint expression of distaste flickered over his face. 'There's nothing to choose between one girl and the next when you get down to it. They're all the same.'

'I see,' Mark said, feeling a little sick.

'We'll have another chat about it all later,' Mr Crompton said, getting to his feet. 'But you'll be too jolly busy with school for the next five years to bother your head over girls.'

I wish I could tell him about it, Mark thought. I wish he was the sort of father you *could* talk to, I mean over the real things. Dad's just like old Waggers when you get down to it, though. Hopeless. He'd blow his top, he really would. Probably whip me off to a reformatory or something. No, not a reformatory, he's too stuck on his reputation. Treasury officials in Pinner have got to be above reproach, haven't they? Like old J. Caesar's wife. But there'd be the father and mother of a row, all right. He'd make it all nasty, too, somehow. Ask me what I did and what it felt like. Nothing that a cold bath and plenty of exercise, ah, wouldn't cure. Take your mind off these morbid preoccupations. *Mens sana*, etcetera. Keep your bat straight and your bowels open.

'I'm going up to see how your mother is, Mark,' Mr Crompton said, glancing ostentatiously at his watch. 'Are you coming? It's getting late.'

'Can't I stay up just a bit longer, Dad?'

'To make a fool of yourself with that Randell girl, I suppose.'

'I *like* dancing, Dad.'

'Extraordinary. I really don't approve of such activities. I had hoped that after our little discussion you might feel the same.'

Mark looked down, scuffing the carpet with the toe of his shoe.

' I only want to have a bit fun,' he said.

' It depends what sort of fun.'

' Honestly, Dad! Babs is just a kid.'

' She looks physically mature enough to me.'

' Oh, *that*! She's a joke when you start looking at her seriously.'

' A joke? ' Mr Crompton said, warily, suspecting some sort of trap.

' Look at the silly way she walks.'

' I thought you liked her.'

' She's fun to dance with, that's all.'

Mr Crompton ran the tip of his tongue round his thin lips.

' There's something funny about you these days, Mark,' he said at length. ' I don't understand it. You're talking as though—as though—' He broke off, defeated.

' Is it all right, then? '

' Yes, I suppose so.' Mr Crompton made an effort to sound magnanimous. ' You're to be in bed by half past ten sharp, though. And that's far too late.'

' Thanks a lot. Oh, by the way—Miss Page said she might see me this evening, too.'

Mr Crompton's manner relaxed. ' Ah, you'll be in good company, then.'

' Yes, Dad.'

' I believe Miss Page is going soon, isn't she? '

' Day after tomorrow.' Mark's voice was neutral.

' You must be sure to thank her for spending so much time on you, Mark. I hope you appreciate how kind and thoughtful she's been.'

' Of course I will, Dad.'

' You'd better ask for her address. Mummy thinks it would be a good idea to drop her a little note when the holiday's over.'

' I won't forget,' Mark said.

His father sighed. ' Miss Page is—' he hesitated—' a very pleasant person. Good athlete, too, I'm told. It's not every boy who has a grown-up so ready to devote time to amusing him.'

' No, Dad.'

' You don't sound very enthusiastic. I suppose you took it all for granted? ' There was a sharp, querulous note in Mr Crompton's voice.

Mark shrugged.

' Your manners are the despair of me sometimes, Mark. You've got a rude surprise awaiting you at Rugby.'

Mark said, suddenly: ' Dad, why haven't I got any brothers or sisters? '

' Eh? What? ' Mr Crompton looked somewhat taken aback.

' It's not much fun being all on my own,' Mark said.

' I've told you before. Mummy was very ill when you were born. The doctors said she couldn't have any more children. Why do you ask that now? '

' I don't know,' Mark said.

His father stared at him, blinking defensively. ' Well, then. I'm off.'

' Night, Dad.'

' Remember, half past ten. Not a minute later.'

' Right-oh.'

Mr Crompton walked out of the lounge with his quick, nervous, fussy step. Mark took a deep breath, and let it trickle slowly out of his lungs. He stretched his arms till the muscles cracked. From next door there came a burst of laughter, and the high, frenetic yelp of a trumpet: Barbara Randell and her friends were losing no time in getting down to business. Barbara. Mark picked up a copy of *Country Life* and began to leaf through it in a vague, half-abstracted way. Fancy paying £5,000 for a *house*, he thought. Fancy having £5,000 at all, come to that.

In the empty room the clock above the mantelpiece ticked away, gravely disapproving. It was surrounded by a series of garish gilt rays, in the centre of which its foolish face shone like a tepid sun.

Mark sat there, fingers turning the glossy pages of his magazine, mind absorbed by an unthinkable image of his father and mother behaving as he and Brenda had behaved that afternoon. Ever since he could remember, there had been separate bedrooms. Mr and Mrs Crompton circled one another cautiously, like alien animals, edgy, irritable, quick to spurts of irrational temper. Love, Mark realised with sudden astonishment, was a word that had been banished from his father's scheme of things. He paused, feeling himself on the brink of some intolerable emotional abyss.

'Mark,' Brenda said, 'I thought I'd find you here.'

He looked up eagerly. Brenda had changed into a yellow corduroy dress; she wore a green paisley scarf knotted round her throat, with an old-fashioned cameo brooch pinned into it. Her hair shone, burnished copper. Mark could smell the gin on her breath. She did not meet his eye.

'I've come to say goodbye, Mark,' Brenda said, in a low voice. She held her hands clasped in front of her: Mark, looking at them, saw that they were trembling.

'But there's another day,' he said, bewildered.

Brenda shook her head.

'I've changed my plans. I'm off by the early train to-morrow morning.'

'No,' Mark said, panic-stricken. 'No, you can't.'

'I must.'

'Oh Brenda—why?'

'I can't explain. Please don't ask me.'

'Is it because of this afternoon?' Mark said.

Brenda made a hopeless gesture with one hand, and swayed rather alarmingly. It suddenly occurred to Mark that she was drunk, and a feeling of instinctive horror swept through him. In his family's circumscribed world drunkenness was virtually non-existent, something to be spoken of with disgust and unacknowledged fear. Once when he and his mother had been waiting for a train on Harrow station they had been forced to watch while a porter on the opposite platform threw up all the numerous pints of beer he had put away over the lunch-hour. For years afterwards Mark had remembered that spreading pool of dark liquid vomit, the hideous hiccoughs and retchings that had heralded each fresh spasm, the porter's greenish, vacuous face. Disgusting, Mrs Crompton had hissed, like an outraged goose. Don't look, Mark. But he had looked, he couldn't help himself.

Brenda caught the expression on his face, and grinned crookedly: an agonised rictus, as though her hand had closed on broken glass.

'Don't worry,' she said wearily. 'I'm not going to make a scene.'

'I'm not worried,' Mark said, dry-lipped.

Brenda said: 'Haven't you ever seen anyone a bit under the weather before?'

Mark nodded, thinking sickly of the porter. Try as he would, he couldn't get that memory out of his mind.

'No one would have guessed,' Brenda said. She took out a cigarette and lit it with exaggerated care.

Funny, one part of Mark's mind said. She's talking quite ordinarily. I thought drunk people were supposed to say things like 'Jolly old Palsh' and see double. I wonder if Brenda's seeing two of me?

'Are you cross because I went off like that?' he asked. 'I'm sorry. Really I'm sorry, Brenda.'

'It's not that,' Brenda said. She looked sick and exhausted. For the first time since he had met her the fact of Brenda's age was brought home to Mark. He felt as though someone had sluiced him with icy water.

'Then what's wrong?' he asked, his voice thick and strained.

'Nothing to do with you, Mark. Nothing you've done.'

'Is it something Major Ferguson said to you?'

Brenda nodded.

'You've just been seeing him, haven't you?'

'Yes.'

'Is that why you've been drinking?'

Brenda grimaced. 'Yes,' she said again.

'Brenda, you don't—you couldn't——'

'The *Major*?' Brenda burst out, and for the first time Mark caught the slur in her voice. 'Major bloody Ferguson,' she said, enunciating each word with great care, 'is a creep and a queer and a filthy blackmailing bastard. Major Ferguson, if you want to know, is the biggest fucking shit it has ever been my misfortune to meet.'

The hard, ugly words took Mark in the solar plexus like physical blows. He knew them, or most of them, from giggling exchanges in dormitories after lights-out; to hear them from a grown woman, from Brenda, shook the entire foundations of his universe.

'I don't understand,' he said, faintly.

Brenda's mouth twisted. 'You don't understand. You don't understand. How the bloody hell could you understand? You're only a kid. I've run the risk of losing my job because of you, can you understand that? I've gone out on a limb for a schoolboy who's so wet behind the ears he jumps when I have three gins too many or use an ordinary four-letter word.'

Mark stood quite still, unable to believe what he had heard, lips parted.

'Oh God, Mark, I'm sorry,' Brenda whispered. Her face seemed to crumple; tears glittered at the corners of her eyes. 'Forget what I said, love. I didn't mean it. Truly I didn't mean it. Things just get too much for me sometimes.'

Mark said: 'But you're going tomorrow.'

'Yes, I'm going tomorrow.'

'Because of Major Ferguson?'

Brenda sniffed and nodded. 'Please, Mark, *please* don't ask me to explain. You'll understand later, I promise you. Oh yes, you'll understand.'

'When I'm grown up, is that it?'

'Don't make things harder than they need be.'

'I'm old enough for some things, aren't I?'

'I've said I'm sorry, Mark.'

Mark stared at her as though seeing her for the first time and said: 'You're frightened.'

'Yes, I'm frightened,' said Brenda. 'Frightened, and ashamed.'

'Ashamed? Because of me?'

'I don't know. I just don't know.'

Mark said, desperately: 'Brenda, what did Major Ferguson say to you?'

'No. Please. Let it go, Mark. You've had your fun. Now forget about me.'

'*Forget* about you?'

Next door a trombone solo wailed out, muted by thick walls, accompanied by a faint susurrous of shuffling feet. Beads of sweat stood out on Brenda's forehead.

'Yes, Mark. Forget me. This was a holiday affair. Don't spoil it now.'

Mark gave a hysterical giggle and said: 'My father asked me to get your address. My mother wants to write and thank you for looking after me so nicely. I'm to express my appreciation—I think I've got it right—for your having taken so much trouble over me.'

Brenda rubbed her eyes and said: 'No dice, Mark. Sorry.'

'But——'

'Let it go. Just let it go.'

Somewhere a door slammed noisily. Voices were raised in the passage outside.

'We can't stay here,' Brenda said. 'I'm going to bed.'

'I'll see you to your room, ' Mark said, suddenly proprietorial.

'Bless you.'

Half-way up the stairs Brenda said: 'Oh Christ, I feel awful.'

Mark pushed one hand through his fuzzy hair, swallowed, and guided Brenda into the lavatory on the first floor landing. He locked the door, and held her heaving shoulders while she was sick into the pan. When the last spasm died away she stood up, tears in her eyes, and said:

'Mark. Oh my darling Mark. I'm sorry. I'm so bloody sorry.'

'It doesn't matter.'

At the door of her room she paused and said: 'I'm better now. You've done your duty.'

She leaned forward and kissed Mark on the mouth.

'Goodbye, Brenda,' he said, steadily; and then he broke away and ran wildly down the stairs again, not looking back, a dazzle of tears in his eyes. He slipped out by a side door and stood in the warm summer night, sobbing helplessly. The sour taste of Brenda's kiss still lingered on his lips: for a moment or two he felt sick himself. Then, slowly, the violent churning in his stomach subsided, the clenched muscles relaxed.

There's nothing left, he thought. Nothing. Dad was right. What difference does it make?

He shivered. The bruising contact of this raw, cruel, unpredictable adult world, so violent and baffling in all its manifestations, had knocked down all his flimsy defences with contemptuous ease. He remembered a nightmare end-of-term boxing match he had been forced to fight against a bigger boy, a beetle-browed Welsh tough who danced round him dervish-like, long arms thudding home on face and body, till Mark, numb and winded, had retreated to his corner and prayed for the liberating bell. There had been a taste of blood in his mouth; the spectators had jeered in the cruel, ferocious way that only small boys know.

He shook his head, dazed: his mind felt numb, as though it had been injected with cocaine. He stood there, breathing in the warm hydrangea-scented air, unable to think or move. In front of him a smooth lawn stretched bright under the moon, with one thin black bar, the sundial's pencilled shadow, ruled neatly across it. Beyond the lawn rose a little dark coppice, secret, owl-haunted.

Mark took out a rather grubby handkerchief and wiped his eyes. A crumpled piece of paper came with it, and fluttered down on to the gravel. Stooping, he picked it up: it was the ten-shilling note he had saved to buy tea for Brenda and himself that afternoon. He carefully smoothed out its creases. The moonlight drained it of all colour, reduced it to a severe pattern in black and white.

From the other side of the hotel came some soul-splitting *obbligato* work on a trumpet—Beiderbecke? he wondered idly, Satchmo?—followed by a burst of applause and laughter. Mark hesitated a moment longer, still clutching the note. Then, his mind made up, he went back inside and marched into the lounge-bar.

It was fairly full: a wave of conversation and cigarette-smoke hit him as he opened the door. He looked round quickly for any sign of Major Ferguson; but the Major was clearly otherwise occupied.

Mark squeezed up to the counter, between two honey-mooners sipping at babychams and an enormously fat parson, a jolly whale of a man, who was holding forth at interminable length about his latest sea-fishing expedition.

Freddie the barman, forehead glistening with sweat, hands busy shaking a dry martini, said: 'Wotcher, Mark boy. Anything I can do you for?'

Ice rattled briskly in the chromium shaker. 'I'm telling you,' the parson said, in a fruity, all-boys-together voice, 'trolling for bass is a mug's game.' He lit another Wood-bine, coughing wetly. The back of his chimney-pot neck turned an interesting scarlet over its encompassing clerical collar.

Mark said: 'Mummy's not feeling too good. Could I have some brandy, please?'

He pushed the ten-bob note across the beer-splashed counter.

'Sorry to hear that,' Freddie said, splashing dry martini into three glasses. 'Quarter bottle do you?'

Mark nodded. It was easy once you began. Easy as pie.

He took the flat bottle of Three Star and elbowed his way out again. He locked himself in the downstairs lavatory, sat down, and carefully removed the tinfoil from the cap. Then he eased the bottle open.

'Well,' he said, 'here goes.'

The first large mouthful he nearly spat out again. It was worse than that Madras curry Uncle Ned had made him eat at half-term. But somehow he got it down, choking and spluttering.

'Golly,' he said, wiping tears from his eyes. The raw stinging in his throat slowly turned into an anæsthetic and rather pleasurable sensation. A blossom of glowing warmth unfolded in the pit of his stomach. Gingerly he swallowed another mouthful. It went down like silk. Ten minutes later he threw the empty bottle out of the window, pulled the plug twice, *con brio*, and set out, rather unsteadily, to find Barbara Randell.

A record was just beginning as he walked into the dance-lounge. Despite his father's prognostications most of the people there were clearly still in their teens. All the lights, except one standard lamp by the gramophone cabinet, had been turned out. The couples gyrated slowly, oblivious and entwined, jive now abandoned for the more leisurely joys of a popular waltz. Fish in an aquarium, Mark thought. What a crummy bunch.

At first he couldn't see Barbara. Then he realised, to his surprise, that she wasn't dancing. She sat cross-legged against the wall, sucking coca-cola through a straw, and talking to a lanky youth with sideburns and a fine crop of what, on closer inspection, turned out to be acne.

Mark slid down beside her.

'Babs,' he said, 'what on earth have you done to your face?'

Barbara turned and inspected him with black-encircled panda eyes.

'Well, dig this,' she said. 'Daddy's let it off the chain.'

Mark said: 'You look like something out of a zoo.'

'Oh Mark, how square can you get?' Then she sniffed suspiciously. 'Coo,' she said, a certain note of awe in her voice, 'don't strike a match, anybody.'

'Barbara,' said the lanky youth, 'I don't think we've been introduced.'

'Sorry, Nigel. Mark Crompton, Nigel Bland-Evesham.'

'No kidding,' said Mark.

Barbara tossed her hair. 'Nigel's at Eton,' she said.

Mark burped discreetly.

'*Mark!*'

'I say, old boy,' said Nigel Bland-Evesham, forgetting his sideburns.

Mark got up. The room tilted very gently as he did so. 'Come on, Bab's, let's dance.'

'Actually,' said Nigel Bland-Evesham, 'Barbara promised——'

'Nuts,' said Mark. He grabbed Barbara's hand. Blinking, she followed him on to the floor.

'Aren't we masterful all of a sudden?' she said.

Breathing rather fast, Mark got hold of her left hand,

put his right arm round her waist, and pressed her hard against him. His cheek was buried in her hair. After a moment he found her ear and, remembering a trick Brenda had taught him, ran the tip of his tongue gently round it.

Barbara jumped like a startled gazelle.

'Mark, what *are* you doing?'

'For heaven's sake, Babs,' Mark said.

'You smell of drink,' Barbara said, a faint note of panic in her voice.

'Pure kangaroo milk.'

'Mark, you're *different*.'

'Everyone seems to be telling me that today.'

Barbara said, bridling: 'You haven't been near me for a fortnight.'

'Sorry, Babs.'

Barbara giggled, warming to Mark's mood.

'Pretty cool, aren't you?'

'Red hot,' said Mark, nuzzling in Barbara's ear again. 'Try me and see.'

Barbara said, tentatively, 'It *is* a bit stuffy in here.'

'Come on, then,' Mark said. They slipped out hand in hand through the french windows.

The moon hung high and tranquil in the sky: a soft thunder of surf drifted up to them from the shore below.

Barbara's hand sought Mark's: her eyes were shining.

'Oh Mark, it's *lovely*,' she whispered.

They walked slowly across the lawn to the coppice, not saying anything.

In the shadow of the trees Mark drew Barbara close to him again. 'I never thought this would happen,' she said, happily. 'I thought you just didn't care.' All her slang and affectation had peeled away like a transfer. 'Mark, oh Mark, I do love you, really I do. I've been so miserable.'

The brandy fumes mounted wreathing inside Mark's brain. Barbara clasped her arms round his neck and, very gently, kissed him on the lips.

'There,' she said.

'Let's sit down,' Mark said, thickly.

The leaf-mould was warm and dry. For a moment they lay quite still, clasped in each other's arms.

Barbara said: 'Aren't you going to kiss me, Mark?'

Mark still made no movement.

'Mark, you're trembling.'

He shook his head like a dog coming from the water. Then his mouth closed hungrily on Barbara's, and he kissed her as Brenda had taught him to kiss.

Shattered, Barbara arched and stiffened, writhing frantically under the pressure of his body. But the spark had fanned to a flame at that contact. Mark's hands ran hungrily over her body, seeking, tearing.

She wrenched her mouth away.

'No, Mark, *no*, let go, you're horrible, horrible, what are you trying to do, *Mark*, let go or I'll scream——'

Panting, Mark kissed her again, altogether out of control now. His left leg was jammed between her thighs, his left hand inside her T-shirt. Barbara twisted her head from under him, sobbing hysterically now, mouth a wide terrified square, tears streaming down her cheeks, make-up smeared and ridiculous. 'A-a-a-ah,' she moaned, 'a-a-a-ah——'

Mark sprang up at that inhuman sound, leaf-mould scattering around him, dizzy, bewildered. What had gone wrong? What on earth had gone wrong? He stood there, helpless, suddenly more terrified than he had ever been in his life, while Barbara crouched in front of him, shirt out, hair all awry, racked with terror and shock. Slowly the horrible grinding sobs died away: she staggered clumsily to her feet. Mark took a step forward to support her.

'Get away from me,' she whispered. 'Get away, you filthy beast. If you touch me I'll scream and scream and scream till everyone in the place comes out. You—you——'

She shook her head helplessly. Mark felt his stomach turn over, cold and queasy. With shaking fingers Barbara tucked her shirt back into her jeans and stumbled away across the lawn.

I don't understand, Mark told himself, blinking his own hot tears back. I don't understand. Everything's gone wrong. He pressed his hands to his face. A strident rock-'n-roll tune blared out from the hotel, mocking, relentless, unreal. Mark took a deep breath, straightened his coat, picked a few stray twigs out of his hair, and slowly walked back round the gravel drive, footsteps crunching. Once inside the hotel he made straight for the nearest lavatory. He sat there for about five minutes, while the blood pounded in his head and recurrent waves of nausea gripped him, his whole mind concentrated on the one major objective of not being sick. After a little the throbbing queasiness died away. Mark got up, swallowed once or twice, and ran the hand-basin full of cold water. Then he sluiced his face again and again, gasping and spluttering. As he dried himself he caught sight of a shock-haired staring ghost in the mirror, and blinked incredulously. Oh Brenda, Brenda, he thought. Why did this have to happen? *Why?* The ghost shook its turnip head in sympathy.

Mark glanced at his watch. Just after a quarter past ten.

He gave a cold, hard little grin and emerged from sanctuary.

As he reached the end of the first-floor corridor a door opened and his father's head appeared round it.

'Well, Mark,' Mr Crompton said, 'you're certainly punctual.'

Mark paused, one hand on the knob of his own door, face half turned away.

'Yes, Dad.'

'Did you enjoy yourself?'

'Yes, thanks.'

'I hope you remembered to get Miss Page's address.'

Mark's fist clenched tight on the door-knob. 'Sorry—I forgot.'

Mr Crompton sighed, a small gust of controlled irritation. 'Was that one little request really too much for you to remember?'

'I said I was sorry.'

'I will not tolerate lack of manners, Mark. Especially when that lack is coupled with plain ingratitude.'

Mark said, dully: 'Is Mummy's headache better?'

'What? Oh, she's asleep.'

'She's lucky,' Mark said.

Mr Crompton considered this remark, and decided to let it go. He cleared his throat and said: 'Oh, by the way, Major Ferguson says he'd be very glad to give you a round of golf tomorrow if you've nothing better to do.' The final words carried a heavy load of sarcasm. 'It's about time you realised, Mark, that a lot of people go to considerable pains to make your life more pleasant.'

'Yes, Dad. Can I go to bed now?'

'You haven't answered my question.'

'What question?'

'About golf tomorrow,' said Mr Crompton, testily.

He knows something's the matter, Mark thought, and he's dead scared of my telling him.

'I didn't think it was a question,' he said.

'Really, Mark. Sometimes I think your tiresomeness is deliberately calculated.'

Mark turned and stared at his father. Mr Crompton saw a white expressionless mask like a sleepwalker's.

'Are you feeling all right?' he asked, rather sharply.

'Just tired, Dad. I'll be all right in the morning.'

Mr Crompton nodded. 'That's what comes of late nights,' he said sagely.

'Goodnight, Dad,' Mark said again, opening his bedroom door.

'Goodnight, Mark.'

'Oh, and Dad—' Mark turned, casually, 'you can tell the Major I'll meet him on the first tee at nine o'clock.'

'Nothing better to do, eh?'

Mark shook his head, the same cold little grin at the corners of his mouth. 'Nothing at all, Dad,' he said. 'Nothing at all.'